"A gripping, thoughtful story that delivers the scares in spades."

—*Rue Morgue*

"With *The Reach*, Nate Kenyon has come into his own, and staked his claim in the ranks of suspense writers. He has given his characters and his world real texture, and created a tense, twisted, and finely written novel full of betrayals, secret agendas, and lost innocence. Bravo."

—Christopher Golden, author of
The Boys Are Back in Town

"One hell of a book . . . very detailed and well written. Kenyon is quickly rising to the top of the genre."

—The Horror Review

BLOODSTONE

"Stephen King's influence is apparent in Kenyon's debut spooker . . . an impressive panoramic sweep that shows the horrors manifesting subtly and insidiously through the experiences of a large cast of characters."

—*Publishers Weekly*

"Crisp prose and straightforward storytelling make *Bloodstone* a must-read!"

—Brian Keene, Bram Stoker Award–winning
author of *Dark Hollow*

"Reminiscent of *'Salem's Lot*, *Bloodstone* is a terrifying horror novel that is action oriented yet doesn't neglect the development of the characters. . . . This is the kind of horror novel that will make readers want to sleep with all the lights in the neighborhood shining brightly."

—*Midwest Book Review*

"Kenyon's debut evokes an atmosphere of small-town claustrophobia . . . [a] tale of classic horror."

—*Library Journal*

THE PREDATORS

His face was missing. That was my first reaction. I could see white bone and gristle where his nose and eyes should be. It looked like something had been chewing at him and had gotten a good bellyful before losing interest and moving on to something else.

As we all stared in silence and shock at the body, something moved at the edges of my vision, but when I glanced at the spot, whatever it was had disappeared.

If I'd been thinking more clearly, maybe I would have wondered what exactly had made those scratching noises, and what the hell had moved the handle on that door. I might have said something if Sue hadn't let out a shriek right then and run into the tunnel. I grabbed at her arm and missed, but Dan was quicker than me and before I could move he was after her. She got maybe five steps before he had her around the waist and held her back.

This was a good thing, because even before I heard Sue screaming his name, I knew that the dead man was her grandfather, had recognized him even without his face. Whatever had happened to him, it was clear he was beyond saving. But Sue wasn't going to hear that now.

I stepped out into the hallway too, Tessa right behind me, and as impossible as it sounds, I thought I saw Sue's grandfather's leg twitch.

That was when they attacked. . . .

Other *Leisure* books by Nate Kenyon:

THE BONE FACTORY
THE REACH
BLOODSTONE

NATE KENYON

SPARROW ROCK

LEISURE BOOKS   NEW YORK CITY

A LEISURE BOOK®

May 2010

Published by

Dorchester Publishing Co., Inc.
200 Madison Avenue
New York, NY 10016

Cover art by:
Stephanie Dugener, "Don't Open That Door"
Kelsey Skrobis, "Clawing For A Way To Get Out"

ISBN 10: 0-8439-6377-8
ISBN 13: 978-0-8439-6377-9
E-ISBN: 978-1-4285-0852-1

Visit us online at www.dorchesterpub.com.

*To Karin "Grease Pot" Claus, contest winner
and overall good sport.*

ACKNOWLEDGMENTS

I'd like to thank my agent, Brendan Deneen, for his fine advice and enthusiasm for my work; my editor, Don D'Auria, and the rest of the Leisure team, for all they do for me; Stephanie Dugener and Kelsey Skrobis for their fine contributions to the cover art of this novel; my "first readers," Donna Russell, Daniel Garay, Donna Johns, Leslie Rosenberg and Marilyn Blakley, for their fantastic feedback on an early draft; and DearReader.com and Suzanne Beecher for running the contest to select them. And, last but not least, I'd like to thank my family and friends for their support, now more than ever. You know who you are.

SPARROW ROCK

"We are close to dead. There are faces and bodies like gorged maggots on the dance floor, on the highway, in the city, in the stadium; they are a host of chemical machines who swallow the product of chemical factories, aspirin, preservatives, stimulant, relaxant, and breathe out their chemical wastes into a polluted air. The sense of a long last night over civilization is back again."

—Norman Mailer, *Cannibals and Christians*, 1966

PROLOGUE

We were all just sitting around the table playing cards, the pack of dog-eared ones that Big Sue found just before It Happened, when all of a sudden Jimmie stood up and started hollering at the top of his lungs, pulling at that scraggly hair of his and scratching at his hives, screaming stuff that didn't make any sense. He wasn't into the game, and we should have known he was about to finally lose his marbles, with the wound in his leg getting worse and the goddamned fever and the way he'd been handling the cards, his fingers all shaky, his thumb bending over the corners and straightening them out again one after another. After all, we'd been seeing the signs for days, and I of all people, with what happened to my father, should have known. But for some reason we didn't see it now until it was too late.

We were all on edge—who wouldn't be after so long in the ground—and maybe that's why Dan did what he did. He sat there for a moment and stared at Jimmie, and it would have been okay if he'd held on to his temper. But when Jimmie started raving about the rats again, Dan couldn't seem to take it anymore. He just stood up and belted him right in the mouth.

Jimmie staggered on his good leg but didn't go down, which meant Dan pulled the punch a little. When the blood started flowing and Jimmie wiped a hand across his lips, smearing it across that scraggly goatee of his that he always thought made him look old enough to drink, Dan said, real quietlike, "We know all about the fucking rats. You don't have to go bringing them up again."

Maybe he thought he had to say something. Me, I just sat there next to Sue and Tessa and tried not to giggle. I mean, it gets funny after a while; sometimes, no matter how serious the situation seems to be, you just have to laugh. You know the feeling? Like when you're a kid sitting in geometry class and someone lets out a fart and you're trying to keep calm about it but all of a sudden you can't control yourself.

Anyway, Jimmie was real quiet, but I could see something in his eyes, dark and stormy the way they got when he was stretched out. Something snapped back in there, all right. It had happened before. We lost Jay just four days ago, and Sue almost clawed her way out after him before we stopped her. Took Dan and me both to hold her down—she's stronger than she looks. She loved Jay, all right. Even now, she won't talk about him, not a single word.

So I knew what I was looking at, with Jimmie. Still, I didn't do anything to stop him.

Jimmie muttered something about his hair falling out. He scratched at his scalp and some more came off in his hand. The stuff spread around topside wasn't exactly perfume, and as far as anyone could tell about a molecule of it could fuck you royally. "I didn't notice," Sue said, which was stupid, because Jimmie was practically bald besides the long patches above his ears.

That was when I couldn't hold it in any longer. I started laughing, really bawling, and everyone looked at me like I was crazy. It's a sickness I have, laughing at inappropriate moments. Jimmie backed away from the table, shaking his head like a dog with a bad case of ear mites, which only made me laugh harder. I mean, tears were streaming down my face.

"Shut the fuck up," Sue said, grabbing my leg under the table and squeezing hard. "Can't you see what you're doing to him?"

Jimmie was pressing his skinny shoulders against the wall now, acting like he wanted to go right through it. The blood dripped down over his lip and off the point of his goatee. He kept slipping his tongue out and licking at it, and even that was sort of funny. He looked like one of those little dogs society girls carry around in their purses. I couldn't stop laughing.

"Hey, Jimmie," Dan said. "I didn't mean to hit you, man. It's just, you know, I get tired of hearing . . ."

"Itches," Jimmie said, or so I thought. With the blood in his mouth, it could have been something else. He was feverish for sure, I could see the sweat on his skin, the way his flesh was stretched taut. That bite had done something to him and it was just getting worse; the hives had blossomed all over him, bulging with some kind of sickness.

I didn't want to think about that, what had happened the last time I saw that bulging under his skin. The things that had come out of him.

Jimmie glanced across the little room at the steps heading to the surface. I knew what he was thinking. Maybe Jay made it. Maybe it's not as bad as we think up there. Hell, he wouldn't be the first to wonder about that—I'm sure we all had at one time or another. Once when the rest were asleep, Dan and I had talked about opening up the hatch to take a look, but that was after we'd downed a six-pack of Circle beer and smoked our last secret joint. We never actually did anything about it or anything.

I guess Dan saw the look on Jimmie's face too, because he made a sudden lunge across the table. Dan was a big guy, football type, did 200 push-ups every morning to keep in shape. But Jimmie was fast, even favoring that leg. He slithered away and quick as a flash he was up the steps, and we could hear him turning the hatch wheel. I could just see his stick legs from where I sat frozen, calves white as paint between the hives, and up high on the right where the flesh swelled and turned purple from the bite and the knife blade, his pair of dirty sneakers with drops of bright red blood on them.

As I stared at the hives on his leg, they seemed to pulse outward once again, as if something was writhing inside trying to get out.

Sue screamed. Dan found his footing again but he tripped over his chair trying to get back across the room, and then we all saw the light go on over the shelves and we heard the shriek of the alarm. There was a great whooshing noise as Jimmie broke the seal, and then a sound like the humming of a million bees; that's the only way I know to describe it. Dan swore and started climbing the steps, but by now Jimmie's feet had disappeared, and I knew he was out.

That's when things got a little fuzzy. I remembered getting up from my chair, and trying to move somewhere—whether I was going to help or just trying to hide, I don't know—and then Sue was screaming again and Dan stumbled back with his hands to his face. The first thing I thought was he'd been bitten, that some new kind of creatures had gotten inside. I guess Sue thought so too, because she grabbed my arm and started pulling me toward the bedroom. She was moaning a little in the back of her throat, and it reminded me of when I used to hear her and Jay making love. She had a way of sucking in air and then pushing it out, and it got faster when she was going to come.

All of a sudden the red light went off and the alarm stopped. Dan still had his hands to his face. I didn't know how long we stood there, but it seemed like forever, the two of us just staring at Dan's back across the room, ready to move fast if we saw that anything had latched onto him. Then I saw his shoulders moving up and down, and I realized he was crying. I'd never seen Dan cry.

Big Sue dug her nails into my arm hard enough to draw blood.

"Do something, Pete," she said.

When we'd checked the whole place over carefully and made sure the hatch was tight, I tried to tell Dan it wasn't his fault. Of course it came out all wrong. Guys have a hard time communicating things like that; either it comes out sounding macho, or condescending. Hey, man, don't worry about it, keep your chin up, all sorts of bullshit, neither of you looking each other in the eye like if you did you might want to hug or something.

Dan just shrugged and stared at the floor. You could tell he didn't want to talk about it. Tessa had this look on her face as if she were melting inside, like someone were hunting her down and she couldn't get away. Me, I didn't know what to think. Jimmie was gone. He'd always been sort of a whiner, but I knew I should be feeling sorry. After all, he was a good friend, my oldest friend, and it was at least partly my fault, what with my laughing fit and what had happened earlier between us in the kitchen.

But lately everything was just numb. I was always the joker, even back when the sky was still blue and rats couldn't open latched doors and everything was all right with the world.

Now it seemed like the jokes were gone and I was still laughing, like some kind of crazy-ass clown making pie faces at cancer victims.

I just didn't know when to stop.

Maybe I should go back to the beginning. Back when the world was sane. If that were ever really the case; because if you think about it, sanity never had anything to do with a thing like this, and looking back it's clear to me that we were teetering on the edge of oblivion for a long, long time.

Maybe it just took the right group of crazies to actually push the button.

Hell, maybe I was one of them.

PART ONE:
SPARROW ROCK

"It's the end of the world as we know it, and I feel fine."
—R.E.M.

CHAPTER ONE

It's ironic when I think of how it all went down. I mean, how we ended up in the hole. We weren't exactly channeling Nostradamus. We were nothing but a bunch of horny teenagers, looking for a place to smoke and drink and bitch about our shitty lives. We got together to hang out at least once a week in those days, and we didn't know it then, but we were about to grow up in a hurry.

News flash: I'd had a fight with my mother. Back then it always seemed like she was looking for ways to get on me about something I should be doing. I didn't study enough, didn't focus enough, didn't know what I wanted to do with my life. I didn't see how much she was hurting, how she loved me and sacrificed for me or what a fuckup I must have seemed to everyone else. I was almost eighteen and high school was just about over and all I wanted to do was hang out with my friends and have a little fun before life moved in for the kill.

Lord knows, my life hadn't been all fun and games. The thing was, my mom was sick. She'd had progressive multiple sclerosis since she was in her early twenties, diagnosed before she had me. It's a slow disease, but living with my alcoholic father didn't help matters much, and by the time the bombs dropped, she was in a wheelchair and heavy drugs were all that kept the pain away.

We were close, as close as a teenage boy could possibly be with his mother without turning into Norman Bates or something. During the hard times with my father she was the only thing that kept me sane, and deep down I knew it. But lately things had changed. Maybe I felt burdened by having to do more at home, maybe I just didn't want to listen, or maybe I was just an asshole. But it seemed like the fighting was getting worse and neither one of us knew how to stop it anymore.

That particular night my mother wanted me to write a letter to a professor she knew at Bates College, letting him know how much I wanted to be a "Bates man." I wanted to catch up with Jimmie and debate the quality of the reefer we'd pinched from Jay's older sister. The reefer won.

"It's your *future*," she'd said, pleading with me as we argued in the kitchen. As if I didn't know that. "We've worked so hard—"

"We?" I said. "I didn't see *you* sitting in on any of my classes. Doing the homework, taking exams." The thing was, I knew what she'd been through to get me to this point, and I knew exactly what she meant. But it still pissed me off, and even though I was aware that I was wrong in taking the conversation down this particular path, I couldn't stop myself.

She sighed. "You've been through a heck of a lot more than most kids," she said, rolling her chair closer and reaching out to touch my arm. "I understand that. But you have to rise above it, Petey, and stop being so self-destructive. You have to—"

"Don't call me that!" I said, recoiling away from her. "It drives me nuts." It was her pet name for me, but it made me feel like a child. I wanted to be my own man, and I felt her holding me back, the weight of responsibility like a chain around my neck.

"You never told me that before—"

"Yeah, well, things change. I need space to breathe, Mom. Just leave me the hell alone."

My mother rolled away from me and crossed her arms over her chest. "I'm not going to be around forever," she said quietly. A blush had crept into her cheeks, and I knew I'd hurt her badly. "I want to make sure you're okay."

"I can handle it."

She nodded. "I know you can. I know it. But you were always my little baby. You're fragile too, Pete. Sometimes I need to save you from yourself. I know that too."

After dinner she rolled herself into her room and took the wine bottle with her, and I knew I wouldn't see her again that night (after my father died, she'd taken to doing this quite a bit). So I snuck out the window, figuring I'd be back in again in an hour or two. *Bye-bye, Mom. If the end of the world comes, don't wait up for me.*

Jimmie was down the block in his red and gray Bondo '98 Mustang, tapping his fingers against the wheel to some old song by The Who as Tessa and I arrived. We drove to McDonald's for a shake and fries. Big Sue and Jay were already there, and we all spent the next half an hour sitting around a table and making fun of Dan, who was working the counter.

"Wear the little hat," I told him. "It makes you look really buff."

He flipped me the bird and stomped into the back. "How about the hairnet, then, big boy?" I called after him.

Dan and I met playing baseball for the eighth-grade team. I thought of myself as a dabbler in sports, a utility guy coordinated enough to make the team, not good enough to start, more nerd than jock. But I tried hard enough and wanted to fit in. Dan, on the other hand, was a multisport athlete, the kind where hitting a ball with a stick or throwing a pass seemed effortless. I used to watch him toss from the outfield to home plate as if the ball were on a string, whacking into the catcher's mitt with a sound like a boxer hitting the heavy bag. I admired the hell out of him for it, although I'd never admit it to his face. He wasn't much of a student, but he never pretended to be, and later on when we all entered high school I introduced him to Jimmie and Sue and Jay, and we all just sort of fell in together. Maybe I was the bridge between them, but Dan quickly took on a leadership role, and that was fine with the rest of us, even if I did give him a hard time every once in a while.

If I knew then what I know now, maybe I wouldn't have found Dan so easy to tease. Hell, maybe I would have done a lot of things differently. But I didn't, and I can't exactly take it back. As my mother would say, *what's done is done; work on what's to come.*

"Are those new Vans?" I asked Tessa, while Jimmie, Big Sue and Jay were in line buying items off the dollar menu. She had these cute little doll feet, and I knew her nails were painted red underneath because she wore sandals a lot. I guess you could say I loved Tessa, in some purely wholesome way (I swear), but then again, half the world might say the same, if they saw her the way I did. She was barely over five feet tall, with these huge dark eyes and expressive mouth, and she probably weighed all of a hundred pounds. In those days I often wondered why she bothered to hang with me. She'd moved in next door right around the time of my father's death, and we had become close friends pretty quickly. She didn't seem to mind my weirdness and humor at the most inappropriate moments, and she didn't mind my friends. The obvious answer was that she had a crush on Dan, but she'd never shown much interest in him. Maybe it was the pot.

Anyway, these new shoes of hers were red and black with pink laces, all the rage these days. The sides had a skull-and-crossbones pattern. "Designed them myself on-line," she said with a small half smile. "You like?"

"They're cool. I was thinking of getting some Skechers if I can save up."

She wrinkled her nose. "Skechers are so out, Pete."

"As in 'so out they're coming back again'?"

"Nice try, but no."

"What are you talking about?" Jimmie said. He was back from line with a trayful of Mickey D goodness, looking confused.

"Skechers, dipshit," I said. "I was thinking of getting some."

"Mischa Barton was wearing them on E! last night, eh," Jimmie said. He had this annoying habit of saying "eh" at the end of a sentence as if he were Canadian or something. "They even made a point of talking about it."

"Probably paid her a million bucks," I said. "And what the hell were you doing watching E!?"

"I think Mischa's hot."

"Sure, if you like twelve-year-old anorexic boys."

"Where are we going to get high?" Jay said, plopping back down in his seat. He was all business when it came to pot. He was voted the most likely to end up in rehab. I think he needed it to take the edge off. His parents put more pressure on him than anyone, because he was egghead smart and was headed to Yale. His dad was a grad, and his older sister too, and Yale banners and books were displayed all over the house like a roadmap they'd put up for Jay's life. Talk about pressure, all right. All that was missing was the huge, blinking neon arrow: THIS WAY TO THE PSYCH WARD.

Jay was a conspiracy theorist. If you asked him about

the government, he'd get this glint in his eye and go off on top-secret organizations and futuristic weaponry and spy satellites and plots to control the world. I look at all that pretty differently now; but back then, I just laughed it off or made fun of him, the way I did most everything.

The joker, the class clown. The shrink I went to for a week called that a defense mechanism. I called him a few names bad enough to keep me from going back there ever again. A good shrink might have smiled and nodded and pointed out that my defenses were raised yet again, but this guy was lousy and I think we both knew it. I was probably better off in the end.

We went through the usual locations as we ate, all of them getting vetoed for various reasons. Then Sue spoke up. "My grandfather finished the shelter last week," she said.

The table fell silent. "That crazy bastard," I said. "Someone ought to tell him the USSR is long gone. What's he afraid of, anyway?"

"North Korea, I think. They've got nuclear weapons that can hit us from over there. He read about it on the Net."

"There are worse things than North Korea," Jay said, tucking some of his long, unruly black hair behind his ears and glancing at Sue. Smart as he was, he'd usually say the grass was purple if Sue said it first. But this was right in his wheelhouse. He pushed his large round glasses up on the bridge of his nose, looking remarkably like that actor who played Harry Potter in all those billion-dollar movies (I even used to call him Potter for a while, as a joke, until he told me he hated it. I might be a smart-ass, but I'd like to think I'm not a complete jerk).

"Underground terrorist groups have been secretly testing long-range missiles," he said, "and we already know they've got nukes. And worse than that too."

"So? We've got a missile shield, right?" Jimmie said. "Shoot the fuckers out of the sky."

"It's not that simple."

"Why not?" Jimmie made a noise like a firing rocket, and pantomimed his two hands coming together. "Bam," he said. "Just like that. Gone."

Dan had appeared from out of the back at some point during the conversation. His shift was over, and now he stood over us, letter jacket in hand, like a guy who's ready to bolt at a moment's notice. I knew he hated this job, and only did it because he needed the money. Football was his true passion. But high school was almost over, and he wasn't going to college. No athletic scholarships for players from little Podunk schools like ours, and his grades were lousy. He was like the guy who worked all day in the paper mill and lived for the weekends, drinking himself silly down at the bar with his buddies. I wondered if he might just become that paper mill guy, in a few more years.

He punched me in the shoulder a little too hard, and I pretended not to feel it. It was our little game, I guess. Hurt like a son of a bitch. Some game.

"Who cares about North Korea or a bunch of third-world terrorists? The shelter's probably stacked with food and it's empty. Is that your point, Sue?"

"I know how to get in," she said. "He's asleep by now. Nobody will see us."

We looked at each other across the table. Jay nodded. Tessa just smiled. That was the end of the discussion.

We all jumped into Jimmie's car and headed out to the island.

CHAPTER TWO

Sparrow Island. I still think back on that drive, and what might have happened if we'd switched on the radio. Would we have turned back and run home to our families? Would I have died huddled under the dining room table with my mother beside me? Or would we have realized it was too late and just kept going, aware that there was nothing else we could do to stay alive except get to Sparrow Rock?

But we didn't turn on the radio, and we didn't know what was coming, and so we ended up crossing the bridge and turning onto the long driveway that led to the Myers estate about fifteen minutes later.

I want you to understand something here. We'd all known each other for a long time. Hell, I'd known Jimmie since the first day of kindergarten. We sat next to each other in those little plastic chairs, the kind that stick to your legs after coming in all hot and sweaty from recess. That very first day, I'd felt sorry for him when the teacher pointed to a letter on the board and he didn't know it, and so I leaned over and whispered the answer in his ear. Of course the teacher saw it and gave me a lecture. But Jimmie appreciated my effort all the same.

You know about Dan and me already, and the rest of the gang I'd met freshman year of high school in some class or another, and we'd been friends ever since. So we knew each other pretty well, all right. But we were kids. When you're a kid, saying you're friends means you know what kind of soda they like, and the TV shows they watch and whether they want to drive a Mustang or a Volkswagen. You might know something embarrassing they did once, or whom they have a crush on, or whether they pick their nose. But you don't know who they really *are*. The private thoughts they don't share with anyone. The dreams they don't want to let into the world. Things that make them bleed inside.

So I guess I should say we thought we knew each other, but we were wrong. That was the way it was among all of us, before Sparrow Rock.

Sue's grandpa, Scott Myers, had bought the eighty-acre island just off the coast years ago and built a bridge and an entire complex at the foot of the Rock, spending a chunk of the huge pile of cash he'd made in the lumber business back in the fifties. He was slowly losing his grip, but that didn't keep the contractors from taking his money. The latest extravagance was the bomb shelter, which had probably cost him ten times what my father had made in a year, and which would sit, gathering dust, until one hundred years from now someone else saw fit to fill in the hole.

At least, that was the way we saw it then.

We'd all been eagerly waiting for the day they finished the shelter. We'd witnessed various stages of its construction, although none of us had been out here in weeks. But facing it now, as a bone-shivering mist drifted in off the water, I felt vaguely disappointed. There was nothing but a round submarine-style hatch set into a ring of concrete at the base of Sparrow Rock to mark its presence.

On a good day you could stand at the top of the Rock and get a clean look at the mainland. If the air were calm and clear you could make out the faces of the people who would sometimes stop their cars and stare across at the construction on the other side. There was probably no more than a hundred yards of open water between them. But they never came over, these gawkers. They knew that there was nothing but Scott Myers's place over here, and Grandpa Myers did not take kindly to uninvited guests. As far as I knew he had yet to actually shoot at someone who trespassed on his property, but the rumor was there were more than a few who had personally witnessed the barrel end of his shotgun.

There was something strange about Grandpa Myers, I had to admit. He was one of those guys who commanded instant respect, but with a healthy dose of fear mixed in too. When you met him you got the feeling he was capable of just about anything. Something in his eyes, maybe. Some of it was the money, sure. Although we never talked much to Sue about it, we were all pretty sure he was worth more than God. When you had that much money you had to be careful, and you probably developed a pretty severe case of paranoia too. Everyone was after you for something.

I always felt Sue was just a little bit afraid of him, and maybe I understood that a little better than I was willing to admit at the time. She loved him, of course, and he sure did love her. Sue's parents were divorced and her father had been missing in action for years, so maybe her grandfather felt like she needed special care. But he was getting older, and this whole bomb-shelter thing made it seem like he was losing his marbles. What we found out later made everything make some kind of twisted sense, but Sue would have been the last person to talk about any of that then.

We stood now staring down at this metal hatch, and I

couldn't help wondering if this was a mistake. A guy like that catches you out here messing with his stuff, even if he likes you—what might he do to you? The stories about that shotgun came to mind. But Sue was with us, and I guess it made me feel safe enough. After all, she was family. You see, as friends of Big Sue, we were the chosen ones. As far as Grandpa Myers was concerned, we were welcome. Everyone else could go to hell, and the faster the better.

"He tunneled thirty feet down into granite," Sue said. "It's stocked. Fully operational, the lights, air, water, everything. There's enough food in there to feed a family for months."

Sparrow Rock loomed over us, a boulder of immense proportions, the tip of an otherwise sleeping giant buried in the topsoil. Grandpa Myers's house sat silently a few hundred feet away, a hulking, industrial-looking tank of a place on the water's edge, its small, square windows dark and empty.

Tessa whistled softly, her little lips pursed, arms crossed beneath her breasts in the cold. I caught a whiff of the salt air mixed with sweet perfume as Sue touched a keypad set into the rock, and a faint hissing sound rose up into the night.

Dan twisted the hatch and swung it open. Sue leaned down, hit a switch, and several bulbs set into the wall and protected by wire cages blinked on. We faced a short ladder, concrete landing and a set of descending stairs that led to somewhere beyond our sight.

"Age before beauty," I said, and elbowed Jimmie in the middle of his scrawny back. The smell of earth and concrete wafted up now from the hole. It felt vaguely like a crypt to me. Maybe it was that smell, or the look of the narrow hole, or the huge rock looming over us all in the dark, but I suddenly wanted no part of our little plan. I think

Jimmie had the same feeling, because he took a step back. But Jay just pushed his way between us, swung onto the ladder and dropped to the top of the steps.

"What a bunch of pussies," Dan said. "No offense, Sue." He followed Jay into the hole. Big Sue followed him, then Tessa, and after staring at each other for a minute and feeling like idiots, Jimmie shrugged and we went down too.

The steps led down to a carpeted and paneled room maybe fifteen feet across, with a farmer's table and six chairs in the middle. A row of shelves held blankets, pillows, clothing, books, a first-aid kit, flashlights, batteries and a bunch of other stuff all stored in clear plastic containers. A thirteen-inch LCD television with DVD player had been mounted in one corner of the ceiling.

"All the comforts of home," Dan said, ducking back through a doorway with the TV remote in his big paw. "Cable works. Tons of food in there too. Munchies, anyone?"

Sue gave us the full tour. The kitchen was pretty small but held everything the most demanding bomb-shelter owner might require: tiled floor, refrigerator, stove, microwave, toaster, sink, even a dishwasher and trash compactor. A huge pantry off the kitchen was crammed with (among other things) flour and sugar, protein drinks and energy bars, cans of soups and vegetables, tuna and Spam, dehydrated military meals, dried meat and fruits, crackers, hard candy, powdered milk and gallons of water. Another room held three twin bunk beds, and the single bathroom contained a handicapped-accessible shower, toilet and sink.

"There's an underground water tank to supply the bathroom and kitchen," Big Sue said. "It recycles, I think. This place has its own septic system too."

"No shit," I said. Nobody seemed to get the joke, or if

they did they didn't want to give me the satisfaction of a reaction.

I didn't know jack about bomb shelters, but this one seemed like the deluxe model to me. I had the vague idea of little tin cans buried in the ground with a hole in the floor for a toilet and jugs of warm water that tasted like plastic. The kind of place you wanted to leave as soon as possible. This was like a five-star hotel by comparison, and would suit our needs for the evening just fine.

The smell of pot had started wafting in from the other room. We wandered back in that direction. Jay was sitting at the table, joint in one hand, eyes closed, half smile on his face. Smoking pot was the only time I ever saw him relax, and he was getting his groove on good this time. Must have been a bitch of a day.

Big Sue dug around the shelves and found a pack of cards, while I went into the pantry and started rifling through the food. When I returned with a bag of chips, beef jerky, a bottle of soda and plastic cups, the gang had already started playing a hand of poker around the table. "Deal me in," I said. "Prepare to be annihilated."

I got a pair of threes in the first hand. Just my luck. But then things got a bit better. The joint made the rounds several times, and less than an hour later we were all feeling pretty good.

"You're all straight guys, right?" Sue said, after winning a hand with a royal flush.

"Last time I checked," Jimmie said.

"All right, Jimmie. If you and your girlfriend were the last people on earth, would you make a baby?"

"Obviously a hypothetical question," I said. "What with the girlfriend and the possibility of sex and all." Jimmie threw a piece of jerky at me.

"No, seriously, would you bring a child into a world like that?"

Sue was always coming up with this stuff. She was a philosopher and an environmentalist, which I thought was probably the most dangerous combination imaginable.

"Come on, Sue," Dan said. "That's shit. You're making my head hurt."

"I don't know," Jimmie said. "What's the world like? Where'd everybody go?"

"Let's say it's been wiped out by a disease and you're immune. But you don't know if the baby would be."

"That's a different question," I said, getting into it. My brain buzzed slightly, my mouth coated with fuzz. "You're talking about risking the child's life."

"It's a question of moral responsibility," Jay said. "You owe it to the human race to procreate."

"Something like that isn't a duty," Tessa said. "And what if one person wants to and the other doesn't? You can't just force it. It takes two people to make a child, unless you're talking about rape."

"Deal the fucking hand," Dan said irritably. "'Moral responsibility' my ass. I have to be home by midnight. I don't have time for this bullshit."

"Pot's supposed to mellow you out," I said. "So, let's say you both agree to go for it. If the baby survives, it has to grow up in a world without people? And Jay, fucking genius that you are, you fail to point out that you'd have to make two babies, a boy and girl, to save the human race, and then you'd be asking a brother and sister to do the nasty."

"That's disgusting, eh," said Jimmie. "You've got a fucked-up mind, you know that?"

"Somebody has to think of these things. I just elected myself king of the pervs."

We all looked at Jay. A bunch of students looking to the teacher for the correct answer. "I'm telling you, you'd end up having the child," Jay said. "It's human nature. You can't stop it, even if you wanted to."

A look passed between Big Sue and Jay, just a moment of eye contact, but it was there. They'd been gravitating closer together lately, and I wondered if something might be going on. Sue was tall and a little overweight and Jay was a serious geek, but stranger things have happened.

That was when the slight tremor ran through the shelter.

CHAPTER THREE

I felt the tremor low in the core of my body, a vibration that coursed down my arms and legs and made my fingers and toes tingle. Then it was gone.

"What was that?" Dan said. Nobody answered him. I mean, it could have been anything. We all waited in silence for about a minute. Another tremor rattled the shelves. Something crashed to the floor in the kitchen and rolled across the concrete.

I've never had a feeling of dread like I did at that moment. Like I said, I couldn't figure out why, but I knew that something was seriously wrong. Looking back now, it seems like I already knew then that the world was ending, that we'd never see the clear skies or calm water or smell fresh-cut grass again. Maybe that's what ESP is all about; simply a low-level feeling of unease just before the shit hits the proverbial fan. But I suppose it's more likely that it was nothing more than the cannabis rearing its ugly head.

The crazy thing was, coincidence or not, this time that paranoia was dead-on.

"Turn on the TV," I said. Dan stood on a chair and the television blinked on. The pleasantly warm buzz from the pot was gone now. My whole body had suddenly gone into fight-or-flight mode. Every hair stood on end.

We all sat and stared at the static on-screen, looked at

each other in silence as the weight and impact of that one simple image sunk in.

I checked my cell phone; no signal. "Maybe it's not hooked up," I said.

"I checked it before," Dan said. He flipped through the channels, one by one, faster and faster. They all held nothing but snow.

"What's going on, man," Jimmie said. A whine had crept into his voice.

This time the whole shelter shuddered. Dan tumbled from the chair and my heart leaped into my throat and thudded so hard I could barely breathe. The lights flickered. A strange purplish glow filtered down from the direction of the stairs. I heard a roaring, rushing sound that was somewhere between river rapids and a jet engine. The light from the stairway turned bright pink, then blindingly white.

Someone screamed. Maybe it was me.

"The hatch," Dan shouted. He reached out and shook me hard, screamed spittle into my face. *Did you close the fucking hatch?*

I shook my head no, and Dan pounded up the stairs and into the teeth of that sound like some terrible, angry god rising above us. I followed him and we climbed to our feet in the dirt and stared off over the water.

I don't know exactly how to describe what we saw. Night had turned to day. It was like the inside of a lava lamp, mixed with one of those static-electricity plasma globes. The sky at the horizon line was a mixture of bright whites and purples and blacks. The center of the light burned so brightly I threw up an arm to shield my eyes. A huge cloud mushroomed skyward like a pulsing bruise; I turned and saw another, and another. The air was unnaturally hot and humid, and the sound we'd heard downstairs continued to swell. Now it sounded like a thousand tiny voices screaming.

I stood there, at the edge of the abyss, at the end of all time, and I laughed. What are the odds, some part of my mind was thinking. Nuclear Armageddon, and we happen to be holed up in a bomb shelter. The voice sounded hysterical to me. It went on and on. I laughed into that hot wind, but it swallowed up the sound of my voice until I could not be sure I was there at all. I did not know if I even existed anymore.

Finally I realized that the voice was no longer in my head, it was coming from me.

"Oh my god Oh my god *Oh my god Ohmygod ohmygod-ohmygod—*"

"Get inside," Dan said. He didn't say it loud but I heard him anyway. I realized that I hadn't been laughing out loud at all. My face was wet, my eyes burned as I blinked away spots of light. A hot breath of air rushed across my skin as everything seemed to be sucked away from us, like the retreating tide just before a tsunami approached at hurricane speed.

"Get the fuck inside now!" He gave me a rough shove. I scrambled clumsily back down the ladder until my hands lost their grip and I fell off the last few rungs onto my back. The impact rattled my teeth and snapped my skull back hard enough to make stars swim across my vision. Dan swung the hatch shut from the ladder and locked it, cutting off the sound and light from above all at once. In its place was a faint humming sound like high-tension wires on a summer day.

I blinked up into the swirling dust as he landed on his feet next to me.

"Tell me we did not just see that," I said. My voice shook with the effort of speech. My tongue had thickened in my mouth. "Please tell me this is a joke. *Please*. Please, please, Jesus God."

"No joke, Pete. Now get up. We need to get downstairs."

"We've got to do something, we've got to get help—"

"There's no help!" he screamed at me. "Nothing we can do out there now, understand? The only thing we can do is stay where it's safe, and see about the others."

I stared at him, and he stared at me. Something shook the earth above our heads. I opened my mouth and closed it again. My whole body trembled so violently my teeth chattered. I felt like laughing hysterically. I felt like I needed to say something, but I didn't know what.

Ultimately there was nothing to say, nothing to do except go back and try to explain to the rest what it was we had seen. Suddenly I had to be with Tessa, had to make sure she was all right. Nothing in the world was more important at that moment, and I jumped and stumbled down the stairs.

Sue and Jay were huddled together, arms around each other. Tears streaked Sue's face. Jay's glasses sat on the table and his eyes were closed. Jimmie stood on a chair and kept pressing the television's buttons, cycling through channels, over and over, muttering something I couldn't make out.

Tessa sat hugging herself. She looked up at me as I came down, and it almost broke my heart. I wanted to move, wanted to say something to comfort her, but I couldn't speak.

"It's a nuclear strike," Dan said, to nobody in particular. "Multiple hits. I counted at least three from where we stood."

I will never, as long as I live, be able to understand how he could be so infuriatingly calm when he said it.

A high keening noise slipped from Sue's mouth. Her

knuckles turned white as she gripped Jay's shirt. "No. Oh, no. *No*."

"You're wrong," Jimmie said in a voice that cracked and rose just slightly. He jumped down from the chair. "What are you, fucking crazy? It's just thunderclouds or something. You dumb fucking shit. Lemme see." He moved toward the stairs. Dan stepped in front of him.

"Dan's right," I said. "Oh, God. *God*. I mean it. You can't go out there. You *can't*."

"Fuck off." He tried to elbow past us. Dan grabbed him in a bear hug and pinned his arms to his sides. Jimmie let out a choked sob and thrashed like a netted fish as something rose up within him and tried to break free. "My father, he wants me home. My dad—he, he needs me. My *father*—oh, Jesus, *Daddddeeeee*—"

"Shhhh," Dan said, as he held the other boy tightly in his arms. "Easy, Jimmie, take it easy."

Something hurt deep down inside my belly. My shaky legs gave out and I sat down heavily on the bottom step as the world tilted and slipped into gray, watching them struggle with each other, engaged in a strange sort of dance made in hell. Tessa came over and sat next to me. I felt her arm slip around my waist and I leaned into her, my heart pounding, my mouth full of cotton.

Then the lights went out.

Sue screamed. In that absolute blackness the terror seemed all the more real, the heaviness of the air close and suffocating, and I snapped back to life. There was sudden, immediate panic within the group. I lost track of where people were, heard a body hitting the floor.

But a few moments later a battery-powered lantern flickered on, and Dan placed it in the middle of the table, bathing us in a slightly bluish light. How he'd remembered where it was in all the confusion, I'll never know. I went to where Jimmie had fallen like a crash-test dummy from Dan's embrace and pulled him to his feet again. We all huddled around the light like moths drawn to flame.

Within my own shock I had a terrible sense of helplessness. I kept trying to picture what was happening up on the surface, and Tessa probably did too, because she kept asking me if it was true, over and over again. She wanted to know what it looked like out there; she begged me to tell her. I don't remember what I said, but whatever it was she didn't believe it. She started hitting me and I sat down on a chair and let her do it. I watched her tear-streaked face lit from the side by the light of the lantern as she swung at my head and body. Days after that my cheeks were still swollen and my arms and shoulders hurt when I moved them.

Eventually she pulled away from me. I grabbed hold and hugged her so tightly it probably looked like I were trying to fold Tessa's body into my own. Then we went over to Jay and Sue and put our arms around them, and we all rocked together, trying to draw strength from each other while the world crashed and burned around us.

It was all we could do, this simple, grasping act of humanity within such madness. If we had known that this was only the beginning, perhaps we would have ended it all right there.

But we didn't, and so we clung to all we had left, and tried as best we could to shut out the truth for just a few minutes longer.

CHAPTER FOUR

"We need a radio," Dan said. "Maybe someone's still broadcasting."

"A fucking radio," Jimmie muttered in a flat, dead voice. "That's the big plan?" He was just a dim shape rocking in the corner under the TV, knees drawn up to his chest and his back against the wall.

We'd left our group embrace and had been sitting silently in our own places in the room for maybe twenty minutes. It felt like forever.

"No, he's right," Tessa said, hope blooming in her mascara-streaked face. "My God, he's right. I think I saw one in the bedroom. *Someone's* got to still be alive."

"What about more light?" I asked. The shadows were getting to me; I kept thinking I saw things moving in them. My mind was up to its old dirty tricks again, and I kept thinking I saw my father's face in the twists and folds of light and dark among the shelves. It used to happen to me a lot right after his accident. I'd see his twisted, broken body lying somewhere close and it was like I was dreaming while I was awake. I thought he was gone from my life the day he died, but I was wrong. He never really left.

"There's a . . . a backup generator," Sue said. I didn't have the heart to ask her why she'd waited until now to tell us. "A buried tank with enough fuel to keep it running for weeks too, if we conserve it well enough."

"There'll be a switch," Jay said, nodding. "Like an oil-burner cutoff. Located near the electrical panel. Maybe in a closet."

We went at the search with a single-minded determination that barely concealed the desperation we all felt. A minute or two later, Jay let out a shout, and we all piled into the little kitchen, where he stood in the near darkness by a small access panel set into the wall inside the pantry. He flipped a switch and something hummed into life. The overhead lights blinked on, and we cried and screamed and hugged each other with relief. Light was life; light meant power, and strength, and my God, it was human. A little bit of control had just been returned to us and it felt damned good.

Dan went around and turned off everything that didn't absolutely need to be running. Sue found the radio and we sat at the table and went through the frequencies, but got nothing except static.

"Do it again," Jay said. "Slowly."

"Maybe there's too much concrete," Sue said.

"They're dead, you fucking cow," Jimmie said, without looking at her. His voice held the same dull and flat and mean tone it'd had before. "They're all dead, eh? Everyone's gone."

Nobody said anything to him, and nobody defended Sue, not even Jay. We sat without speaking, listening to the static and feeling the hope that had bloomed with such suddenness slowly fade away, until I started hearing ghost voices through the hiss.

They weren't real; it was like seeing patterns of the Virgin Mary in grilled cheese sandwiches. But all the same, it seemed like they were talking to me, in a voice just a fraction too low to make out. I thought I heard my name. I thought, for just one moment, that it was my mother.

. . . Pete . . . hurts . . .

Guilt washed over me. Guilt for my father, and for me leaving my disabled mother alone. Guilt for the terrible fight we'd had just before I left, for leaving her with that final memory, and for generally being such a shitty son. I blinked away more tears, reached over and flicked off the radio. The silence that followed was worse.

"You were talking about the end of the world," Jimmie said. "Just before it happened. About raising children after everyone had died. Why, Sue? *Why would you say that?*"

"I don't know," she whispered. "God help me, I don't."

"It's like you jinxed us or something. The fuck—"

"Leave her alone," I said. I didn't like the strain in his voice, the way his eyes kept darting around the room without fixing on anyone. Jimmie shrugged and licked his lips, but he didn't say anything else.

"If it was al-Qaeda, they had help," Jay said, as if to fill the empty air. "My money's on a Russian-based terrorist group. Their military doctrine has always stressed striking first. They feel that a nuclear war can be won. There have even been rumors that they've been preparing something ever since Bush started building a missile defense system."

"But their economy's shit," Dan said. "We tore down the wall and they went to hell. They're a fucking third-world country."

"In some ways, maybe. But they've still got a lot of warheads, and there's a terrible resentment against the United States. Put that together with a larger terrorist network, and you've got big trouble."

"What difference does it make?" Tessa said. "I mean, seriously, why do we care who it was?"

Jay took off his glasses and rubbed the lenses with his shirt. The effect was ludicrous, really. I mean, here we were, sitting around discussing the situation like a bunch of fucking preppies in a Starbucks, only we weren't talking about the latest 3-series from BMW, we were discussing a nuclear strike.

Jimmie looked like he might start screaming at any moment.

God, it was so *quiet*.

"Hey," I said, "we don't know anything for sure, okay? We don't even know how far it went. Maybe the strike just hit New England. Hell, maybe it's not a strike at all, maybe Seabrook Station went up. There's no point in doing this right now, not before we know more."

"What color did you see out there, Pete?" Jay asked. He'd put his glasses on again, and except for the dirty streaks on his face he looked like the old Jay, seriously bookish. I felt some sort of comfort in seeing it.

"The sky was purple, black and a pinkish white," I said.

"Does your face feel sunburned?"

"A little," I admitted, touching the skin of my cheeks carefully. Of course, Tessa had been beating on me pretty good, so it might have been her too. I kept that to myself.

"An electromagnetic pulse would disrupt radio traffic," Jay said, almost to himself. "It'll be getting dark now. Dust and radioactive waste is in the atmosphere, blocking out the sun. Mass fires. Near the point of impact nothing's left standing. Craters a few hundred feet deep by a couple thousand feet wide. I'm guessing that the closest strike was at least ten miles from here. Much closer and you'd have second- or third-degree burns on your faces. But the shock waves still would have reached this far, blown out windows, started fires. The hatch may be buried in debris." He paused, looked at Dan, then at me. "You may have been exposed."

"How bad?" I said, my mouth suddenly filled with cotton. I wanted to go find my mother and bury my head in her lap, like I did when I was a little boy. The thought of my mother again made me want to cry. I hadn't thought of her in that way, as a source of comfort, in a while. Now it hurt so much I couldn't stand another second.

I didn't want to listen to him. But I had to know.

"It's hard to say. Minimal levels, probably. Not enough to kill you. May lose some hair, or get a few skin sores. Or maybe not." Jay sighed, rubbed at his eyes under his glasses. "Depends on the type of blast and the size of the warhead. But nobody can go outside. It was fairly calm today but once the radioactive waste gets up into the atmosphere it will spread out for miles. The fallout will kill a lot more people."

"How long are we talking about being down in this hole?" I said. "A couple of weeks?"

Jay seemed to struggle with his control, and when he spoke the strain was clear. "I don't think you understand, any of you. One warhead would destroy a city, cause hundreds of thousands of deaths for miles around. Fallout would make the area uninhabitable for weeks, maybe more. But what you described up there—three, maybe more hits at once even in this area—that's Armageddon. Full-scale nuclear war."

He looked at each of us in turn, shook his head. "We're talking about the end of civilization."

CHAPTER FIVE

Until that moment, when Jay brought it home for us, I don't think we had a real idea of what we were about to face.

In the adrenaline rush of a life-threatening situation, there's no time to think of the implications. It is only afterward, in the long silence that follows, that nightmares really begin.

But we were just children really, and maybe that saved us from losing our minds that long first night. We didn't know what death was, or how close it could be. We didn't have a grasp of our lives having a clear end point and finite length. Life is funny like that; just about the time you're able to fully appreciate the accommodations, you're checking out of the hotel.

We really didn't know if there were survivors out there. We didn't know if they'd be looking for us. But then Sue told us about the beacon that her grandfather had installed. Set to go off automatically when it sensed a severe atmospheric shift on the surface, it would broadcast a repeated SOS until someone came to shut it off.

We found that lifeline and we clung to it. It gave us a reason to go on, to prepare for some kind of rescue.

Still, as the first few hours passed down in the hole the

idea that we didn't really know what was happening top-side kept eating at me. I didn't doubt that some sort of nuclear attack had occurred; after all, I'd seen the evidence with my own eyes. My brain kept trying frantically to scrub it away (*maybe I'm imagining how bad it was, maybe I'm going crazy*), but the images remained, burned into my memory.

I wondered whether humankind had survived at all, and if so, whether cleanup had already begun. With the confusion they would surely face in such an effort, would they really come for us? Isolated as we were down here, how would we know the truth?

It was the ultimate irony: we couldn't know for sure unless we ventured outside. But we could not risk opening that hatch.

Sue and Jay huddled together for a while that night, holding each other and whispering things I couldn't make out. Dan fiddled with the radio for a long time, looking for a signal, and then he paced the room, as if deep in thought. I sat in a chair and tried my best not to think at all. But that was impossible, and I found myself going over the last few hours before the strike, my last words to my mother, our time at the restaurant, the drive to Sparrow Island. I kept searching for something we'd done wrong, something we might have changed, a clue we should have caught. But, of course, there was nothing. And what good would it have done, even if there had been a warning?

And there was something else, something I was trying to avoid facing at all costs. That I could have been exposed. That I could be, even now, dying one cell at a time.

Sometime later Tessa came over to me. I stood up. She didn't say anything at first, just touched my cheek where a purple bruise had spread. Her fingertips were hot and dry as she traced the pattern of my flesh. "I'm sorry I hit you," she whispered. A tear trickled down her face, and she pressed her lips together. Then she hugged me. We stood there for what seemed like forever, just holding on to each other.

When I was six years old, a blizzard hit White Falls and covered our house with nearly three feet of snow. The power had gone out about an hour into the storm and with our nearest neighbor a half mile away, and nobody moving from where they'd dug in, we had no idea how long we would be stranded. My mother estimated that the plows wouldn't come through until the middle of the following morning.

I didn't like being locked up in the house. From the haunted, blood-starved look on her face, I could tell my mother didn't like it either.

But my father was a different story. It was as if the storm had breathed life into his otherwise pale existence. Jeff Taylor's eyes grew brighter and his face flushed a healthy pink. He went around sipping his usual rum and Coke and humming a Beatles tune, his steps speeded up and more purposeful than before. The cruelty that was normally present in him was gone.

That day might have been the most excited I'd ever seen him. He went from window to window, staring out into the swirling blizzard and grunting his approval. He pointed out several times how the ice clung to the branches of the trees, and the snow drifted and swelled against tree trunks and brush. I think he liked the idea that there was nothing else alive and moving around out there.

Apparently we weren't enthusiastic enough for him. After a while he took a lantern and went down into the basement and picked up one of his endless woodworking projects, leaving my mother and me upstairs to face the storm alone. We could hear him hammering away down there in the near dark. The moment, that hint of some sort of a connection, had fled.

What is it about isolation that brings certain people to life? What does it say about them? I remember wondering if my father might have been better off if my mother and I had never existed. Maybe it was the pressure of having to provide for his family that pushed his self-destruct button, or maybe it was the thought of someone cracking his shell and finding out who he really was underneath it.

Or maybe, just maybe, he knew he was mortally wounded, and like an animal with a broken leg he was just looking for a place to crawl off by himself and die.

CHAPTER SIX

It was Dan who finally pulled us together and gave us focus. I'd always thought of him as a born leader, mainly because he seemed to lack the imagination the rest of us had, but I realized later it wasn't quite that. Dan was all about action. To make decisions quickly, you couldn't think too much about the consequences, you just had to move fast and keep from second-guessing yourself. It was the same instinct that had served him well on the athletic fields, I suppose.

Of course, nobody is exactly the way others see them from the outside, and I didn't really have a handle on him at all. But at that point, it didn't matter. What mattered was that he was willing to act.

Early the following morning (we knew it was morning only by the clock mounted to the wall), he called us all together. We all sat but he remained standing at the head of the table, assuming a natural position of authority.

While we were all watching, he took a screwdriver from the little toolbox on the shelf and scraped a small, vertical line into the wall near the entrance to the other room. "Day one," he said. "If we're down here for a while, we'll need to keep track."

Day one. We all sat there and thought about that, the implications of lines on the wall, building up day by day until there were groups of six vertical lines with slashes through them, groups of seven at a time marching across the wall and marking the passing of days, weeks, maybe months. It was a pretty primitive way of marking a calendar, but maybe that was Dan's point. If all else failed, power, water, if the batteries all died and we were sitting in the darkness, if we used the last of the paper and pencils, we could still scratch lines to keep track of time passing. Even without all those conveniences, we were still human beings. We were civilized, conscious and capable of order and structure. We were strong.

"Listen up," he said. "We need to approach this situation rationally. Take stock of our supplies and estimate how long we can survive down here. Try to figure out the extent of the damage outside, and who might or might not be coming to help us."

"You forgot praying," I said. "Now's a good time to find God." I was only half kidding. I wasn't particularly religious, but that sounded pretty smart to me at the moment.

"Dan's right," Jay said. "We've got to keep our heads. Disaster-response experts would say the same thing. We should make a list of our options, with all the pros and cons for each. What are the risks for each action? How can we make an informed decision?"

"My grandfather would have thought of everything," Sue said. "He's careful that way. He'll have what we need to keep alive down here."

"But not forever," Dan said. "We have to know how long he planned for, and exactly what we've got. Maybe there's some kind of supplies list. If not, we'll have to make one. Sue, will you do an inventory when we're done here?" She nodded. "Okay. So, assuming we have enough supplies to keep us safe for at least a month, our options are pretty simple. One, we remain where we are for as long as possible, and wait for the radio to work or for someone to come get us. Two, we open that hatch ourselves, stick our necks out and take a look."

"No fucking way," I said. "We both saw what happened out there, Dan."

"I didn't," Jimmie muttered. He'd been so quiet I think we'd all half forgotten he was there. That wasn't like Jimmie at all, and it made me very nervous.

Now he looked up and met my eyes. I saw a mixture of unreasoning hope, anger and pure fear. "How do I know?" he whispered. "You think you're so funny, eh? Maybe you're lying. Maybe this is some kind of big practical joke."

"Believe me, it isn't," Dan said. "What kind of sick fuck would do that?"

Jimmie looked away from me. "Pete, maybe," he said. Then he looked at Dan. "And anyway, who died and put you in charge?"

Ninety-nine percent of the human race, I thought, but didn't say it.

Jay spoke up. "Martial law," he said. "In times of crisis, there must be a clear chain of command or everything will break down. Dan wants the job, I'm not going to stand in his way."

"Me either," I said. "You want it, Jimmie? You think you can do better? And for the record, I may be a joker, but even I know when to stop. This is no joke."

"Fuck you," Jimmie said, and stood up. Veins popped in his skinny neck, and his eyes bulged. He looked around the table. "Fuck all of you."

"Yeah, that makes sense," I said, and I stood up too. "We're the enemy here. We're the ones who blew up your house."

I knew I should have kept quiet but he was pissing me off. As soon as I said it Jimmie sprang at me, hands out and going for my face. It happened so fast I hardly had time to get my arm up to ward off the blow, and the momentum from his body knocked me backward over my chair. I hit the floor hard and my head thudded against the carpet.

Jimmie was like a spitting cat, clawing at me as I tried to push him away.

Then he was gone. I looked up in time to see Dan picking him up by the back of his shirt and slamming him into a chair. "Knock it off!" he shouted. "We're not gonna fight each other, you hear? You hear me?"

Jimmie struggled for a moment, but Dan had him pinned, one big hand on the back of the chair, the other against Jimmie's chest. He gave one final heave and then went limp and started crying, sucking air in great, whooping gasps. Snot hung from his nose. "Sorry," he said, "sorry, I'm sorry . . ."

Dan let him go and turned away to help me up. "I'm all right," I muttered. "I'm okay."

Jimmie wiped a forearm across his face. "Sorry," he said again. His chest hitched like a little kid's after a tantrum. "It's just . . . I just freaked out."

"You're a quick little son of a bitch, you know that?" I said. I made a big show out of squinting at him and rubbing the lump on the back of my head. "And now there's two of you. Great."

Jimmie stared at me for a moment and then he burst out laughing. So did Sue and Tessa. The tension broken, Dan shook his head and sat down.

"Let's take a vote," Sue said, after we'd all calmed down. "Wouldn't that be fair? Who thinks Dan should be in charge?"

We all raised our hands. Even Jimmie.

"Okay," Dan said. "Enough of this horseshit, then. Let's

get down to business. We all heard what Jay said last night. The fallout alone will kill anyone stupid enough to go outside. We can't risk everyone's lives just to take a peek. So that leaves option one."

"What if there was, I don't know, some kind of protection around here?" I felt stupid as soon as I said it, but the words were out. "A suit, something."

"Hazmat suits don't protect against radiation," Jay said. "Biological warfare, yes, but not this kind of attack."

"We stay inside as long as possible, then," Dan said. "But that doesn't mean we can't stay busy. We need to explore every inch of this place, and keep working the radio. We need to conserve food, starting right now, by keeping track of everything we eat. We should make a note of anything we might be able to use, anything at all. Are you with me?"

We all nodded. "Good. Now let's start that list."

CHAPTER SEVEN

We did, indeed, find hazmat suits in a garment bag in the little bedroom closet, and we found a bunch of other stuff too: some spare T-shirts and shorts, a fire extinguisher, rodent and insect killer, more spare batteries, three toothbrushes and six tubes of toothpaste under the bathroom vanity, a pretty extensive medical kit with potassium iodide tablets, Geiger counter, notebooks and pencils, some DVDs and a stack of books. But the most important thing we found hidden behind some blankets on the top shelf in the closet: a .38 snub-nosed Smith & Wesson revolver with two boxes of bullets.

Dan took the gun down and brought it to the table. We stood around staring at it for a while. It was hard to imagine that we suddenly lived in a world where a weapon was a necessity. But I think we all finally realized that the people who came to open our hatch (if anyone came at all) might not be friendly.

Then Dan put the gun away again and we all sat down at the table and talked. We talked about what we would do when the world went back to normal, even though we knew things would never really be normal again. Big Sue said she wanted to go right to Dairy Queen with her mother and get a Blizzard full of peanut butter cups. Tessa said she would cook a big dinner for her friends and then sit around the fire drinking hot chocolate. Jimmie (who seemed to be handling things a little better now) said he would play catch with his dad in the park across the street. Dan wanted go to an action movie with his baby brother and eat a tub of hot buttered popcorn. I wanted to drive to Six Flags and ride the roller coaster.

We all picked things we liked to do as little kids. Maybe that meant something.

Jay didn't say much. He looked different. I saw something in his face that made me think of time passing, as if he had continued moving ahead while we fell back on memories. I don't think he liked what he saw there.

Sometime later, when we had gone over the list of inventory again, separating it into categories and trying to get a handle on how long we could last down in that hole, we all sort of hit the wall at once. I looked around the table at glazed eyes and slack-jawed faces. We were all most likely still in shock, and our brains and bodies were shutting down. We'd been awake, more or less, for over twenty-four hours now. All we had seen, all we had been through, was overwhelming us.

I grabbed a blanket and pillow from the storage shelf and took one of the lower bunks near the closet. Jimmie climbed into the bunk above me, Dan and Jay to my right, and Tessa and Sue in the bunk near the bathroom.

As dead tired as I was, I lay there blinking up into the darkness for a while before I fell asleep. I dreamed I stood on the edge of the water and watched the sky bloom red. Naked people waded toward me. Everyone I knew was there; teachers, family members, friends and neighbors, and their faces were melting like soft clay against a blast furnace. They were screaming at me as their flesh dripped and ran but I could not move. I looked to my right and saw Jay and Dan embracing, and the flesh of their arms ran together and started smoldering. Then they burst into flames.

I woke up and watched Jay climb quietly down from the upper bunk next to me, cross the room and get into the lower bunk with Sue. It was dark, but there was enough light from the lantern in the other room to see shapes. Jimmie was snoring in the bunk above me, and Dan's bed was empty.

Jay whispered something and slipped under the blanket. Sue reached up and traced a pattern on his face as he held himself above her. He leaned down and kissed her, and I heard her sobbing softly as he rocked her in the dark.

I must have drifted off again. When I woke up, someone was sitting on the edge of my bed. The shape was too large to be Tessa. *Sue.* The others were asleep in their beds again. I could hear them breathing.

"Are you scared, Pete?" she asked.

I sat up and touched the tender skin of my cheeks. It was tingling slightly, like a sunburn. "Of course I am. I'd have to be crazy not to be."

"The whole world is crazy! Our lives have been ripped apart and there's nobody to stitch them back together again. And we all just went to sleep."

I glanced around at the huddled forms of my friends. Then I looked at Sue. She looked so vulnerable sitting there. They all did. I guess I was grasping for something, anything that would make her feel better.

"We have each other, Sue," I said. "That's got to count for something. We're going to be fine."

Maybe I wanted her to think I was strong, that I could handle it. But I could tell immediately that I'd made a mistake.

"Fuck that," she said. Anger had bloomed in her plump

face. "You show me how we're fine. How are you fine? You think we're just going to wait a few days, then walk out of here and start rebuilding the world?"

"No, I don't," I said. "I'm sorry. I didn't mean to make it sound like nothing happened. It's just—"

"Everything's changed. *Everything*."

Her voice had ticked up a notch. Someone shifted in one of the other bunks. I reached out to touch her arm. "Sorry," I said again. "We're in trouble. Big trouble. But we're alive. That's all I meant. We're alive."

"He should have been here," she said. "My mother would have been with him. She would have driven to my grandpa's house, and they both would have come down here to the shelter. I don't understand it."

"Maybe they couldn't get here, but they found somewhere else to hole up," I said. "We have to try to stay hopeful, you know!"

Sue nodded. "I'm worried about Jay," she whispered. A tear slipped from one eye and trickled down her cheek. "We've been . . . seeing each other. I know some things about him that are important. But I don't want to . . . betray him." She waved her hand as if to wipe something away from her face.

"I think we're past stuff like that," I said.

"His medication," she said. "Oh, God, Pete. What's going to happen to us, really?"

When you're the class clown and the end of the world comes, you're kind of out of a job. Or, maybe not, after all; maybe your job becomes even more important than ever, and more difficult. There's a razor-thin line between hilarious and offensive when you're talking about death. Think about it: some of the funniest jokes in the world are about dying. A priest, a rabbi and a lawyer go to heaven . . . that sort of thing. Or worse. Humor is a way of facing the pain without the fear, or breaking it down in ways we can handle.

I guess maybe that's why I ignored the medication line for now. I probably should have pushed it, but I was way past rational thought by then. And anyway, knowing Sue, she wouldn't have told me anything more until she was ready. That girl was stubborn.

"I know one thing for sure," I said. "If we get out of here, there's going to be some plum jobs opening up at Walmart."

Sue didn't say anything at first. Then she started chuckling. It began low and slowly in her belly, and grew from there, until it became the kind of gripping-your-stomach-with-both-hands, rolling-on-the-floor-crying sort of laughter. She did it all silently enough, but before long she got me going too, and both of us were rocking back and forth on the bed like idiots, laughing our asses off at the end of the world.

Ain't life grand?

Part Two:
Fallout

"The world is very different now. For man holds in his mortal hands the power to abolish all forms of human poverty and all forms of human life."
—John F. Kennedy

CHAPTER EIGHT

Days passed, and what can I say? We just kept going, kept busy. I waited for my hair to start falling out, or sores to grow in the palms of my hands and roof of my mouth, and every time I went to the bathroom I looked for blood in the water. But nothing happened, and after some time I started thinking that maybe I'd dodged a particularly nasty bullet. Maybe the big guy upstairs had decided that being trapped down in a hole while the world crashed and burned was bad enough.

But it wouldn't be long before I found out that God was just getting started—and he had one hell of a sick sense of humor.

We only had a few outfits between what we'd brought and the spare stuff we'd found in the closet, so we found ourselves washing our underwear in the sink each day, and trying to keep clean enough not to start to stink. There was deodorant in the bathroom, at least, and things like sanitary napkins for the girls when it came to that. As time went on, as strange as it sounds, we spoke less and less about what we were facing. It was a survival mechanism. After the inventory, we knew that we had enough food and water to last us several months or more. Judging by the notes and logs we found in a notebook on the shelf, there was enough fuel to keep the power on for at least that long, longer if we were careful. We checked the radio several times a day, but there was never anything but static.

Intent on living as if we were dealing with a small inconvenience, we played cards, drank what beer there was to drink, smoked pot and listened to the CDs that we found on the shelf in the bedroom. Most of them were classical or jazz, stuff that none of us had ever cared about before. The music seemed more complex by that point though, deeper and more meaningful. I don't know how the others felt, but I began to listen for the individual instruments in each recording, separating the strings from the percussion and the winds until I could hear each note. Then I would begin to reconstruct the music by adding each sound in, one by one, until the symphony was whole again.

I suppose the cracks in each of us were showing even then, although none of us was with it enough to notice. These cracks were all different, of course, based on what we feared the most. Let's face it, we're all a product of our own pasts, and more often than not, it's the past that trips us up when we face down a crisis, rather than the crisis itself. I know that's true for me, as much as anyone.

Maybe that's where the jokes come from too. Understanding people. You have to know what makes them tick, before you can make them laugh. But I missed the warning signs with Jay, and some of them with Jimmie too. Hell, I even missed them in myself, I guess.

We were all waiting, you understand. Waiting for Godot. Waiting for some kind of sign, some kind of miracle. Waiting for the sound of someone knocking at the hatch. What eventually came for us was nothing like what we'd expected, but a nightmare that was a hundred times worse.

* * *

It was a little over a week after the strike when we heard the scratching in the kitchen.

That day I was sitting in the front room with Tessa and trying to remember what the sun felt like. The walls seemed to be closing in lately, and my hands and feet had begun to tingle. I didn't like that feeling at all, and so I tried to imagine the exact opposite of where we were. The sky, stretching out in a great blue expanse far above my head, and the ocean reaching up to meet it at a distant horizon.

"Did you hear that?" Jimmie said, coming into the other room from the kitchen. I knew he'd been scrounging for food, even though our schedule strictly prohibited any eating beyond the set mealtimes. We were trying to make everything last now, and Jimmie knew damn well that he was breaking the rules. Still, I didn't have the heart just now to say anything to him. The beach was still in my head, complete with rolling surf and the cry of gulls wheeling overhead.

I touched the CD player. "It's called music, numb nuts," I said. Tessa laughed.

"Don't be a jerk, eh," he said. "I thought I heard something in the walls. You didn't hear it?"

I shook my head and Tessa did too and I wondered, privately, whether this was the moment his mind had finally snapped for good. But I went to get the others anyway, and we all gathered in silence in the kitchen.

For a few moments there was nothing, and then we all heard a sound like something chewing. It seemed to move around behind the cabinets.

We all looked at each other. "Mice," Dan said. But it was too loud for that, and I think we all knew it. We stood and listened to the thing moving around inside the walls.

The concrete must have been two feet thick, so I don't think any of us were really worried that whatever it was might get in, at least not at that point. But the sound of something else alive after all this time was strangely unsettling.

Finally the sound seemed to focus in an area behind the fridge. It would stop, as if listening, and then start again, a deliberate sort of scratching.

Like something trying to get at us.

I felt a chill. I looked at Dan, and he nodded. Sue put her hand on my arm, as if to stop me, and then let it fall.

We each took one side of the fridge and slowly slid it out from the wall, a few inches at a time. What we all saw took our breath away.

Behind the fridge was a steel door. It was riveted into the concrete like the entrance to an airlock.

"What the hell," Jimmie said. His voice had a strained, choked quality to it that I didn't like. Being down in this hole had changed him; already high-strung, now he was beginning to look not quite right, as if there were thoughts going on just beyond those eyes that would leave us all screaming if he spoke them out loud. Like I said, the cracks were showing, and I wish to hell now that I'd paid more attention. Maybe things wouldn't have turned out any differently, but then again, maybe they would have.

"My grandfather would have built another entrance that came from the house," Big Sue said from behind us. "A tunnel. He would have kept it from everyone. I know how he was. It would be just like him." Her eyes brightened. "Maybe that's him, the noise I mean. He's hurt, trying to get in." She looked around at all of us, and I could see the hope blooming within her.

Jay shook his head. "Sue—"

"No, listen," she said. "It's possible, isn't it? He survived the initial blast, but he was injured. He got into the tunnel but couldn't make it to the door. Until now."

Nobody said anything. I mean, it was crazy. There were countless reasons why it couldn't be Sue's grandfather behind that door. Even if he had survived the multiple hits from the warheads that Dan and I had witnessed, there was the matter of clean food and water, the days that had gone by without a sound.

Plus, if it were he, why didn't he just open the door?

We heard the scratching again. It was close. I picked up a fire extinguisher attached to the wall and held it like a club, feeling like an idiot. We all watched the door. Silence for a moment; muffled thumping; then the handle moved just slightly, as if someone were on the other side, testing the latch.

"*Grandpa?*" Sue said. Dan told her to be quiet, but she was beyond hearing anything now. "Grandpa!" she shouted, pushing past us. "You hear me?" She pounded on the door. "We're in here!"

She reached for the handle.

The next few seconds seemed to pass in slow motion. I heard the handle click and a slight sucking sound as the door's seal was broken; someone shouted, and Jay lunged at Sue, but he was too late.

The door swung outward, revealing a narrow concrete hallway. With it came a surprising amount of light cast from fluorescent bulbs set into a drop ceiling, and a moment later, a slight puff of air carried in the sticky sweet smell of rot.

A man's body lay on the floor of the hallway about twenty feet away.

He lay on his stomach. He wore a black T-shirt and jeans, and they were soaked with the liquid of decay. The body had swelled up like a purple balloon. One arm was stretched out toward us, as if reaching out for help, the hand puffy and nails broken in several places.

His face was missing. That was my first reaction, looking at him. I could see white bone and gristle where his nose and eyes should be. It looked like something had been chewing at him, and had gotten a good bellyful before losing interest and moving on to something else.

As we all stared in silence and shock at the body, something moved at the edges of my vision, but when I glanced at the spot, whatever it was had disappeared.

If I'd been thinking more clearly, maybe I would have wondered what exactly had made those scratching noises, and what the hell had moved the handle on that door. I might have said *something*, sounded a note of caution if Sue hadn't let out a shriek right then and run into the tunnel. I grabbed at her arm and missed, but Dan was quicker than I was and before I could move he was after her. She got maybe five steps before he had her around the waist and held her back.

This was a good thing, because even before I heard Sue screaming his name, I knew that the dead man was her grandfather, had recognized him even without his face. I thought about her cradling that stinking, slimy head in her hands and wanted to be sick. Whatever had happened to him, it was clear he was beyond saving. But Sue wasn't going to hear that now.

I stepped out into the hallway too, Tessa right behind me, and as impossible as it sounds, I thought I saw Sue's grandfather's leg twitch.

That was when they attacked.

It all happened blindingly fast. One moment we were alone, and the next the hallway just beyond the body was full of rats.

At least it seemed full to me. There were probably at

least thirty of them. They were huge bastards, about the size of small cats, and their fur was matted and missing in places so that their grayish pink flesh showed through.

I didn't know where they'd come from, or how they had appeared so suddenly out of nowhere. Sue was still screaming and struggling in Dan's grasp, and strong as he was, she was nearly free. I don't think either one had seen the creatures yet. I shouted something at them and then turned to go back inside the shelter, only to find that one of the little fuckers had flanked us and was now standing on its hind legs in the open doorway, baring its rotten teeth.

Jesus. The thing actually took a hop-step forward like that, and I tucked Tessa behind me and held up the fire extinguisher like a weapon, glancing back in time to see a whole battalion (that was what I thought then, that they looked like hundreds of little animal soldiers) moving in tandem to surround Sue and Dan and cut off my retreat.

We all froze. They were so goddamned *quiet.* At the sight of those things moving like that I almost lost it. My bowels felt loose and my legs began to shake. I'd never seen anything like it before, the way these animals were acting. One rat is bad enough, thirty of them are even worse; but to see all thirty act as if they had a plan for you, and it involved turning you into steak tartare: that was enough to make any man want to run away screaming like a little girl.

I looked at the open door and saw Jimmie standing just inside with Jay right behind him. I caught his eye for only a moment and saw the pure, naked fear there before he swung the door shut, and I heard a thunk as the latch clicked into place.

"You *fuck,*" Dan said from behind me. I turned to look at him. He'd seen what Jimmie had done, and his face was purple with rage. Sue had stopped screaming now, but it wasn't because she'd calmed down; she'd seen the rats. She stood rigid in the center of the hallway, not moving one muscle, staring bug-eyed at the things slowly advancing on us all. The closest one was less than five feet from her leg and I could tell she was about to bolt.

Dan noticed it too. "Stay calm, both of you," he said in a low voice. "Don't make any sudden moves. They're just hungry."

"That's what I'm afraid of," I said.

Tessa had her back pressed up against me, and she reached down and clenched my free hand with a grip like a vise. I looked back down at the one closest to me, near the shelter door. It had dropped back down to all four feet and had closed half the distance between us. I could have reached out and tapped it with my foot.

"We look like lunch to you?" I said, taking another couple of steps backward until I was close enough to Sue and Dan to touch them.

"Knock it off, Pete," Dan said. "They might be carrying some kind of disease."

"They're *huge*," Sue said, her voice high and trembling. "Do something, please."

When the actual attack came, they moved so swiftly and with such purpose it was almost impossible to believe. Several of the largest rats broke rank and skittered along the edges of the hall, making us instinctively step closer together, while the center of the pack actually moved backward like a wave, drawing our attention for a split second longer. I didn't understand what they were doing at first until I heard movement above us and realized that more of them had crawled into the space above the drop ceiling.

We'd been herded like sheep into a tight ball, then

distracted long enough for some of them to move into position.

"Dan," I said, "I think maybe—"

A ceiling panel above our heads exploded downward, and half a dozen furry, writhing bodies with slippery tails came along with it. Sue screamed and ducked. I raised the fire extinguisher like a club and batted one away, but it was hard to swing freely with Dan and Sue and Tessa so close to me. Two of them bounced off my shoulders to the floor, where they scrambled to their feet. Dan slapped at others as they fell and grabbed one that had landed in his hair, tossing it against the wall where it hit with a splat and slid down, leaving a wet streak of gore.

One of them had managed to grab hold of the back of Sue's shirt, its claws digging in, and I almost creamed her with the extinguisher before coming to my senses. Instead I held out the hose and tried to pull the trigger, but nothing happened.

Dan shouted something and swatted it off her back, and at the same time I felt them at my feet. I glanced down. The others had moved in from all sides now, and the floor was a seething, writhing carpet of fur and teeth and claws.

I stomped down on two of them, feeling the crack of bones snapping and soft internal organs popping like water balloons, then kicked out at more. I felt myself slipping into total panic, adrenaline lighting up my body like an electrical shock.

The smell coming off these creatures was like a sewer filled with rotten meat, and they were everywhere. I was gagging with it, the stench filling my nostrils and making my eyes water.

"Don't let them trip you!" Dan shouted. "They're going at our legs. If we go down, we're finished!" He and Sue kicked and stomped on more of them, and Tessa got her share too, but others just moved in to take their place. They were relentless. I saw a huge one leap over the backs of the others and fasten itself against Dan's right pant leg before he pulled it off and hurtled it down the hallway.

As I watched it bounce away and quickly regain its feet, I saw something else: all around us, those rats we had crushed underfoot were still moving. But they weren't trying to get away. Even now, with cracked bones and burst organs, they were trying to get at us.

The pin. I'd forgotten I had to pull it from the extinguisher before it would work. I grabbed the yellow ring and yanked it free, then held the hose out and pulled the trigger.

This time, a fierce shot of white mist and foam covered the backs of the rats on the floor. I aimed more carefully and pulled the trigger again, and this time the spray knocked them back a couple of feet and slowed them down. I stepped into the opening and sprayed in a wide circle and in brief, concentrated bursts right into their little rat faces, as many as I could hit.

It gave us room to get out from under the hole in the ceiling. I glanced up and saw more of them getting ready to leap at us, and I gave the little bastards a blast with the hose to push them back before clearing a space to the shelter door. "Stay behind me," I said. "And move fast."

It was like the sons of bitches heard me. They came at us with renewed fury, like a hundred furry little robots with a single, focused purpose. There was something else strange about the way they moved, but I couldn't put my finger on it right then. We'd probably squashed at least half of the original group by now, but more seemed to appear out of nowhere. I knew we wouldn't be able to hold them off much longer.

I let Sue and Tessa go ahead and then turned to spray the rats again. Dan kicked and stomped beside me, keeping them away while Sue pounded on the door. "Open up!" she shouted. "Please!"

I could only imagine the struggle that was probably going on inside between Jimmie and Jay. I knew Jay wouldn't let Sue stay out here, but what if Jimmie had done something to him? Was that really all that crazy a thought? After all, he'd locked us out here alone to cover his own ass. Didn't seem like much of a stretch to imagine him putting a broom handle across Jay's temple.

Just then I heard the door open, and Tessa's whimper of relief. I glanced back to see Jay grabbing Sue by the shirt and hauling her inside. His face was sweaty and his glasses sat crookedly on his nose. There was no sign of Jimmie.

"Go," Dan said. He gave the nearest rat one more vicious kick and we backed to the door, still spraying the foam, before ducking inside and slamming the door shut.

Just like that, it was over. The sudden silence engulfed us. I collapsed against the closed door, my chest heaving and tears blurring my vision. My legs were shaking so badly I slid down to the floor and cradled my head in my hands, staring at the clumps of fur and gore streaking my shoes and feeling like I was going to be sick.

I'd only felt like this once in my life before we ended up down in this hole, and I never wanted to feel it again. Except I had the sinking feeling I would, and soon.

"Jesus, Jesus," Big Sue was sobbing, over and over again.

"Is everyone okay?" Dan asked. "Sue? You hurt? Did they bite you?"

I looked up as Sue shook her head, tears streaking her face. "I'm . . . okay," she said.

Tessa smiled weakly at me. "I'm fine too," she said. "I don't think those rats are doing as well as we are though."

I thought my heart might burst hearing that. I knew she was brave, but right now she seemed almost too calm. I wondered what I ever did to deserve her. I wondered what else she was hiding behind that supercool exterior.

"Pete? What about you?"

"I'm . . . fine," I said. I didn't trust my voice to say anything more.

"Good. Now where the fuck is he?" Dan said to Jay. "I'm going to kill him."

CHAPTER NINE

It didn't take long for Dan to find Jimmie. Sue and Jay followed him out of the kitchen, and I heard a commotion from the bedroom, voices raised and a sudden crash. I struggled to my feet with some help from Tessa. My legs still felt wobbly and my stomach threatened to return the energy bar I'd eaten an hour earlier. I couldn't get the smell of those things out of my nose and throat; it had settled there, it seemed, the stench of rot.

I smelled Tessa instead, leaning impulsively into her hair and breathing in deeply. We were alone in the kitchen. She stopped still, not leaning into me, but not moving away either. Beyond the surface her hair smelled slightly dusty with the hint of lilac shampoo, just like I'd expected it to smell. I wondered if she'd known I might do that, or whether she was so shocked she couldn't make sense of it. Did it matter? We'd known each other so long now, it was like she was my better half. And yet we'd never discussed anything other than friendship, as if both of us understood that this thing between us was something unusual, something that could not be explained or understood by anyone not in our shoes.

I thought of us mingling together, becoming one with each other, like two halves made whole once again, and I swear to God this had nothing to do with sex, but more of a spiritual oneness, something I hadn't experienced before in my life.

Or maybe I was just crazy and coming down from an adrenaline high, and all this would seem like a dream tomorrow. Either way, I didn't want it to end.

But just like that, it did. I heard Dan dragging Jimmie into the main sitting room. "We better . . ." I said leaning away again. Tessa nodded, her eyes meeting mine. For a moment it seemed she might speak, but I heard Jimmie's voice, and then Jay's asking Dan to stop, and I hurried out of the kitchen to see what I could do.

They were at the far end of the room. Jimmie was in nylon shorts and his bare thighs were pressed up against the table while Dan had him by the shirt, shoving him backward until he was leaning over the table, Dan holding him up. One of Jimmie's eyes was swelling shut and turning purple, and at first I thought Dan had hit him, but I saw Jay rubbing his fist and figured maybe the struggle for control in the kitchen had gone further than a few harsh words.

Thank God Jay had been inside, otherwise maybe we would still have been out there. He wasn't much of a fighter, but with Sue on the other side of that door, I guess he'd done what was necessary.

"Tell me why I shouldn't kill you right here," Dan said. "Rip your fucking heart out."

"I . . . I was just trying to keep them from getting in—"

"Bullshit. You locked us out in that tunnel to save your own ass."

Jimmie licked his lips. I noticed how cracked they were, and flecked with white. "I would have let you in, I swear. I just wanted a chance to *think* for a second."

Dan glanced at Jay. "He put up a fight?" Jay nodded

briefly, then looked away. "Okay," Dan said. "Maybe I've got a better idea. Maybe we lock you out there with them."

Jimmie's eyes went wide. He shook his head. "No, man, fuck you. You can't do that to me."

"I can do whatever I want," Dan said. His face was about one inch from Jimmie's nose now. The veins in Dan's neck were standing out and a muscle in his cheek was jumping. I started getting a very bad feeling about this, watching that muscle jump.

Jimmie looked away first.

"You listen to me, and you listen good," Dan said. His voice was low but we could all hear it clearly enough. "If we're going to make it through this, we all have to act like a team. We all have to have each other's backs. That means we lay down our lives for the good of the group, if need be. Anyone who doesn't understand that is a liability. You just showed me you can't be trusted."

"Hey," I said. "Just take it easy."

"Fuck that." Dan shook Jimmie by the shirt. "We can't risk it."

I forced my rubbery legs to march, walked over and took Dan by the arm. His bicep was like a knob of wood. *Mental note: do not piss Dan off.*

He glanced at me and I gave him my biggest, widest smile. It felt like a shit-eating grin, but right then, it was all I had. Sincerity was in short supply at the moment.

"Hey," I said, "you could do that, you could. But you should know that he's an awfully good lay."

I heard Tessa snicker behind me. Dan didn't move, and for a second I thought I'd badly miscalculated. But then he smiled and shook his head, and his grip relaxed and he took a step back. "Hate to deprive you of that," he said. "I forgot you two were hot for each other."

Jimmie shot me a look and I couldn't tell whether it was grateful or pissed off, and to tell the truth, I didn't much care.

"He was moving," Big Sue said. That snapped us all back pretty damn quick. She'd seemed pretty out of it, I thought, and Jay was holding her arms and rubbing them, as if to warm her. Now she spoke up as if waking from a particularly bad dream. "I saw it. Before they came. He was *moving.*"

"Sue, listen to me," Jay said to her softly. "His face . . . he was gone. He's been gone for a while."

I nodded along with him. But inside I wondered. I'd seen something too, hadn't I? Her grandfather's leg—that corpse's leg, I corrected myself—had twitched. And what about the other weird stuff that had happened out in that hallway? Were we going to face any of that now? Or was it too soon?

"I . . . saw it too," Tessa said. I looked at her, surprised. She didn't usually speak up like that with the group. A bit shy, I'd always thought, though not with me.

"It was a rat," Dan said. "Must have been underneath him, you know, wriggling around. Made it look like that."

"Then what about the handle, eh?" Jimmie muttered. "It was moving too, remember? That's how we found the door in the first place, the noise. How do you explain that?"

We all looked at the archway to the kitchen. It yawned before us like a big, hungry mouth. We couldn't see the steel door from where we were, but I imagined it right now, everything still and silent in there, and then the handle ticking softly back and forth as something tried to get inside.

I shivered. "Not helpful," Tessa whispered to me. I didn't think I'd said anything out loud, but then again, she had this way of understanding me that slipped north of creepy sometimes. I never knew whether she was actually inside my head, but it sure as hell felt like it.

"Rats don't open closed doors," I said, "and dead men don't either. So unless you're suggesting we fell into an *X-Files* episode, there has to be some other explanation. I'm more concerned with the way those little bastards attacked us. Did that seem strange to anyone else, or was it just me?"

"They're smart," Jay said. He looked at me and I saw something in there, some glint of recognition. "Smarter than your average rat, anyway."

I nodded. "They had a *plan*. Didn't it seem that way? And the way they moved, together like that, was just flat-out whacked."

"Well, they're not getting in here," Dan said. "This is reinforced concrete. It's a fucking bomb shelter. Nothing's getting in if we don't let it."

I glanced at Jay again, and he wouldn't meet my eyes. *He knows something*, I thought. "Jay? Something to tell us?"

"We should double-check that door," he said. "And make sure nothing snuck by while we were . . . busy."

That brought another chill down my spine, and by the look of the rest of them, they felt the same. We all fell into line behind Dan, moving toward the kitchen. I wished I had my trusty fire extinguisher now, but I'd left it on the floor in there, and to be honest, it was so streaked with gore I was probably better off without it.

But something else . . . I grabbed a couple cans of creamed corn from the shelf and hefted them in my hands. They'd make a pretty mean weapon to throw in a pinch, but I'd rather have something I could keep a grip on, so I put them back and took a thick-handled flashlight about a foot long and full of D batteries. Better.

The kitchen was empty. The lights shined brightly

down on silent appliances and the short countertop speckled with pickle juice and powdered milk from our last meal.

God, I was already so sick of powdered milk. Made me want to puke.

But what really made the gorge rise in my throat was seeing the bloody footprints our shoes had left in the tile. Bits of fur and guts painted the floor nearest the steel door, which was firmly closed.

"See," Dan said. "Nothing here." The kitchen was small enough that with all of us in there, it felt a little too claustrophobic. I turned to look at the pantry. The light was off inside, and the light from the kitchen reached only an arm's length into the six-foot space, so that the back was deep in shadow.

As I stared into the darkness, I thought I saw something move.

A sound like claws scrabbling on tile.

I jumped back as the rat leaped out of the shadows. Jay pulled Sue out of the way just in time as the thing landed with a slapping sound and then turned and leaped again, this time directly at Jimmie's bare legs.

There was no time for the rest of us to react. The entire thing had happened in the blink of an eye. But still I felt this terrible helplessness as I stood just a couple of feet away and watched this thing dig its dirty claws into Jimmie's flesh just below the knee, bare its teeth and bite down.

Jimmie shrieked and shook his leg, but the goddamned thing held on, digging its teeth even deeper into his flesh. Then it clawed higher and bit again, burying its snout in Jimmie's knee.

Bright red blood wet the rat's fur and splashed across the tile. Jimmie started doing this disjointed, crazy hopdance, shaking his leg and slapping at the rat's body as if he could just wipe it off him like the slime of a dead bug. Still it hung on. I was reminded of once when I saw a boy in our town step on a ground hornet's nest, and the things swarmed up his pant legs; he'd done the same thing, gone white as a sheet and performed this dance that was half panic, half purpose.

No more than five seconds had passed, but it felt like forever. Dan was on the other side of me, and he hadn't moved. So I raised that flashlight I'd taken from the shelf in the main room and a swung it at the rat as hard as I could.

If this were a cheesy B movie I probably would have hit that one right out of the park, but in reality I missed by a mile. Jimmie hopped around again and I swung upward in a backhand tennis swing, and this time I clipped the little fucker's skull.

I thought I'd hit him pretty good, and, in fact, it looked like half his head was caved in, but it didn't seem to do much. "Stop goddamned moving," I said, but Jimmie didn't hear me. I whacked the thing again, this time square in the back, and heard bones crunch. The smell hit me again and I gagged. God, it was like a dead animal rotting away in the sun.

Jimmie grabbed hold of the rat's body and ripped it off him, taking a chunk of his leg with it. He threw the thing to the ground, where it lay convulsing, teeth still snapping open and closed. I stomped down, flattening its hindquarters to mush, and I could see the damned thing twist its head trying to get at me.

Foul black fluid spread out over the tile under my shoe. I stomped down again, this time on its head, and felt the rat's skull pop.

Jesus, did that stink. When I stepped away again, breathing hard, what was left was still twitching, as if trying to get up.

As all this was happening, everything else had faded away, but I could hear Sue crying hysterically now. I felt Tessa's hand on my back. Dan swore and stepped over the carcass to where Jimmie lay against the wall. "We're going to need the first-aid kit," was all he said.

I didn't have the heart to tell him, but before too long, I had a feeling we were going to need one hell of a lot more than that.

CHAPTER TEN

We carried Jimmie to the sink and washed out his wound, then sprayed it with antiseptic. It was ugly, an inch-long chunk missing from the area just to the right of his knee-cap. I thought maybe the rat had gotten some of his ligaments or something too, but once we'd cleaned it out and the blood had slowed to an ooze, it looked a little better. Still, there was a lot of damage and I wasn't sure whether he'd be able to put much weight on it for a while.

We wrapped it in gauze and tape from the first-aid kit. Tessa had taken a course one summer when she was a camp counselor, and she did a halfway-decent job nursing him. Jimmie bitched the whole time; you'd think he were getting his leg cut off the way he carried on.

After that we carried him into the bedroom and put him in the lower bunk I'd been using, gave him some pain-killer from the kit and washed it down with a shot of Jack Daniel's we'd found in the pantry a few days back. Dan seemed to have forgotten his plan to throw Jimmie out in the tunnel to fend for himself, and I was glad for that. Jimmie could be a pain in the ass, and he'd proven himself a coward to boot, but he was my friend, and he'd been one longer than any of the rest of them. I didn't want to have to face making a choice.

With the way he bitched at Tessa while she was dressing

the wound, she would have had good reason to snap back at him, but she never did. I admired her for that. Seemed like I spent a lot of time admiring her lately, which was understandable. She was cute and smart and there wasn't much she couldn't do. But I swear to God this wasn't a romantic thing. It was more like how you'd admire an older sister. Someone you looked up to and wished you could be like.

Once Jimmie was settled Tessa and I went back into the kitchen to take a closer look at the corpse. Dan and Jay were already there, but Sue had begged out of the whole thing, volunteering to stay back and keep an eye on Jimmie.

Looking down at the mess on the floor, I hardly blamed her. It was barely recognizable as a living creature anymore; I was reminded again of a particularly bad roadkill I'd had to scrape up with a shovel last summer outside Blue Moon Restaurant where I'd been washing dishes for eight bucks an hour. An eighteen-wheeler had hit a possum and dragged it about ten feet before releasing what was left, a pile of blood and guts and shards of bone steaming in the sun.

That was about what we had here, and the smell was just as bad too.

Dan was standing about five feet away at the sink, one hand clutched over his nose and looking like he might puke any second. But Jay was a different story. He'd found a pair of latex gloves somewhere and was crouched over the remains, a pencil in one hand and a look of concentration on his face. I saw him poke gently at what had been the rat's head. It looked like a rotten apple that someone had stepped on and smeared across the ground.

"Jay," I said. "What the hell are you doing?"

"Watch," he said.

At first, nothing happened. He poked it again, and this time, what was left of the rat's jaws snapped together.

Dan made a sound like water gurgling in a drain and leaned over the sink, gagging. I took a step back, my heart pounding hard.

"Normally you don't see this kind of reflex in a mammal," Jay said. "Insects, sure. You ever pull the legs off a grasshopper and watch them twitch? But this is unusual."

"Call the Smithsonian," I said.

"Maybe it's still alive," Tessa said. She crossed her arms over her chest and hugged herself, as if for warmth, although the kitchen was almost too hot for comfort.

Jay didn't answer her. "How about it?" I said. "Could it still be alive somehow?"

"No," he said, and this time he did look up, his eyes bloodshot as if he'd been crying, although I hadn't seen it. "Actually, it's exactly the opposite. It's been dead for days."

Nobody said anything for a long moment. Then Dan turned from the sink, wiping his mouth with the back of his hand. "What the fuck are you talking about," he said.

"Look." Jay pointed at the now-congealing pool of black fluid that had run from the body. He poked at the thing's slimy blue-black guts that had burst from its stomach. "This is rot. After death, bacteria living in the stomach start to eat the intestines from the inside. Digestive enzymes help things along. Once the bacteria break down cells, you get fluids and gas and bloating, which you see here. Putrefaction. That's the smell."

"Okay, professor," I said. "Let's say it was already dead when I stomped the shit out of it. Solves my lingering sense of guilt over taking a life so young. But how do you explain it walking in here and chewing a chunk out of Jimmie's leg?"

"I can't," he said. "But there's no other way to figure it.

This is the start of decomposition. An animal couldn't be alive in this condition."

"Could something have made the decay move along faster, after we killed it?" Dan asked. "Like maybe the radiation or something?"

Jay shook his head. "I don't see how, and anyway, there's no way it could have rotted to this point in the past twenty minutes, while we were in the other room."

"You think they were *all* dead, out there? What about Grandpa?"

We all turned to look at Big Sue, who stood in the doorway. She was shivering, and her eyes were wet. "He *moved*," she said again. "I know he did."

I thought about what it must have felt like to her to see her grandfather lying there in that condition, and it made me think of my own mother, alone and scared as the bombs came down. Helpless to get away, a prisoner of that wheelchair, screaming for her boy to save her as the shock wave washed over our little house, imploding the windows and cracking walls, heat melting plastic bowls stacked in kitchen cabinets and turning my mother's flesh to ash.

Everyone was looking at me now. "Sorry," I muttered, wiping my own eyes, realizing that I must have made some kind of sound. "Sorry." There was a hiccup in my voice that I couldn't control and didn't like. I'd suffered from panic attacks for a while after my father died, and I always knew they were coming by the way my breath caught in my chest and everything felt tight and strange. Then my heart would start to flutter and my palms would sweat and I would know for certain I was about to die.

The only thing that would help was a quiet, dark room, away from other people, and time. I hadn't had one in a while (pretty much since Tessa showed up on the scene, actually), but if there ever was a reason for them to come back, it was now.

As if in answer I felt Tessa's warm hand sneak into mine, and the warmth spread through me until I was able to breathe again.

"Thanks," I whispered. She squeezed my hand.

CHAPTER ELEVEN

When I was a boy of about seven, my father took me hunting for the first, and last, time. Even in my short time on earth I hadn't known him as much of a family guy, as I guess you know; the most warmth I tended to get out of him was a grunt when I'd bring him one of my drawings or a misshapen ashtray made out of Play-Doh from school. He wasn't the read-aloud type, or much of a sports guy either. I never saw him watch a Red Sox game like the other dads I knew, or go fishing on a sunny summer day with his friends and a cooler full of cold ones.

But one thing my father did like to do, other than his woodworking projects in the basement, was shoot things. He'd go out back and aim at beer bottles he propped in the crook of an apple tree down by the fence line, enjoying the cracking sound and the tinkle of glass, the shattering.

But if the things he shot at were alive, all the better. I remember being afraid when he'd pick up his rifle that he might just decide to turn it on me sometime. That was the thing about my father; you never could tell what he might do, which kept everyone around him on edge.

That day he decided, for a reason that's escaped me, to bring his son into the woods with him. Maybe he thought it would be a teaching moment, or maybe he thought it would be amusing to see what his sissy boy Peter would do when faced with a little blood. Or maybe he was just drunk. If that last were true, he hid it well, because his face never got beyond deadly serious, and I think I knew early on that this was not a trip I was going to like.

We walked for a while into the woods beyond our home, crossing a little stream and continuing on through a meadow with grass that came up near my waist and burrs that stuck to my clothes. We followed a faint path that seemed to disappear completely for stretches, but my father never wavered.

Eventually we came to a platform and wall built into the arms of a large pine tree, looking out over a clearing with a stump in the middle and a deer-food plot nailed to the top of it. The grass in the clearing was all trampled down, like a lot of animals had been there already. My father helped me into the blind, and then climbed up himself.

"Look right here," he said, and he pushed my face against a slot in the wood wall, mashing it just a little too hard so I could feel the roughness biting into my cheek. I could see the clearing from here and the stump with the deer bait. "Watch for anything that moves. You see something, you tell me. Quietly, understand?"

I nodded, and he proceeded to pull a silver flask from his pocket and sit down against the tree trunk, where he took a long pull. I turned back to watch through the slot, knowing better than to disobey him.

It seemed like hours before I saw something. A flash of white at the edge of the clearing, then nothing for a minute, and the deer materialized like a ghost from emptiness, head up and sniffing the air, black eyes wide, nostrils flared. She was beautiful, long-legged, coltish, with a white belly and brown spotted back. I turned to motion to my dad and then turned back excitedly, wanting to see more. I caught a glimpse of her fawn stepping knock-kneed and timidly out into the clearing behind her before my father pulled me away from the wall and peered out himself, the smell of the alcohol on his breath bathing me with its sour sweetness.

He grunted softly. There was an energy to him now, an excitement that mirrored my own. But his was for a different reason. I watched him raise the rifle and poke the barrel out the slot.

"Cover your ears," he said, and that was all.

The rifle barked twice, and then he took me by the arm and half carried, half dragged me down the ladder to the ground again. When he set me on my feet and I looked across the clearing I could see the beautiful doe down on her side near the stump, her mouth and nose bubbling with blood. Two dark holes bled on her side, and her chest heaved once, twice, and she kicked hard. She was bleating low in her throat.

That was when I learned that death was ugly. I smelled oil and gunpowder and the coppery smell of blood. The doe shivered, kicked again, and was still.

My father didn't stop there. The fawn was running in circles, calling like his mother. My father took the rifle and kneeled in the dirt beside me, placed my hands on the stock and wrapped my finger around the trigger.

"This one's yours," he said, and his voice was deep and rough with something dark and vicious that had gotten hold of him. I knew it well enough by then to understand that to disobey or even to hesitate meant a beating with a sapling branch. Other boys might have just gotten to work. Some might have even learned to enjoy it. That wasn't me, and as I stared at the dead doe lying in the grass and her baby running around and around her the scene seemed to shatter into a million brilliant, broken pieces, a prism of wavering light.

Still, as my father bent my head to the sight, and directed my hand to aim, I did pull that trigger.

I'd like to say the fawn died quickly. But that would be a lie. The first shot went wide by five feet, but the second hit him in the hindquarters. He went down, writhing and bucking.

My father dragged me over, pointed the rifle at his head and instructed me to finish him. I shook my head. Disgusted, he took the rifle from me and put a bullet between the creature's eyes. Then he came back to where I'd curled up in a ball, and crouched down next to me.

"That there's a mercy killing," he said. "Without a mother, it would have been dead by nightfall. Understand? It's one hell of a stretch better getting a bullet in the brain than ripped apart by coyotes." He scratched his cheek where a tiny fleck of blood had settled. "Life ain't civilized. That's a human creation, rules and order and compassion. Nature doesn't care about any of that. Things kill, they eat or they die. You think a wolf worries about how his dinner feels? It's survival. You don't learn that in school, and your mother won't teach it to you. That's a father's job. It's why we're out here today."

I wiped away my tears and tried to look strong. It wasn't because I wanted him to think better of me, it was out of fear. I knew what he was capable of, and I wanted to avoid the pain. That was all.

I think he took it differently though. He nodded at me, as if we'd shared an understanding. "There's hope for you yet," he said. "You tell your mother I shot the both of them. This is man's work, out here. You did good. We'll eat well this week."

Then he tousled my hair and stood up. I remember feeling the touch of his hand long after he'd turned away, a burning that slowly faded like a bulb that's been flicked off into blackness.

CHAPTER TWELVE

The next few days passed in a blur. Jimmie recovered enough to limp around the shelter without much assistance, and he kept his distance from all of us, Dan in particular. Dan didn't threaten him again, but he didn't get all warm and fuzzy either.

To tell the truth, for a while Jimmie simply ceased talking entirely, and had the look of someone holding his emotions in only through a supreme effort of will. It was the beginning of his break with reality. We avoided him as much as possible, but it wasn't easy, and maybe we did him no favors by ignoring the problem. Maybe what he really needed was a punching bag, the way I'd been for Tessa that first night, but none of us was in any kind of shape, mentally or physically, to oblige.

I never thought I'd miss him talking at me, the annoying way he ended every few sentences with "eh" like a god-damned Canadian, even though he was from southern Maine, the way he rambled on when he got excited about anything until we told him to shut up. But I did now.

On the third day after the attack he developed a fever. The bite had swollen and infection had probably set in, but he hadn't let Tessa look at it, just changed the bandages himself. The only way I knew for sure that it was ugly was because I caught a glimpse of the old bandages before he threw them in the trash compactor that third day, and they were soaked with pus and blood.

Even then, I didn't force him to let us help. Looking back now, I wonder what kind of friend I'd turned out to be. Whatever he'd done, he was still a human being, still the same Jimmie I'd known since kindergarten, and yet I refused to do anything about it. Maybe more of my father had rubbed off on me that I realized.

When the fever hit, Tessa argued with me to force him to let her dress the wound again, and this time I agreed. Jimmie was in bed, moaning to himself and not entirely lucid. We tried to look at his leg, but he kicked and thrashed. I went to go get Dan and Jay.

"Jay, hold his legs," Dan said. "I'll get his shoulders. Pete, you get that bandage off fast."

I made way for Tessa, the expert, and Sue held back and watched. I felt pretty helpless, I have to admit. But Tessa was good; she worked quickly enough.

The wound made us all gasp. The flesh around it had puckered up and turned purple, it was weeping whitish fluid, and an ugly red line traced its way under his skin up his thigh.

"Infection," Tessa said. "Heading for his heart."

"What can we do?" Sue asked.

"He needs antibiotics. If this infection gets worse, it could lead to gangrene. If that happens we might have to amputate his leg."

Jimmie stopped struggling, seemingly passed out, and we all stood there, taking in the implications of the situation. There was no hospital down here, no doctors, no real medical supplies. If the infection got that bad, there was really nothing we could do. We all knew we couldn't take off a limb. It just wasn't possible.

"Okay," Dan said. "There's antibiotics in the first-aid kit. We should have given some to him in the first place."

"There's only one bottle," Jay said.

Nobody spoke for a moment. "How many treatments?" Dan asked.

"I don't know," Tessa said. "It looked pretty full. Maybe two or three people could get enough to help them, if they were sick."

"We can't just let him die," I said. "Not when we have the pills that could do the trick. We don't know when we all might need this stuff. Could be never."

"Fat chance of that," Jay muttered. He'd been on edge the past couple of days, preoccupied by something, and I'd assumed it was from the thing about the rat and the lack of pot. We'd run out over a week ago. But I thought again about what Sue had said when she sat on my bed that night; something about his medication.

I wondered now exactly what she'd meant.

"Pete's right," Dan said. "We can't let him die. Sue, go grab the kit, and get a cup of water."

Nobody said anything about the fact that just a few days ago he'd been this close to throwing Jimmie out to the rats. Sue hurried off and returned moments later with a cup and the bottle of antibiotics, and Dan and Jay helped prop Jimmie up in bed. His head lolled on his neck and for just a moment I flashed back to a dark basement and a childhood nightmare and I shivered. But then he opened his eyes slightly and took the pills we offered before falling back into a fitful sleep.

A couple of minutes later Tessa pulled me out into the kitchen. I stared at the spot on the tile where the rat's body had been crushed. Even though we'd cleaned up the mess and disposed of the remains in the compactor, I felt like I could still see the outline of that pool of black fluid.

It made me think of those deer and my father, and I shook my head as if to clear it.

"Take it easy," Tessa said. She knew about the deer story, and a lot more too. Tessa knew just about everything about me. Sometimes I forgot that.

"If we have to cut off his leg—"

"We won't." She moved closer and put her arms around me. "He's going to be okay." She squeezed gently and then released me, holding my elbows and looking up into my eyes. "When that thing attacked him, right after . . . you had one of your panic attacks, didn't you?"

I shrugged. "I might have, if you weren't there. But you were."

"I'm worried about you, Pete," she said. "I know what kind of pressure you put on yourself, believe me. But you're not your father, and you can't keep blaming yourself either."

"What about our families, Tessa? My mother? If we could just find a way out of here—"

"She's gone," Tessa said. "You know that. She couldn't have survived."

"She *could* have," I said, warming to the subject. "Maybe if there was enough warning, maybe she could have gotten to a shelter or something, the basement of the high school, I don't know. She was pretty good about her emergency rules, she had people she could call. Or even if that didn't work, our own basement . . ."

"Don't think about the basement," Tessa said. Her hands were still on my arms, and she squeezed. "Just don't."

"Sorry," I whispered, tears flooding my eyes. "You're right. I don't want to go there, do I?"

"Hey, Pete," Dan said. He was standing just outside the doorway to the kitchen, staring at me, and I knuckled the tears away. I had no idea how long he'd been there. "You okay?"

"Sure."

"Can I talk to you a minute?"

I glanced down at Tessa, who nodded and released me, and I followed Dan back into the bedroom, where Jay stood somberly at the foot of Jimmie's bunk. Sue was lying on one of the other top bunks, sleeping.

"We need to show you something," Dan whispered. "Stay quiet, okay? Don't wake Sue. She doesn't need to see this."

For some reason the hairs on the back of my neck raised up, and I felt too cold. Suddenly I didn't want anything to do with what they were about to show me.

Jay nodded at Dan. Without another word, Dan went to Jimmie's side and lifted his shirt.

Bright red hives had broken out all over his torso. They were about the size of quarters, swollen and with irregular edges like port-wine stains.

"What the hell are those?"

"Shhh," Jay said. "I don't know. Some kind of rash. We figure it has something to do with the infection, but they're not like anything I've ever seen before. We thought maybe you'd have a better idea."

Me? Why me? But I didn't ask them any more questions, just stepped closer, drawn as if hypnotized to the marks on Jimmie's body and unable to help myself. Thin red lines ran like thread from one to the next, making him look like some bizarre human version of connect the dots. The centers of the worst of them looked slightly white and puffy as if they were filled with pus.

There were more on his legs too. As I stared in horror, I saw one of the largest hives on his thigh pulse and bulge slightly outward and then grow still again.

Jimmie turned and muttered in his sleep. He raised a hand to his stomach and pressed his fingers against the hive, and his eyes opened into slits. "Itches," he said, his voice hoarse and thick. Then he closed his eyes again and went back to sleep.

CHAPTER THIRTEEN

"Jay's claustrophobic," Sue said.

We were sitting at the big wooden table. It was early in the morning, and the others were still asleep. Sue had come to get me from my dreams, finger to her lips, and the look in her eyes made me get up immediately and follow her without a second thought.

I sat now in my boxers and T-shirt, the chair too cold against my back and buttocks, and considered how to respond to that.

"You're kidding."

She shook her head. "He's always been embarrassed by it, but it's true. He's terrified of small spaces. Says it used to be impossible for him to ride in trains, even cars. Sometimes if a building he entered was too dark, the roof seemed to close in on him, and he'd panic. I think it was the pressure his parents put on him, and he put on himself. Remember when he got sick with the flu last year?"

I nodded. "He was out of school for a week."

"It wasn't the flu, Pete. He had a nervous breakdown. It was pretty serious, he was in the hospital under observation."

"I had no idea."

"Not many people did. His parents got him on medication and it helped. But now . . ."

"He's run out."

She nodded again.

I shifted in my seat. "Forgive me for asking, but why are you telling me this?"

"I remember when you were younger, before your father died . . . you used to get these looks in your eyes sometimes, and I could see you tighten up, clench your fists, breathe faster. You'd start to sweat, and sometimes you'd have to go to the nurse. It was panic attacks, wasn't it? I figured maybe you'd understand." She inched her chair closer, hunching over the tabletop toward me. "Then, after the funeral, you were gone for a few weeks and I thought—"

"We went to my grandmother's house in Miami," I said. "Mom had to get away from our place, away from the people."

"And when you got back you seemed different somehow. How'd you beat it, Pete? I haven't seen you do that in a long time now."

I thought of Tessa. When we got back from Miami, she'd been there. The girl next door. It was such a cliché, but I couldn't help being fascinated by her from the very first moment. I remembered the first time I saw her, standing out in the rain in her backyard, just letting it wash her clean, her hands and face up to the sky. I remembered wondering how good that felt, and when I went out to join her, she didn't think it was weird at all. We stood there together for a long time, staring up into the raindrops. She knew who I was, and what had happened to me, she told me later. But she didn't ask about it then. Somehow, that made it bearable.

"I don't know. Just grew out of it, I guess. It's really bad, with Jay?"

"He's holding on, but it's like, I don't know, a coiled

spring. It's taking every ounce of energy he has. Maybe you could talk to him?"

"That would probably screw him up worse," I said, trying on a smile. It felt wrong and I dropped it quickly. "There's no magic formula, Sue. I wish there was, but there's not. And I'm not a psychiatrist."

"I know. But if you told him what you went through, if he knew you understood . . ." The look in her eyes made me ache for her. "Maybe it would help. Please. I—I love him. I don't know what else to do. With what's happened, and being locked down here . . . I'm afraid he'll try to hurt himself."

"Okay. I'll try." I reached across the table and took her hand in both of mine. It was big and soft and felt too warm to me. I didn't know Sue as well as the others, but what I did know I liked. She was a good person, concerned with others, helpful and kind. But she was in an impossible situation here, and I knew it. I wanted to help her, I just didn't know how.

"I'm sorry about your grandfather. I know you were pretty close. It's hard enough down here, you know? Without seeing that. I'm really sorry."

Her eyes welled with tears. "You understand that too, don't you, Pete? You know how I feel." She sniffled and wiped her free hand across her nose while I clutched her other hand more tightly. "God. I still think I saw something out there, something I can't explain. And I can see how that might be my mind playing tricks, I really can. But maybe there's another reason to hope. We never found out for sure. Maybe it wasn't him, after all. Maybe it was a—a neighbor or a friend or something. Maybe he's still alive up there, and my mother too. His house was built to withstand a hurricane. And that tunnel, it would have protected him too, right?"

"Sue—"

"No, listen to me. We don't *know*, do we? We don't really know anything."

I shook my head. "No, we don't. But we can't just open up that door again and take a look." I didn't tell her about my nightmares about my own mother, about her turning black and blowing away in the wind and flames, or my unreasoning hope that somehow, some way, she had survived it, and was waiting for me to come get her.

Or my feeling that somehow, some way, I was going to do it.

"I do know one thing," I said. "Jay's going to need you. If this thing he has is the way you've described it, he's going to need someone to lean on, and lean on hard. It might not be fair, but you've got to be strong for him."

"We've all got to be strong, don't we?" she whispered. A tear ran down the outside of her nose and hung there, trembling, until she wiped it away. "We all need each other. But for what, Pete? What kind of life is left out there for us?"

I wondered what world would come out of something like this. That is, if humanity survived at all. Would it turn everyone into a violent criminal, a survival-of-the-fittest situation when resources were so scarce? Or would the same people who were naturally kind and helpful build a society from the ashes of the old, and cast out those who were more naturally prone to murder?

I thought about the secrets we all held; keeping Jimmie's rash from Sue, Jay's illness from the rest of them. My own secrets kept from everyone except for Tessa. And all the other secrets they each had from me, those I'd probably never know. We acted like friends, and maybe we all really were; but when it comes down to life and death, friendships change. You begin to see the cracks in some, and the strength in others. You find out who your real friends are, which might just surprise you.

"I'll talk to him," I said again. "I'll do my best." I squeezed her hand again and smiled at her. This time, it felt more natural. She smiled back.

"What's this?"

I'd been concentrating so hard on Sue's face that I hadn't seen Jay emerge from the shadows of the door opening behind her. Now he stood there staring at us, looking ridiculous with his hair sticking up in clumps, owlish glasses slightly askew, Creed concert T-shirt clinging to his bony frame, bare legs and white socks pulled up over his ankles. He kept scratching nervously at a red patch on his arm and glancing around the room, then back at us.

Sue spun around in her chair, pulling her hand from mine like it had been scalded. Someone caught with her hand in the cookie jar. That probably made it worse. I saw the muscles in Jay's jaw tighten.

Something about the look on his face made my blood boil. He had no right to think this; we were only trying to help. Looking back on it now, I guess it made sense that I would get angry, considering the amount of pressure we were all under; and when I get tense, I tend to say something stupid. It's my way of dealing with the stress. But I never expected Jay's reaction.

"We're planning a spring wedding," I said. "Sue wanted to elope but I said we simply had to have it right here, in the backyard. Wouldn't it be beautiful?"

Me and my big mouth. "Shut up, Pete," Sue said. "Jay, I was upset and Pete was trying to make me feel better. That's all."

"How long have you been screwing her?" Jay said

abruptly, stepping forward. "A few days? Or has it been going on for a while?"

"Jay, Jesus Christ—"

"I asked you a question!" he shouted. "Answer me, damn you!"

I'd never seen Jay lose it like this, ever. It was like someone had just opened up an emotional fire hydrant. Sue reached up to touch his arm. "Calm down—"

"*Don't* touch me." He yanked himself away from her. "I've seen it, don't think I haven't. The way you two look at each other. And then the other night, Sue sitting on your bed and the two of you whispering in the dark? I heard you."

"That was nothing," Sue said. "I'm just scared. Nothing's going on."

"She's worried about you," I said. Sue turned and shot me a look, and if looks could kill, I'd surely have been dead right then and there. But I kept going. "She asked for my help. I know about your claustrophobia and the meds. I know you must be going nuts down here, dealing with this."

Wrong choice of words. Again. Jay crossed his arms over his chest and looked from one of us to the other. "So that's it now? You two talking about how to deal with poor crazy Jay?"

"Look, this is getting out of hand," I said. "I get it, okay? You think you're the only one who's dealt with bad shit in his life? Come on. I've looked into that darkness, I've been there. And now we're all locked away down here, and we have to deal with it somehow. But if we end up attacking each other—"

"You have no idea. You really don't." Jay ran his fingers through his hair and started pacing back and forth. I could feel the nervous energy streaming off him in waves, and I wondered whether he'd been sitting in the dark in his bed, obsessing for hours before coming in here. "You're worried about us attacking each other? You don't know what we're in for, but I do."

"Really? Why don't you enlighten me?"

"Don't start," Sue said. Maybe she was just trying to avoid him slipping into full-blown paranoia. But I glanced at her pleading face, the way she looked at him, and I had to wonder. You ever walk into a room where there was something else going on, a hidden conversation or deeper meaning that left you feeling out in the cold? That's the way I felt now. I kept thinking I was missing something important here.

"You'd never believe me," Jay said.

"Try me."

He took a deep breath, let it out slowly in a long hiss of air. "I know what was wrong with that rat."

I sat back, unable to process the sudden shift. "What the hell are you talking about?"

"Jay—" Sue said.

He waved her off. "No, listen to me. It's time someone around here started *listening* to this. *She* won't. For God's sake, you people don't even have a clue!" Jay's hands were shaking as he ran his fingers through his hair again. "There've been rumors of experiments like this circulating for a while now in the online chat rooms. I used to read about them all the time. If you went to a place like whispers dot com, you'd see threads about it. Most people talked about al-Qaeda bankrolling them, but nobody ever seemed to know for sure."

"Bankrolling what, exactly?"

"Biological weapons. But not the ones everyone thinks of when people say that, like anthrax or smallpox or Ebola. These are quite a bit more sophisticated."

"That attack was nuclear," I said, as calmly as I could. "I saw it. Atomic-bomb mushroom clouds, the works."

"I *know* it was nuclear, damn it," Jay said. "But that was only the first wave. Computer simulations clearly show that even in the event of a full-scale nuclear war, human beings would survive. And not in the organized way that people who would plan something like this would want. Humans would survive in pockets here and there and grow like weeds again. There'd be no controlling them and we'd be back where we started eventually. If you really wanted to do the job right, you'd need a second wave. And to do that, you'd need to make weapons carriers out of the creatures most likely to survive the first attack."

"You know how crazy this sounds," Sue said. "We've talked about this. Why would anyone want to wipe out every single human being from the face of the earth? It makes no sense."

"You know why," he said.

There was silence for a moment between them; then Jay looked at me. "It makes sense if those planning it know it's coming. They can prepare a place to hide out and wait, a kind of Garden of Eden. They can engineer it so they can control the plague. Then once everyone else is dead, they can begin to reshape society on their terms, in their image. Start from scratch."

"Sounds sort of like eugenics," I said. Jay and Sue glanced at each other again quickly, but I caught it. "You think that's it?" I asked. "Ethnic cleansing?" I shook my head. "Okay, I'll bite. What exactly is most likely to survive a nuclear war?"

"Insects," Jay said. "They make the best disease carriers too. Our own government used insects in field tests of biological weapons way back in the Korean War. Fleas, for one. But there were other programs. The point is, insects are best equipped to survive. They're tough, difficult to find, and they can move quickly over pretty large distances."

"So al-Qaeda snatches up half the nuclear warheads in existence, figures out how to drop them all at once across the world, then follows up with a plague of disease-ridden bugs? I don't buy it. These are the same assholes who spent ten years planning how to fly a couple of planes into some buildings. This sounds like it's a little beyond their abilities."

"I didn't say it was al-Qaeda." Jay ran a hand through his hair again, and I swear to God, he looked like he might just blast off at any moment right through the ceiling, he was so hopped up on adrenaline or something. I started to wonder if maybe Sue didn't have a point about him being about to lose his mind. And that would be a very nasty thing down here. It was bad enough with Jimmie's leg, and no doctors or hospital to take him to for treatment, but what about mental illness? What the hell do you do about that?

You stay out of the way, that's what. Try to contain the damage. But if he got violent, with himself or others? Paranoia could lead to all sorts of trouble. I used to see it in my father often enough.

"So if it's not al-Qaeda, then who?" I said. "What, the Russians again? That's what you said when it first happened. And what does this have to do with the rats, anyway?"

This time the look Sue shot Jay was loud and clear. *Keep your mouth shut.* Why she would feel that way, I had no idea. She'd come to me for help, after all. It made no sense. And yet I couldn't have gotten it wrong. Sue might as well have reached out and smacked his face, it was that obvious.

Jay shrugged, looked away, then back at her again. He opened his mouth and shut it. "I-I don't know," he said.

"Come on, guys," I said. "I might be a little thick, but even I can see that something's going on here. You're not telling me something. Spill it."

If things had turned out differently, maybe I would have gotten some answers right then, and there would have been no turning back. But the silence was shattered by Jimmie's bloodcurdling scream from the other room.

CHAPTER FOURTEEN

I'm the first to admit that sometimes my mind goes to pretty dark places. In the depths of my anger and fear after my father's death, there were times I wanted to hurt everyone, myself most of all. It's a natural function of what happened to me, or so I'm told; but to be honest, I think it's more than that. I think we're all hardwired to the tendencies that show up later in life. Sure, our moods and habits can be influenced by our experiences, but there are too many instances of a person going through terrible trauma, rape and torture and horrible violence and coming out the other side with more compassion than ever, while someone else who has a perfect upbringing in suburbia with a caring mother and father, lots of friends and plenty of money ends up killing people for fun. Some are wired for empathy, and some are not.

When I went to these dark places in my mind, I tended to feel pretty insignificant. I wondered about the meaning of life. We see a fly on the wall and we smack it dead, and don't give it another thought. Why? Because it's nothing to us. And yet, as small and unimportant as that fly is to a human being, imagine how much more so a human being is when compared to the universe. Here we are, living and praying on earth as if we matter to God, as if he exists and actually can spare the time to pay attention to us, when the reality is that our planet is like a grain of sand in a nearly infinite beach, and we are specks of dust in a hurricane.

And if we're hardwired to be the type of person we are, what of free will? We like to believe that we choose the paths we take, but our psychological tendencies choose for us, more often than not. Even if we could change our own lives, our destiny, so to speak, why would it matter? If the entire human race just blinked out all at once, the universe would keep on expanding and God would keep on laughing, if he noticed at all.

My mind had gone to a pretty dark place right then, when Jay was talking. I didn't know exactly what he was trying to say about all this, but whatever it was between him and Sue, whatever secrets they were sharing, I knew it wasn't good. The look that passed between them was enough to tell me that. Still, Jay was the smartest of all of us, the smartest kid in our school, maybe the smartest one to ever come through White Falls. As crazy as he seemed to be, I still wanted to believe him. And if we really were facing some kind of biological warfare, the sliver of hope I'd been holding on to since the strike would disappear in an instant.

Nuclear war was bad enough. There was no way we could survive something like that.

When Jimmie screamed we all rushed back into the bedroom. Dan had jumped out of bed by then and turned on one of those portable lanterns, so that Jimmie was lit from the side as he writhed and kicked in his bunk.

Dan was standing in the middle of the room now, staring. Tessa stood just inside the door with her arms at her sides. She didn't make a sound but I could see her hands clenched into fists. I wanted to go to her but did not, just stood there with the rest of them watching the bizarre scene in the lower bunk.

"Make it stop!" Jimmie screamed, convulsing upward until I thought his spine might break. He raked his nails down his chest. "It itches . . ."

I could see the sweat pouring off him. His shirt was damp and his head . . . there was something wrong with it, but for a moment I couldn't figure out what. I moved a step closer, close enough to see clumps of hair on his pillow.

What I was seeing were patches of scalp.

My stomach was churning. We all looked at each other. "He's going to hurt himself," I said. "We better tie him down somehow."

Dan nodded and pulled a couple of belts out of the closet. Sue went to her bed and found a robe she'd been using and pulled the white cloth belt from it. Together Dan and I went to the bed where Jimmie lay, and Dan took his arms while I grabbed at his legs.

Jimmie kicked out at me and almost caught me in the chest. I dodged and then grabbed at his leg again. His skin was slippery with sweat and burning hot, and as he twisted and writhed I wrapped both hands around his lower thigh, just above the bandage that, so far, was remaining in place. Tessa had done a good job of wrapping it. His entire leg was red and swollen. I forced it down with my own weight, pinning it to the bed as Dan quickly lashed the belts around the slats of the headboard and secured his wrists.

As I looked up to see Dan finishing the job, I felt something move in the flesh of Jimmie's leg.

It felt like a snake or worm wriggling under his skin. I let go and fell hard off the bed onto my back, stunned from the blow.

Jimmie kicked the top bunk so hard one of the slats snapped.

"Jesus, Pete," Dan said. "What's the goddamned problem? Get his legs."

I shook my head and scooted backward on the floor. All I wanted to do was get away from whatever that thing was under Jimmie's skin, the slick flesh against my hands and the clumps of hair on his pillow. *Jesus Christ.* I felt like I might be sick.

Jay stepped forward, as if to help, and I shook my head again. "You don't want to touch him," I said. "There's something . . . inside."

Jay looked at me oddly. Then he reached out and grabbed Jimmie's foot, yanking it toward him. Jay's not a strong guy, scrawny and pasty white, actually—your prototypical nerd. I was afraid he might get a heel right in the face and break his glasses. But he surprised me, wrestling both of Jimmie's legs down quickly, using his own body's leverage well. Sue moved in to help with the white belt, and before long they had him tied by the ankles to the cross piece at the end of the bunk.

I realized I was still in boxers and a thin shirt, and I glanced at Tessa, but she hadn't moved or taken her eyes off what was happening in the bed. Jimmie was contained now, but he had enough slack to keep thrusting his body up off the mattress and pull at the bindings on his wrists and feet. They wouldn't last long.

Since we'd entered the room he had kept his eyes mostly squeezed shut, but now he opened them, lifted his head from the pillow and stared right at me. "Help . . . me, Pete," he said, his voice thick and hoarse, as if it took every ounce of energy he had. Tendons stood out in his neck, and spittle flecked his lips. "It itches . . . my leg . . . so bad."

I stood up and inched closer to him, ready to bolt if he

made any kind of move. My skin was crawling, thinking about touching him again. But we had been friends for so long. No matter what he'd done recently, he didn't deserve this. Jimmie had never been particularly brave, and he was lousy under pressure. But he was great at picking you up when you were feeling down, and he'd stuck by me when I was at my darkest point.

A lot of things had changed, but he was still the same Jimmie in so many ways. I remembered building tree forts in the pine woods behind my house, pulling crawfish out of the stream in the ravine, tossing a ball in the field near the school, or just watching TV. Normal kid stuff. He always got the best toys for Christmas—*Star Wars* figures and long-range radios and iPods and video games—and he never hesitated in sharing all of them with me.

And on those days when my father got too drunk and violent and my mother couldn't stop him, Jimmie would be there, ready to slip me out the back door to safety.

"What do you want me to do?"

"Cut it," he said. He closed his eyes and moaned. "Crawling. Get it out, please!"

My stomach did a slow, lazy flip, and I looked around at the others. "No way," Tessa said, stepping forward. "No, uh uh. Bad idea."

Jimmie went berserk, yanking his wrists against the belts and trying to kick his legs free. He screamed again, and the sound was so loud inside the confines of the shelter I thought my ears might pop. I could see him straining with every muscle to reach down and scratch his wound, his hands stretched out like claws.

The belts had begun to cut into his wrists. Blood seeped from underneath and began to spatter the bedsheets as he twisted back and forth.

Dan shook his head. "The fever's made him nuts."

"I don't think so," I said. I stepped even closer, keeping my eye on that area of his thigh just above the wound in his knee. There were more hives now, bright red and angry-looking against his skin. Some of them were as big around as a baseball.

"Jimmie, wait. Can you hear me? Just stop a minute."

Incredibly enough, he did. I could tell the amount of effort it required by the way his muscles remained taut and trembled slightly. *Imagine that unbearable itch between your shoulder blades that you just can't reach. Imagine that, only a hundred times worse. And it just goes on and on . . .*

Just when I thought I must have been mistaken, there it was: a bulging line under his flesh, running from about two inches above the wound, under several of the largest hives along his thigh, to his boxer shorts.

As if something alive was moving around inside him.

"There's something under his skin," I said. "There. Right there." I pointed at the spot.

The keening began low in his throat, and grew until it was a constant, high-pitched squeal. I was reminded of a documentary I'd seen on Egyptian wailing women at funerals, only this was worse. There was so much pain in the sound.

Jimmie started thrashing again and the blood from his wrists started to flow faster. "Get it out get it out getitout-getitoutgetitout—"

"Sue, get me a knife from the kitchen," Dan said. His face was set and grim.

"I—"

"Just do it." He walked over and put his hand on Jimmie's forehead. "Easy, buddy. Hang in there. We're going to help you."

"I can't do this," Jay said abruptly. He was sweating too, and breathing hard. I knew how he felt.

"Then don't," Dan said. "Go wait in the other room."

Jay nodded and backed out. Sue returned a moment later with a serrated kitchen knife with a black plastic handle, the kind you use to cut steak. She handed it to Dan, then looked around for Jay. I pointed to the other room. "You better check on him," I said. "Besides, you might not want to be in here either."

I turned back to where Dan stood. Tessa came forward to stand next to me. I thought about asking her to leave too, but she was the closest thing we had to a doctor in this place, so I kept my mouth shut.

The two of us approached the bed. "This is going to be bad," I muttered. Dan shot me a look.

"Jimmie," he said. "I want you to try to listen to me. I don't know what that is in your leg, but we're going to try to get it out. You have to be absolutely still. Do you understand?"

Jimmie nodded violently. Blood was running freely down his arms now, and I winced at the raw, angry lines the belts had dug into his skin. He clenched his teeth. "Please, just do it. *Do* it."

Dan nodded. I rarely saw him looking indecisive, but he did now. He swallowed hard and bent over Jimmie's leg.

I took Jimmie's ankle in both hands, trying to ignore the crawling, itching sensation I got when touching him. Together we held him still against the mattress. "I'm going to do this as fast as I can," Dan said. "Pete, we might need a tourniquet or something. You can use one of the belts when we're done."

Then he set the blade of the knife against one of the big hives and sliced down.

Yellow pus spurted up and splashed his hands, followed by a reddish brown fluid. Jimmie screamed and his leg jerked against my grip. I felt the sickness rise up in me, and

I gagged. The smell was intense. It reminded me of the rats in the tunnel, and I flashed back to the weight of them falling on top of me, their slippery tails against my face and hands, their matted fur and coarse whiskers.

Tessa put her hand on my back. "I don't know if I can do this," I said thickly.

"Stay with me," Dan said. "Jimmie, I'm going to—"

All at once Dan leaped backward, the knife clattering to the floor. I looked at the wound he'd made and I stumbled back too, unable to tear my eyes away, my chest getting tight and my breath coming faster.

Some kind of insects were crawling out of the deep slice in Jimmie's leg. I watched as they emerged one by one, their antennae poking through and wiggling before they forced their way out in a perfect line. They looked like small black ants, the kind you see in every backyard and at every picnic in the country.

Except these ants had just burrowed a hole in my friend's body, chewed him up from the inside.

"What the fuck is that?" Dan said. He had his hand cupped to his mouth and spoke through his fingers. "Jesus Christ, Pete, are you seeing this?"

Jimmie picked his head up enough to get a look, and when he did he started screaming again and yanking so hard against the belts I thought his wrists might break. The line of ants ran down his leg and over the mattress to the floor.

Insects. They make the best disease carriers.

I turned and threw up. My stomach convulsed again and again, as if it were trying to rip itself from my body. The smell of my puke mixed with the smell of rot coming from Jimmie's wound made me heave again, this time coming up with strings of mucus. My eyes watered and my nose stung, but it helped clear my head.

When I wiped my mouth and turned back again, I resumed my position next to Tessa by Jimmie's side. Quickly she used the top blanket to wipe away the pus and blood and remaining ants from the cut, then picked up the knife and sliced lightly along the bulging line up his thigh.

His skin parted and more ants poured out, wriggling and dropping to the floor. There must have been hundreds of them. Jimmie's screams went on and on, filling the room until I thought I might start screaming myself. I couldn't register what I saw with reality anymore; it was as if I had stepped outside myself and into a dream where anything and everything could happen.

One of the belts snapped. Jimmie reached down with his free hand and ripped at his own skin with his nails, opening up the wound and causing fresh blood to pulse out. He dug at himself furiously, seemingly unaware of the damage he was causing.

That unbearable itch . . . I swallowed hard and went to help, grabbing his arm and holding it down. He fought me, but I was determined this time not to let him go. Everything was slippery and sticky with blood and pus. Dan came around and helped too, as Tessa pressed the blanket to his wound to stop the bleeding. Ants were crawling everywhere now, over the bed and the bloody blanket, across the slats of the headboard, on the floor. I watched them return to eerie formation, drawing back into a single line as if pulled there by invisible strings, and marching over the bed and down to the floor.

My stomach heaved again, but I swallowed it down.

Slowly Jimmie began to lose strength. I felt him go limp, and his head lolled to one side. I didn't know if he had passed out or was simply playing possum. "Get his arm tied again," Dan said. I took the other belt from around his wrist and used it to tie both hands together.

Then I felt for a pulse in his neck. It was erratic and faint.

"Shock," Tessa said. "We have to clean him up and get him warm. Hold this." She put Dan's hand in place over the blanket. "I'll be right back."

A moment later she returned with a bottle of iodine and cotton pads from the first-aid kit. She pulled away the bloody blanket to expose the ugly wound, then poured iodine all over it. Jimmie didn't move, even though it must have hurt like a son of a bitch. Gently she patted the wound clean with the cotton pads. It still bled, but more slowly now, and the ants were gone.

I looked around the bed and the floor again. They had all vanished.

"This should have stitches," she said. "There's a needle and thread in the kit. Anyone know how to sew?"

I swallowed hard. "I think Sue took a quilting class once," I said. "I bet she could stitch it up." Dan nodded, and I went to go get her.

She and Jay were in the kitchen, sitting on the tile. Big Sue had her arms around Jay and was rocking him like a baby in her lap. She looked up at me, the pain in her eyes obvious.

"Is it done?" she asked.

If I hadn't been so distracted I might have found that odd; no *what happened* or *I heard him screaming*. But I just shrugged.

"We need your help," I said.

"I can't leave him," she said, looking down at Jay. His eyes were squeezed shut and he might have been asleep, except for the way his right foot kept jittering against the floor.

"You're going to have to," I said. "Just for a couple of minutes."

Sue sighed. Then she hugged him close. "I'll be right back," she said. "I promise."

When we left him he was curled up on a ball on his side, eyes closed, that foot still jiggling against the kitchen tile.

CHAPTER FIFTEEN

Sue did a pretty decent job sewing Jimmie up, considering the circumstances. He never regained consciousness, even as the needle was being threaded into his flesh. After it was done we dressed the wound, wrapping it with layers of tape so he couldn't get it off easily. Then we released his arms and legs and wrapped him in a blanket. He seemed to be breathing pretty evenly and his pulse was stronger. There was nothing else we could do at the moment.

The room smelled like puke and rot, but nobody was up for a good scrubbing, and I doubted we could get it all clean anyway.

"Group meeting," Dan said. "Dining room."

We filed in and took seats around the table. Sue went into the kitchen and helped Jay come out to join us, where he huddled in a chair, clutching his knees to his chest and rocking. Then she disappeared back into the kitchen and came out with the bottle of Jack Daniel's and a stack of cups, and poured a round for everyone.

The alcohol burned my throat and stomach going down, but it felt good. Every muscle in my body was shaking with exhaustion and I didn't know if I'd be able to get up again.

"Okay," Dan said, standing at the head of the table. He threw down a shot of Jack and grimaced. "That was weird."

"Understatement of the century," I said.

Nobody laughed. Nobody said anything. Dan scrubbed his face with his hand. I noticed for the first time how much older he looked, stubble on his chin, a hollowness to his cheeks and a slump to his shoulders. He had always prided himself on keeping in perfect shape, eating well and getting enough sleep. If you were on the outside looking in, he never seemed to fit in quite right with the rest of us. We were certainly closer to nerds than jocks; even if I had played some ball way back before high school, I was no ringer. And yet he'd never made fun of us, never put us down in front of his other friends, had remained steadfast in the face of steadily increasing peer pressure. Eventually we had become more popular simply by association. The rest of the jocks left us alone.

Sports had been his life, or so I thought. What was he going to do now?

Leaders lead. I wondered about that. It made sense that he would become the head of our little pack, but Dan could have hung out with any social group he wanted to in White Falls. Why had he chosen us? Was it because we were weaker than the rest, and he felt safe enough to let his guard down? Or was it something else?

"Tell me what happened," Jay said. "No, wait, don't. Ants, was it? Burrowing under his skin?"

We all looked at him. He was even more of a mess, pale as death with black circles under his eyes, thin as a rail, his hair all matted and greasy. That red patch on his arm had gotten worse. He'd been quiet up until then, but now he took the shot of Jack from the table and drank it down. Then he reached for the bottle. Sue went to stop him, but he waved her off and poured another shot. "Did you get them all?" he asked.

"How the fuck should I know," Dan said.

"If we don't, it'll happen again," Jay said. "Hell, it'll probably happen again anyway."

"Let's not jump to conclusions," Dan said. "They must have gone after the wound, the smell maybe, I don't know. We didn't clean it well and it got infected, and somehow they got in there."

Jay laughed, but there was no humor in the sound. It sent chills down my spine. "It's all planned," he said. "All of it." His leg had started jumping again. He looked like a guy who needed to go into detox, all jittery and twitching. "The world's gone to hell, and we're the last ones left standing."

Dan stared at Jay, then at Sue and back again. "What's going on?" he said. "What's wrong with you?"

"Nothing," Sue said. "He's just exhausted. We all are." She moved around to stand behind Jay and put her hands on his shoulders, kneading lightly. When she touched him, he jumped. "Maybe we should just try to get some sleep, and regroup in the morning."

"They were inside the rats too," Jay said. "You guys weren't paying attention, but I saw them, little tiny ones. Don't you get it? That rat in the kitchen was *dead*. They all were. But they attacked us. How do you think they did that?" He looked around at everyone.

"What the hell are you talking about?" I asked.

"Like pilots of an airplane, Pete. The rats' bodies became a means to an end, an inanimate object, nothing more. Puppets getting their strings pulled."

"That's impossible."

Jay shook his head. "They're smarter than you think. Honeybees fly in formation, one by one, obeying precise commands and able to find their targets hundreds of yards away. Ants can build these amazing palaces underground, moving one piece of dirt at a time, all working together in the most complex kind of dance anyone has ever seen. They have social roles. Some take other ant species into slavery for their entire lives. How do they do these things? Nobody knows for sure. But if we could somehow find a way to harness that, the hive mind, use it for our own ends . . ." He shook his head. "Little armies of super soldiers, going places and doing things humans can't do."

"I thought you said they were carrying a plague."

"In a way, that's exactly right."

"But they're not big enough to do any real damage—"

"There are over a billion insects for every single person on earth," Jay said. "You like those odds? How about throwing together some of the most dangerous ones, like the Japanese giant hornet? Three inches long, vicious and deadly to humans? The army ant swarm that'll shred anything in its path? Or the bullet ant, an inch long with the most powerful stinger on earth? They say it feels like getting shot. Oh, and did I mention they live in trees and drop on top of you when you walk by? Try running across a few hundred of those."

His voice had raised in pitch and intensity, and he was sitting up ramrod straight now. Sue took her hands from his shoulders and took a step back.

"Jay," she said, "I don't think—"

"But what really worries me," he said, ignoring her, "based on what's happened here, is the botfly."

"Bot . . ." Dan shook his head. "Jesus Christ, Jay, you're off the deep end, you know that? What the hell's a botfly?"

"They lay their eggs in human flesh," he said. "The larvae eat their way through from the inside."

I heard my father's ghostly voice, from so many years ago: *Life ain't civilized. That's a human creation, rules and order and compassion. Things kill, they eat, or they die.*

You could have heard a pin drop in that room. I don't

know what the others were thinking, but that one got to me. Giant hornets and ants with vicious stingers were bad, sure, but a worm that eats its way through human flesh? Maybe it had something to do with what I'd just witnessed in the other room, but that one, I couldn't stomach.

And then, suddenly, it all came together for me.

"Biological weapons," I said. "You don't mean a virus. You mean those ants we saw in there are genetically engineered insects."

"That's what I'm saying, yes. Taking the worst of different species and blending them together. They'd be natural killers, and smart too. Probably able to be controlled in some way, that would be built in. Wanderers with highly developed social patterns. There might even be different kinds of them. At least some of them the burrowing kind."

I imagined a world ravaged by a swarm of killer insects, the devastation of the nuclear attack giving way to something else. Anything left alive would be unable to fight back and consumed. Or worse.

"They all disappeared," Tessa said. "Anyone notice that? They were crawling everywhere one moment, and then the next, they were gone. Like they knew exactly what they were doing."

"Let's say I buy what you're saying," Dan said. "Let's say there are armies of highly trained, murderous, designer bugs on the loose, ready to overthrow the world. It's plain crazy, but whatever. Why haven't they attacked all of us by now?"

"I don't know," Jay said. "But Jimmie was bitten. Ants have a highly developed sense of smell. Maybe there's a marker of some kind, or maybe they just smell infection."

We all looked at each other. "They're going to come back for him," I said.

"Maybe they never really left," Jay said.

* * *

Dan and I went back into the darkened bedroom and flipped on the lights. It was shocking to see the carnage in this way, blood splattered across the bed and floor, even up on the walls above Jimmie's head and the bottom of the upper bunk.

We were both jittery as hell, choosing our steps carefully, ready to run at the sign of any movement. Jimmie was still sleeping and hadn't moved. I watched the rise and fall of his chest to make sure he was breathing.

I held my nose against the stench and picked up the bloody blanket from the floor and shook it. No little black armored bodies fell out.

Together we looked around the bed, on the floor, the walls. There was no sign of any ants. The shelter looked airtight. I started to wonder if we had all hallucinated it. Maybe something had gotten into the air in here, some kind of odorless gas from the generator or seeping in from outside, and made us all high enough to see such crazy things. It made about as much sense as anything else.

Finally I lifted Jimmie's shirt. Maybe it was wishful thinking, but the hives looked a little less angry to me, and I didn't see a sign of anything moving under his skin.

I swallowed hard. "We should probably change him or something," I said. "Clean this place up. I think someone puked in here."

Dan chuckled. "You are something else, you know that, Pete?"

I smiled through the lump in my throat. I was so goddamned tired, I felt like my muscles might just turn to mush and I'd collapse where I stood.

Dan got down on his hands and knees, poking under the bed. "Hand me that lantern," he said, his voice muffled. "I want to see better under here."

I set it on the floor next to him. "You think Jay's lost it?" he asked, head still halfway under the bed.

"I don't know. Maybe. Killer ants seem like a pretty crazy scenario." I didn't say anything about what Sue told me about his meds, although I have to admit it was damned hard. Dan deserved to know the details. But I wanted a chance to talk to Jay alone first.

"But we saw them, didn't we?" Dan said, echoing my own thoughts of a moment earlier. "We all saw them." He got back up and stood there a moment, then turned to the other beds and pulled off the blanket and sheets from the top bunk, stripping it down to the mattress. Then he did the same for the rest of them, and gathered the sheets into his arms before stuffing them into the closet.

"Just want to make it easier to watch for them," he said. "Just in case."

"Don't you ever question yourself?" I asked. "You always seem so sure. Except when you decided to cut into Jimmie's leg, but even then, you did it. Don't you ever wonder if you can do something, if you've made the right decision, if you are strong enough or good enough or smart enough?"

I didn't think he'd answer me, but he did. "Sure," he said. "All the time. But successful people make a decision and have the confidence to trust in it."

"What if you're wrong?"

"Then I make it right."

Unless it's too late, I thought, but I didn't say it. What good would it do to point that out? Right now, for better or worse, Dan was our rock. We needed him more than he needed us.

For some reason I couldn't see very well anymore. Things were broken into a thousand different prisms of color.

"We're going to die down here, aren't we?" I said.

Plenty of people have written about the point in your

life when you realize that someday, maybe sooner, maybe later, you will cease to exist. Not when you're a kid and you get the general concept of death, but later on, when you're old enough to *really* grasp that life is finite. You can finally see your life as a complete package, the beginning, middle and the coming end. You realize how random life is—who is chosen, and when—and question why you have been chosen to survive. This realization gives you a new perspective, a sense of appreciation for the time you have, and a sense of inevitability as time races on, faster and faster.

I was feeling that right now.

"No," Dan said. "We're going to make it. I promise you that."

"I don't feel so good," I said. "I think maybe I better lie down."

"That's a good idea," Dan said. "We'll take shifts, to watch out for each other. We should all get some rest. Things will make more sense if we sleep on it."

I seriously doubted that, but I nodded. I left it to him to tell the others, flipped off the overhead lights and crawled onto the adjacent mattress, and, bugs be damned, was almost instantly asleep.

CHAPTER SIXTEEN

I woke up sometime later disoriented and cold, clutching at a blanket that wasn't there. My dreams had been bad, but I remembered very little. Something about bumblebees the size of footballs chasing my mother down a dark tunnel. I strained to remember what had happened to her in the dream, but I could not. It seemed important somehow, as evidenced by the ache in my chest.

I miss you, Mom. I'm so sorry.

My eyes were wet and I had to use the bathroom very badly.

The room was bathed in a soft, dim light from the lantern on its lowest setting. The smell had gotten worse. I could hear someone snoring lightly in the bunk above me, and figured it was Sue.

I lay there for a minute as my mind cleared, thinking about what Jay had said. Some kind of terrorist group experimenting with the genetic code of insects. Creating something that the world has never seen before. *You're fucking kidding me. Nuclear warheads don't do enough damage?*

It meant the possibility of facing things that would make radiation poisoning look like a bad case of the herpes. I remembered reading a Web article a while back about bioengineered weapons and nanotechnology, and rumors that the military was conducting experiments to combine the two and create machines that could rearrange human or animal cells at the molecular level; carry and disperse genetic codes of different species, create mutations, horrible pain, or simply cause the body to dissolve into itself until there was nothing left.

Hell, Jay might have even been the one who sent the link to me. It was probably just the rantings of one of those fringe conspiracy groups he always loved to talk about, but it did make me wonder. A few weeks ago, we would have all laughed it off as Jay just being Jay. But now, it didn't seem quite so crazy after all.

I sensed movement from the bunk next to me. When I looked over, Jimmie's eyes were open and he was blinking rapidly at me.

"Water," he said in a croaking voice. "Please." Then, as if suddenly remembering what had happened, he lifted his head enough to look down at his bandaged leg. "Are they gone?"

"I think so."

His head fell back to the pillow and he closed his eyes. "Thank God."

"I'll get you a drink."

I got up and walked through the other room. Dan was sitting at the table, head nodding toward his chest. He jerked awake as I passed, looking guilty. I wondered how long we'd all been sleeping, and whether he'd woken up anyone else for a shift. Probably not.

"Did you see anything?" I asked.

"No," he said. "I've been checking the bedroom every few minutes. Nothing."

"Jimmie's up," I said. "I'm getting him some water, and then I'll sit up a while so you can sleep, okay?"

He nodded. I continued into the kitchen, poured the

water and found an antibiotic pill, and brought it back into the bedroom.

Dan had climbed into a bunk and was already fast asleep. I helped Jimmie sit up slightly and put a pillow under his back, then helped him take the water. He tried to gulp it down, choked, and then took a slower, longer sip, and swallowed the pill too. His lips were cracked and bleeding. I tried not to stare at his scalp, which was showing through in patches. I don't think he'd noticed yet, and I wasn't about to point it out.

I felt his forehead and sat down on the end of the mattress, ducking my head slightly to keep from hitting the top bunk, where Tessa was sleeping. "Fever's broke," I said, my voice low to avoid disturbing the others. "How do you feel?"

"Like a truck parked on my chest," he said. "And then a meteor landed on the truck." He tried to smile and only managed a grimace of pain. "My leg hurts so bad. You guys . . . cut me?"

"Yep. Tied you up too. Sorry, we had no choice. You were pretty out of it."

"Thanks." He closed his eyes and for a moment, I thought he'd fallen back asleep. But then he spoke again. "Those things . . . I could *feel* them inside me. Chewing." He shivered and opened his eyes again, and searched my own as if he might be able to see the truth in there. "How do you know you got them all out?"

I wondered how to answer that. The honest answer was, I didn't know. "Can you still feel them?"

He thought about it for a moment. "No," he said. "I can't." He sighed. "What a fucked-up world, eh, Pete?" Then he tried to sit up some more, groaned, and lay back.

"Yeah," I said. "You could say that."

I looked around the room. The light was dim enough

that I could almost imagine movement in the corners. Little black lines of something crawling. When I blinked, they were gone.

Insects could get in anywhere. They could *be* anywhere. How could we possibly stay safe from something like that?

Again, I thought Jimmie might have drifted off to sleep, and I was startled when he spoke up. "We have to try to see what's outside that hatch," he said.

"I don't think that's a very good idea. It's too early. The fallout could still be deadly—"

"We don't know that," he said. "We don't know anything about what's happening out there."

"Still, it's too dangerous. We can't risk it."

He shook his head. "I could go."

"Jimmie, that's crazy. It's suicide."

"I'm . . . infected. That rat gave me something. Look at me." He gestured down at his legs, which were blotchy with the hives. "If anyone goes, it should be me."

"It's probably just a virus. Your fever's down already. You're going to be okay."

He shook his head again, and squeezed his eyes shut, hard. There was a catch in his voice. "I'm sorry I'm such a fuckup. I'm sorry about what I did in that tunnel. I don't know what I was thinking." He sighed and wiped tears away from his eyes. "I didn't mean to hurt anybody, least of all you, Pete. You're my best friend, you know that? We've been together ever since we were kids, and now, down here, I've just been acting like a spoiled brat, getting into that fight the first night, then the tunnel . . ." He was crying hard now, tears streaming down his face, his nose running. "I'm just so scared, man. That's it. I'm so scared. Ah, God." He wiped his nose with his hand. "I'm such a pussy." He laughed. "I can't even cry right."

I remembered the day when we were ten years old and we'd gone sledding on the hill outside our elementary school. It was a brutally cold day, and it hadn't snowed in a while. The hill had gotten so packed down it had nearly turned to ice. I took my first run, my teeth snapping together over the bumps, my face aching from the wind, then another. On the way back up the hill, another larger boy lost control of his sled and ran full speed into my legs, flipping me over so I landed on my shoulder. I could feel the bones crack, the pain like an electric shock running down the entire side of my body.

Jimmie told the other boy to get help. He stayed with me until the teacher came, and then he rode with me in my mother's car to the hospital. He insisted on staying there until I went in to get my bone set, and then he was at my house when I got home.

I was going to do what I could to be there for him now.

I got up from the bed and I hugged him, and it was a real hug, no quick patting of the backs or whatever, guy code out the window. Jimmie was an only child, like me, and for better or worse, I think that can tend to make you a more selfish person if you're not careful. It depends on how you're raised, and knowing his mom and dad, it was no wonder he acted the way he did. They doted on him, the kind of parents who insisted he wear a helmet and pads when he rode his bike even when he was twelve years old, the kind who walked him across every street and made sure he had his vitamins and called him "our special boy." I always got the sense he was embarrassed by it, especially around me, since he knew the way my father was; but sometimes I thought it was more than that. Sometimes I wondered if he secretly envied some part of my life, as crazy as that sounds. I was forced to prove myself, again and again, while Jimmie was coddled to the point of distraction.

When I pulled away from the hug we were both uncomfortable. "Maybe we should, I don't know, make out or something," I said.

Jimmie laughed, then winced. "You always could make an awkward situation worse," he said.

"It's a rare talent."

"Does Dan still want to kill me?"

"I think he's coming around. Just don't lock him in with a bunch of killer rats again anytime soon."

"I'll do my best." Jimmie touched the bandage over his leg. "What were those things, Pete?"

"We don't know for sure. They looked like ants. Jay has a few theories . . ." I shrugged. "Pretty crazy, to tell you the truth. I think they were going after the infection, and what with the situation aboveground, they're being more aggressive than usual. Let's face it, you're ant bait, man."

"I don't like the sound of that."

"Yeah, well, join the club." I stood up from the bunk. "Listen, you rest a bit more. I'm going to make some coffee and something to eat. You up for that?"

He nodded, leaned back and closed his eyes. "Sure, sounds good. Thanks."

I left him lying there in the semidark, his eyes still wet, or maybe he'd never quite stopped the tears. Either way, I had the funny feeling that Jimmie was never going to be the same, that the Jimmie I'd known was gone. Maybe that was the same for all of us.

I also had the feeling that something terrible was coming, something that would tear us all apart and would make what happened so far look like a day at the beach. No matter how hard I tried, I couldn't shake it.

As it turned out, I wasn't even close. It was far worse.

PART THREE:
THE INFECTED

"The world began without man, and it will end without him."
—Claude Levi-Strauss

CHAPTER SEVENTEEN

My mother was my protector. She got real good at sensing one of my father's moods, and did her best to keep me out of the path of the storm. His drinking wouldn't always deteriorate into violence; sometimes he would just get mellow, even a little nostalgic. Other times he'd just sit and stare out the window at the trees. I knew he'd survived the terrible events that had turned White Falls into a ghost town a few years back, although I was too young to remember much of it, and maybe that had something to do with his moods. But then again, if I'm to be consistent here, I suppose I have to acknowledge that the darkness was hardwired into him, and it wouldn't have mattered much where he lived or what kind of life he led. And if I'm honest with myself, I'd have to admit that maybe I'd inherited some of it from him.

When the drink turned the dark against him, it was like someone had dialed down the thermostat and the air held a charge. Violence was like an unwelcome houseguest who wouldn't leave. I guess I got pretty good at sensing it too. If he was yelling, that was a good sign; it was when he was quiet and still that you had to watch out.

The problem (and it was a big one) was that my mother's way of protecting me was to take the brunt of my father's wrath. Distraction, as it were. It usually worked, but she would be the worse for it. There were plenty of bruises and finger marks and black eyes, and she'd suffered multiple broken bones over the years.

The slow progression of my mother's disease didn't seem to stop him either. I used to wonder whether it was the diagnosis itself that set him off in the first place. Maybe he felt she'd abandoned him in some way, or pushed the focus onto herself and the burden onto him. They both knew that she'd get progressively worse over time, and he would eventually have to bathe her and change her clothes, carry her from bed to chair and back again. My father was not a caregiver, and maybe he felt that he'd married her so that she could do all those things for him.

But as I grew older I realized that wasn't entirely the case. There was something else between them, something that maybe used to be warmer but that had slowly shriveled up and turned black. And I was a part of it. I knew I looked like her, more than I did him, and that it drove him crazy: the lighter color of my hair, the freckles across my nose, the more delicate bone structure.

It did strike me later that perhaps I was not his child, although I had nothing firm to account for that. My mother didn't have many real friends, certainly no male ones, and nobody came around asking about me after my father died in a way that might have been suspicious. I couldn't imagine my mother having an affair, but then again she was my mother, and, of course, it wouldn't have occurred to me back then that she was a sexual being.

Whatever it was about me, it speeded that darkness along. When my father looked at me, I could see the thing that lived inside him all coiled up and waiting to strike.

One of the worst moments of my life happened when I was only nine years old. This was before my mother's wheelchair days, although I remember it was getting more difficult for her to get around, especially in the mornings, when she'd awaken stiff and clumsy and things she touched would tend to spill and break. This particular morning was a bad one, after a night of heavy drinking for my father and the dawn coming crisp and clear. The sun must have felt like shards of glass in his eyes, and I remember him shouting something about the curtains before my mother got up to pull them all the way closed.

I was up by then, an early riser in those days, listening outside their door. It was my way of testing the wind. I had become very good at telling his mood, just from hearing the tone of his voice when he woke up. That night I'd wet the bed, something that had been happening more and more frequently after the deer incident, and I was desperate for him not to find out. I had stripped off my sheets and hidden them in my closet, but the stain had bled through to my mattress, and my room smelled strongly of piss.

I thought I was lucky when my mother came out of the bedroom first and saw me crouching inside my open door as she began to try to navigate the stairs down to the kitchen. She followed me in there and saw my stripped bed, and I recognized the fear in her eyes as quickly as she tried to hide it.

"Give me the sheets," she said. "Go."

I opened the closet doors and she took the sheets in her arms and walked back out in the hallway to the stairs again in her stiffened, shuffling gait. She hadn't closed the door to their bedroom fully, and we could both hear my father's snoring.

Again, I thought that by some miracle I'd made it through, and started to relax.

When my mother reached the third-to-last step, an edge of the sheet slipped from her arms and caught her foot, and she fell.

She hit the floor so hard it shook the house. I heard her cry out and almost immediately stifle herself, but by then it was too late.

I shrunk back into the shadows of my room. My father cursed and came out of the bedroom a few moments later. He shuffled to the top of the stairs and stared down.

"The fuck you doing, Miriam?" he said, as if he couldn't believe what he was seeing. "Get off the goddamned floor." Then he went down to her. I couldn't see them from where I was, but I heard him mumble something to her, then a muffled slap. I crept out into the hall.

"No," she said clearly.

"What'd you say to me?"

"I did it. It was my fault. I was cleaning his room and I fell and I . . . wet myself."

"Fuck you did."

I heard my mother sob once, and then another stinging slap.

"Where is he?"

Terrified, I scurried back to my room, turned out the lights and crouched in the closet, pulling the doors shut behind me. I sat there hugging my knees, the smell of piss from my underwear in my nostrils. I'd forgotten to change them and he would smell it for sure. I took them off, squeezed them into a ball and tucked them inside a box of old baby clothes.

When he opened the closet doors I was sitting naked in the corner, rocking back and forth, thumb in my mouth.

He reached down without a word and yanked me to my feet and into the room. "You pissed the bed again," he said. His eyes were little slits, his mouth set in a thin line. "You're making your mother do more laundry and you're ruining another mattress but more importantly you *woke me up.* I told you to keep quiet in the mornings."

He shoved me toward the bed. I stood and tried to cover myself with my hand. "You got nothing to hide there," he said. "What kind of boy wets his bed every night? You some kind of faggot? You like guys' dicks? That it? Jesus." He spat against the wall, where it hung for a moment, a fat yellow blob, before dripping down. "Sucking your thumb. Christ. You're spineless, boy, always have been. I got a splitting headache, and now I gotta teach you what it means when you wet the bed." He approached me, hands at his sides, looking around the room for something appropriate.

I knew that look, and backed away, whimpering. When he got like this I knew he would hurt me, probably with a belt or strap, and I didn't know when he would stop.

My mother appeared behind him and touched his arm. "Jeffrey, please—"

He didn't even turn, just backhanded her into the wall, the sound of his hand hitting her face like a hammer against wood. She went down to her knees but got back up again as he came at me, jumping and clinging to his back and screaming at me to get out.

He grunted and stumbled slightly as her weight hit him. I slipped past my father's grasp, and the last thing I saw before I left the room was him holding her by the hair with one hand and punching her in the face.

I hid in the trees in the backyard for two hours. The black flies swarmed around my naked body, but I didn't dare go near the house. I was covered in bites and pinpricks of blood. I went to the shallow stream to wash it off, but that only made them worse. Eventually I saw my mother coming out the rear door, walking with a limp. One eye was swollen shut and her lower lip was split in the middle.

She was holding my clothes in one hand, the other arm bent close to her chest. I ran to her.

"Your father's gone out," she said. "There'll be a doctor coming. I fell down the stairs, you understand me? I fell down the stairs with some washing and got hurt, bad."

"He *hit* you." I shook my head, trembling all over, my eyes spilling over with tears.

She took me by the arm with her good hand and shook it hard enough that a day later, I had bruises there from her fingers. She dropped down heavily to her knees and looked me in the face. "Petey, listen to me. I fell. That's all. You didn't see what you think you saw. Your daddy, he . . . he loves me. He wouldn't do that. He was angry, but he stopped. He didn't let it get out of hand."

I shook my head again, tears streaming down my face. My entire body ached inside. "I'm sorry," I said. "I didn't mean to, Momma." I started sobbing and she gathered me to her chest, holding me close and rocking me gently.

"I know you didn't, baby," she said. "Shhh, now, it's okay. It's not your fault. Everything's fine. You'll see."

She got me cleaned up and dressed, and when the doctor arrived the laundry was done and she was lying on the couch with an icepack and I was sitting with her. My father acted like I weren't there. He had been deflated in some way by the violence, and now just looked like a tired old man. I often noticed that with him; it was as if some charge built up over time, a spring winding him ever tighter until the explosion, and then it would begin all over again.

The doctor treated my mother's injuries, spoke to her and my father for a few minutes longer, and left. He never talked to me.

If he had, I don't know what I would have said. I kept out of my father's way for a few days after that and started wearing rubber shorts to bed, and things were better for a while. But even at nine years old, I had a feeling that things were only going to get worse. I sensed a moment coming when everything would come to a head, and my world would change in some explosive, life-altering way.

It took another six years, but the day did come when my father's luck ran out. The fact that I was there to witness it mattered more to the police who came to the house than it did to me, or at least that's what I told myself. He was dead, and our family and the entire world was better for it.

Tessa told me once that I was in denial, that discovering such a thing had to have been a terribly traumatic experience for me and that I needed help to deal with it. This was after we'd gotten to know each other well enough that she could say those types of things to me. I guess she was probably right. Tessa was always right. But back then I wanted only to lock it all away and move on with my life, forgetting my father and all the emotional baggage that came along with him and letting my mother finally breathe without fear.

If I was anything like him, it was just this: I was unable to see my own blind spots, and when I finally came upon them it was with great surprise, as if someone else had been walking in my shoes and only at that moment had I been plopped down into them and begun to see things as they truly were.

My anger ran deep, second only to my denial, and both things together would eventually rise up and drown me in a great sweeping wave of blood, violence and shame.

CHAPTER EIGHTEEN

For about a week after the incident with the ants, it seemed as if Jimmie would recover fully. He got up and started limping around the shelter, using a mop handle that Sue had adapted as a makeshift crutch, then abandoning that shortly after, complaining that it hurt his arm too much.

As funny as it sounds, the complaining made me think the real Jimmie was back again, and I welcomed it. Tessa wasn't so sure. "Sometimes I want to crack his skull," she said, after we all spent hours cleaning up the mess of puke and blood in the bedroom while he sat and watched and occasionally gave us instructions. The smell faded but a ghost of it settled in permanently, leaving the air feeling heavier and slightly polluted. Maybe it was the ventilation system.

The idea of Tessa cracking anyone's skull made me laugh, and she punched me in the arm lightly and smiled when I did. I sensed a change in her lately, and I knew I'd changed too. The laughter was still there, but whatever it had been hiding was bubbling closer to the surface. It was as if several protective layers had been stripped away during the trauma of the past couple of weeks, and we were all feeling raw and exposed. One crack and everything would explode upward like liquid under some tectonic shift.

Those next few days, we continued sleeping in stages, watching for any sign that the insects had returned. We had to assume that they would only attack the wounded; they would have been all over us already if that wasn't the case. But Jimmie was still a target. We kept his wound clean and changed the bandages twice a day, which meant we had to start washing the gauze wrapping or we would have run out before long.

After a while it was easy to slip back into a more relaxed routine. Dan was the last to give up his watch, but even he finally fell asleep in his chair, and nothing happened that night, or the next night either.

We kept living. I wish I could say something significant, how we learned to adapt, how we learned the Great Lesson; but life just went on. Sometimes—now this is funny—I felt like I were alone down there. I mean, I was living in four rooms with a couple of girls and three guys and we couldn't get away from each other if we tried. But every once in a while the walls just seemed to fall away and there was distance, great distance, and nothing but emptiness.

I often dreamed about the way it was up top, as I guess maybe I've said. Sometimes my dreams were about nothing but water—great wide stretches of it as far as you could see. I used to love watching the sailboats when I was a kid, it was a freedom thing, when my father came down a little hard and I yearned for some open space and a way to escape. But now my memories were fading away like fog on a summer morning, and the colors often seemed wrong, as if the ocean in my dreams was just a little too blue.

I didn't want it to be that way. I wanted to remember.

The insects did not return, and Jimmie's hives didn't get any worse, but they didn't fade away. I took to calling him pepperoni for the way they looked scattered across his legs and stomach, until he told me to stop. For some reason I didn't quite understand, I listened. Maybe I felt sorry for him. His hair loss slowed but didn't stop completely, and we all avoided talking about that. I think maybe we felt that with what we were facing aboveground, it could happen to any of us at any moment. After all, Dan and I had been exposed at the beginning and we'd all gone into that tunnel. Even if we weren't showing symptoms now, who knew when they might start appearing?

Dan marked the wall when he woke up, and listened to the radio every morning and every night for about twenty minutes at a sitting—the same schedule he'd kept pretty much since the beginning—checking the emergency broadcast frequency, then dialing up and down the bands looking for anything but static. I don't think any of us actually thought he'd hear something, but it was one of the few possible beacons of hope for us, so we gave him that time and space willingly, and sometimes listened in too.

Those were a few of the things that concerned us as we tried to settle back into some kind of routine. But what I worried about the most was Jay. He was acting more erratic by the day, moving with a kind of frenzied energy, his eyes wild and darting like a trapped animal's, and he kept digging into every corner and closet in the shelter, pulling things out of boxes as if searching for something, although when confronted, he refused to admit it. I often came upon him and Sue engaged in a heated but whispered conversation that stopped as soon as I entered the room. There was clearly something going on between them that was making things worse, but whenever I tried to bring up the subject to Sue, she passed it off as his increasingly paranoid delusions and her efforts to talk some sense into him.

Maybe that was really all it was, but I doubted it. Jay was wound pretty tight, but he'd always given off a kind of honest intent even when talking about the wildest theories. And the look in Sue's eyes was one of guilt, as if she were hiding something too painful or explosive to say.

I did try to speak to Jay about the situation, his meds and how he felt. But he brushed me off time after time, making up things to do, and finally avoiding me completely. At least until the following week, when everything unraveled.

CHAPTER NINETEEN

I'd sensed Jay building up steam earlier that day (watching him reminded me a little bit of my father before one of his explosions), and during that evening it came to a head. I woke up in the middle of the night and heard him having an argument with Sue in the kitchen, their voices muffled, but clearly strained and raised in anger or fear. That time of night was pretty much the only time anyone could get any privacy. We were all on top of each other, and I think the stress was making us all a little stir-crazy.

The lights in the bedroom were dim. I could hear Dan snoring lightly to my right and could just make out his huddled, still form. I glanced at the bed to my left and found Jimmie fast asleep. But Tessa had rolled over onto her side and was staring at me from the top bunk. "You hear them?" I whispered.

She nodded. "I think he's about to lose it. You should do something before things get worse."

I'd explained the situation to Tessa earlier, so she understood everything. I knew I could count on her to be discreet with Dan, who, while well-intentioned, was like a bull in a china shop when it came to things like human psychology.

I was determined to confront Jay now, no excuses. Sue was right. Something had to be done. But there was a right and wrong way to handle a situation like this, and I only hoped I would know which was which when the time came.

The two of us dressed in the semidark and crept into the kitchen. Sue was standing near the pantry door, arms crossed, while Jay paced back and forth before the sink in a black sweatshirt and sweatpants. He was sweating heavily and scratching at his arm again, and his blinking had become more exaggerated as if he was trying to clear his sight. His hands were trembling. If I hadn't known better, I would have sworn he was on some kind of stimulant like meth or coke. We didn't have a lot of the heavy drugs in our high school, but there were always a few users in any school, and I'd seen them high once or twice and knew what those drugs could do.

At first, neither of them saw us, but when they did they both stopped short as if caught in something indecent.

"He can't sleep," Sue said finally, as if that explained it. "Nerves."

"I can't sleep because—"

"You need air," she said. "You need space. I know."

Jay stared at her for a long moment and then looked away, shaking his head. "My sister would be ashamed," he muttered. "You know our little dog?"

I opened my mouth and then closed it again, shocked into silence by this sudden change in direction.

"Sure," Tessa said "T-Bone, right?"

Jay just continued as if he hadn't heard, his voice high-pitched and shaky, the words running together as he paced back and forth in his socks. "My sister, she picked that dog out at the pound—we all went, I was maybe nine or ten and she was a teenager—I wanted a black Lab because our neighbor Holly had one and I loved that dog, played with it when I went to her house on the weekends."

I nodded, as if I understood where all this was going, while in my head I was wondering whether we would have to restrain him or something, and what we could possibly do if he didn't snap out of this obvious psychosis.

"My parents were going to find a Lab breeder but my sister, she insisted on the pound. 'There are so many dogs looking for a home,' she said, 'if they don't get adopted they're put to sleep, killed, because nobody loves them.' So we went and they didn't have any Labs and we walked all over that place and looked at all the dogs and there were a couple of mutt puppies that had just come in that were pretty cute. But she didn't want anything to do with them, she just looked around for the ugliest, meanest dog in the place, 'I want that one,' and there was T-Bone, huddled in the back of his cage, growling, his fur all matted and that one torn ear and his fur stained around his eyes with the gunk he was always producing. My parents tried to convince her to take another one instead, but she insisted, and when they let T-Bone out of his cage, he wouldn't come anywhere near us, he snapped at us and growled, but she didn't give up, and when I started complaining she took me aside. 'If we don't save him, nobody else will,' she said, 'he'll die here, all alone. He's been mistreated all his life, but it's not his fault. Don't you want to help him, Jay?' There were tears in her eyes. That was my sister, always doing the right thing, the smartest, strongest and best person I knew. I could never measure up to that. And you know what? Taking that little dog home was one of the best things we ever did."

The whole story came out in a single rush. None of us said anything. Jay was crying without making a sound, his shoulders shaking in silence, his face screwed up tight. "I miss that dog," he said. Then he turned and swept his arm violently across the counter, knocking the dish drainer onto the floor. The three plastic plates stacked in it bounced and clattered across the tile.

He turned back to us, his chest heaving, hair damp with sweat, nose running with snot. "Tell them, Sue," he said. "They deserve to know the truth."

She glanced at us, then back at Jay. "Calm down, please," she said.

"No. Do the right thing." He clutched his hands to his head. "It's hidden around here somewhere, the truth. Ah, God! My head, it's on fire, I can't stop it, these voices." He grunted, a brief, strange, fierce bark of sound that echoed through the shelter and died away.

"Jay, listen to me," I said. I put my hands out as if that would calm him, then drew them back, thinking better of it. "I hear them too."

That stopped him. He cocked his head at me, not unlike the way a small dog would. I knew just enough about delusional thinking to be dangerous. I remembered a few of the techniques that worked with my father, but they didn't *always* work, and you were never sure when the attempt would backfire.

I looked around the room, everywhere but right at him, avoiding eye contact. I wanted him to identify with me, not feel threatened by me. "Sometimes they soothe me. Sometimes they try to give me advice. And sometimes they don't make any sense at all." I glanced briefly at Tessa, and she gave me a nod and a brief smile as if to say *good job, keep going.* The problem was, I had no idea what to say next. There was a voice in my head, sure, but was that really any different than anyone else? I figured everyone had such a voice. It was called a conscience. I was pretty sure the situation with Jay right now was different.

"I learned a way to tune them out," I continued, fishing for the right words. "But it's hard. You focus on someone else's voice, you put on mental blinders and you find something simple that needs to be done. One thing at a time. That can help. If you ignore them, eventually they start fading away."

"Are you cut?" he said.

"Excuse me?"

"They get into the blood," he said, staring off into space. I didn't know if he was talking to me. "They get inside and they start chewing, and they don't stop until they're in control."

I remembered something Jimmie had said: *I could feel them inside me, chewing.* I didn't like the sound of this at all. "You mean the voices in your head?"

He squeezed his eyes shut hard, once, twice. "These voices aren't imaginary, these are real. I can't understand what they're saying, it's just white noise. But they're getting louder."

"What's going on?" It was Dan, emerging from the other room, wide-awake and ready for action, God bless him. "I heard shouting."

"It's okay," I said. "We're just venting, that's all. Where's Jimmie?"

"Still in bed," Dan said, staring at Jay with obvious mistrust. "He's pretty exhausted. I told him to stay there, I'd check it out."

"I just want to get *out* of here," Jay said, his entire body trembling. He wiped the snot from his nose, his chest hitching. "I feel like someone's tearing my head apart. I can't *think!* I can't *think!*" He turned to Sue. "Tell them, or I swear to God I will."

"Baby—"

"No?" Jay turned to the rest of us. "Fine, I'll do it, then."

"Please—"

"It's no coincidence we're down in this godforsaken

hole," Jay said. "Sue's grandfather knew it was going to happen. He was a part of the whole thing."

"Stop it!" Sue screamed. "Just stop it, stop it, stop it—"

Two things happened in quick succession: the first was that Jay stepped forward and slapped Sue's face. The sound was like a stick snapping in the woods, and it left a bright red, blooming print across her cheek. Her mouth snapped shut, and she raised her fingers to the mark, as if exploring its heat.

The second was a direct result of the first: I leaped forward between them, intent on stopping whatever Jay might do next. As I did, I grabbed for his arms, but caught the sleeve of his sweatshirt instead, and as he yanked and twisted himself away from me, his arm slid out of the sleeve I was holding and the sweatshirt rode up over his head, exposing his belly.

I let go of the sleeve as if I'd been scalded, and Jay pulled the sweatshirt back over his head to cover himself, breathing hard. He clutched his arms to his chest as if to hide it. But the glimpse I'd gotten of his stomach had been burned into my brain forever.

"What was that?" I said.

"Nothing!"

Sue's sobs grew louder.

Twin swollen lines like scratches down his skin . . .

"Let us see," I said. "He's hiding something. Dan, he's burning up. Tell him to take that sweatshirt off."

"No," Sue said. "Leave him alone!"

"Pete, let him be," Tessa said. "He's scared."

"So am I."

Dan looked at me strangely. But he gestured at Jay. "Let's see your stomach, then," he said. "Come on."

I didn't think he'd do it, and I imagined the very unpleasant possibility of wrestling him to the ground. I wasn't sure I wanted him to, either, if I'd seen what I thought I'd seen . . . But slowly, Jay let his arms drop. His entire body was shaking so hard and fast I thought he might actually start chattering like a jackhammer across the tile.

"I'm sorry, Sue," he said. "I love you." He raised the shirt.

Two deep, bright red furrows ran across his chest to his stomach. But that wasn't what made my blood run cold.

Hives had bloomed across his skin like a constellation of blood and pus, spreading outward from the twin wounds. Some were little bigger than dimes, while others were almost as large as Jimmie's had been.

We all stood there staring at him, the silence broken only by Sue's quiet sobs. I felt pinpricks of fear cross my scalp and the nape of my neck, and the idea that we were alone on this planet, perhaps this universe, utterly alone, filled my mind until I felt impossibly small, that grain of sand on an endless beach, the speck of dust in a hurricane.

"He scratched me, when we were fighting over you in the tunnel, and I was trying to let you back through the door," Jay said. "They look for breaks in the skin, for blood, that's how they get in. They smell it. My scrape's not as bad or as deep as his bite, so maybe it took them longer to find me, I don't know. But they did. I'm infected."

The fight about the tunnel had happened over two weeks ago. Any wounds he'd received should have pretty much healed up by now. Unless something was keeping them from healing.

Sue's sobs grew louder. Her cheek, where he'd hit her, was a mass of red, and I could see the swelling growing worse.

"Why didn't you tell us?" Tessa said.

"You should have said something," I said. "We could help you. Jimmie's better now, maybe there's a way to recover from whatever this is—"

"No." Jay shook his head. "Jimmie's not better." He chuckled, but there was no humor in the sound at all. "You just got rid of one version of these things, but the really dangerous ones—they're microscopic, they get in your blood and move to your brain—those are still there. You'll see, soon enough."

"You're crazy," Dan said. "What did you mean, Sue's grandfather knew? He was a part of what, exactly?"

He took a step backward, as if it might be catching. If Dan wasn't on board to handle this, I didn't know what we'd do.

Jay's face scrunched up again as he fought more tears. He looked at Sue. "I'm sorry," he said again. "I didn't mean to hit you. But they should know everything. It might help." His voice broke, and he whined in the back of his throat. "Ah, God. This is hard. It hu—huurts. Something . . ." Then he opened his mouth, wide, wider, and the muscles in his neck stood out, veins jumping in his temples. His head came forward and he stood there, as if trying to force something out of his throat, his eyes leaking tears. I thought he might be choking, and he made a small sound like a cough before his eyes went completely dead. It was the strangest, most unsettling thing, almost as if the Jay we knew was a machine, and someone had just flipped the *off* switch.

Then, without warning, he screamed again, but this was not a human sound at all. It reminded me of the sound an old dial-up modem made when trying to connect over a phone line. The high-pitched, earsplitting, crackling screech went on until I thought my ears might burst.

Finally he stopped.

In the ensuing silence, as we stood in mute shock, an answering sound came from another part of the shelter.

It didn't sound human.

"Holy fuck," Dan said. He did not look at me, kept his eyes on Jay, who stood absolutely still in the center of the kitchen, his eyes still dead and dull, as if whatever essence, whatever life had been in him, was gone. "Pete, go. Now."

My heart was pounding and I had a sickly sour trembling in my stomach. I turned and raced through the dining room to the bedroom doorway.

Jimmie was sitting straight up in bed. He held the same strange pose as Jay had in the kitchen: tendons standing out in his neck, dead eyes looking at nothing, mouth open and head thrust forward. A line of spittle spun out from one corner of his mouth and dripped onto the mattress.

"Jimmie?" I said. "You okay?" I stepped forward and snapped my fingers in front of his face. No response. I reached down and pinched the flesh of his arm. Nothing. I might as well have been dealing with a wooden sculpture, except for the heat of his skin, his chest rising and falling, air passing through his mouth and nose.

I could see the slight pulse of an artery in his neck. But he did not move one muscle, not even a twitch in his eye or cheek, and when I tried to turn his face to look at me I could not budge it.

Again, the strange idea of a sculpture struck me, a hollow machine like the Trojan horse, something that looked like Jimmie and felt like Jimmie, but wasn't Jimmie at all. A shell that hid something far worse.

My entire body was tingling, the hairs rising up across my arms and legs as I took a step away from him, everything in my soul telling me to *leave this place*, take everyone and do it now. But where would we go? There was no escape from what was essentially our tomb. I felt like tearing open that hatch and running until I couldn't run anymore, until my lungs screamed and gave out, and I collapsed in a heap of debris and under the metal gray clouds of the apocalypse, my tears turned to blood and my skin blistering and turning black.

My breathing grew shallow and quick, my heart rate leaping ever faster as stars swirled in my vision, and I realized that I was having a panic attack. I could not risk passing out now, but already I was feeling light-headed. I stumbled, the room spinning around me.

Almost as if I willed it to happen, I turned and Tessa was there, my Tessa, looking for all the world like my guardian angel, and perhaps she was; I fell toward her and she held out her arms to catch me as lightly as a parent would catch a child, but even as I fell I realized that she wasn't there at all and had not caught me, it had all been in my mind, and I hit the floor hard.

The fierce bark of pain brought me sharply back into focus, and I sat up rubbing my head. A sudden commotion came from the kitchen, things crashing to the floor and more shouting, and then Jay scrambled through the dining room and around the table right in front of me, slipping and crashing into the wall and then up again from all fours as objects tumbled off the shelves. His glasses were gone and his skin was shiny with sweat, and he moved with a strange, disjointed gait as if there were something wrong with his legs.

He saw me sitting there, and as we made eye contact I caught a glimpse of the sheer panic and desperation that had hold of him.

"F-f-find it," he said. It took obvious effort for him to speak, the words forced out of him in a stuttering, stop-and-start staccato. "If she won't tell. If she won't. It's in here, s-s-somewhere, the answers to everything. You take care of her, you p-p-promise me. I . . . can't hold them off anymore . . . hurts . . . so bad."

He looked at me again, pleading, then clutched his head as he had in the kitchen and shrieked at the ceiling, the sound of pure agony, not the strange inhuman sound from before, but a person in terrible pain. It looked like he was fighting with himself. As strange as it sounds, it looked like a battle for control. I wanted to believe he was finally buckling under the pressure, the pressure he'd felt his entire life from his family, of not being good enough or smart enough as the rest of them; the pressure of being trapped down here under the dirt and rocks in an eight-hundred-square-foot coffin; the pressure of staying strong for a girlfriend who needed more than any of the rest of us seemed to understand.

But at that moment, watching him clutching at his own head and screaming, remembering the hives on his chest, Jimmie's strange behavior and what we had cut out of his leg, I believed it was something far worse.

They get into the blood . . . they get inside and they start chewing, and they don't stop until they're in control.

I stood on wobbly legs as Sue came out of the kitchen after him, screaming for him to stop. She grabbed for him but he shook her off and went for the steps.

I realized too late what he meant to do.

Dan came through from the kitchen just as I went for the stairs too, and we ran headlong into each other, tangling up our legs and slowing both of us down long enough for Jay to get to the ladder. Sue scrambled up the steps after him as we came around the table toward her, and I could see her reach for him but he kicked at her and she fell back, tumbling down to land at our feet.

Jay started to turn the hatch wheel.

A screeching alarm sounded through the shelter and a flashing red light went off on the wall near the shelves. Above the sound of the alarm I thought I could hear a vast, angry humming sound from beyond the hatch, which frightened me more than anything else. I didn't know what it could be, but I knew it wasn't good.

Jay's feet disappeared as he climbed the ladder up and out and was gone.

I heard Sue screaming again and Dan grabbed her around the waist as she tried to go after Jay. She elbowed him in the face and almost wriggled free, and I jumped on top of them both, but still she fought hard, heaving and twisting against us and nearly getting away even then, calling for him to come back, pleading with him to return to her.

I'm not sure why we chose to restrain her, rather than try to get to Jay. I guess we both realized there was no stopping him now, and losing Sue in the process was only going to make things worse. Still, my heart ached for her and as I felt her body wracked with sobs, a terrible hope-lessness filled my core until I was weeping too, weeping for the loss of Jay and also for the loss of something impor-tant within myself, a part of what made me human.

We held her down as she kicked and clawed and swore at us like some kind of raving lunatic, until we heard the hatch close and that brain-numbing screech of the alarm finally stop.

We were distracted, but that's no excuse. We should have been more careful.

In the middle of all this, none of us realized what had gotten into the shelter while Jay had the hatch open.

CHAPTER TWENTY

When she heard the alarm stop, Sue went limp beneath us, her body shaking, probably in shock. Tessa came out from the kitchen and helped get her into a chair, talking in a soft, soothing voice. Sue didn't seem to hear her, just curled up into a ball on the chair. I got her a damp towel to soothe her red cheek, which had swollen pretty badly now, but she just threw it against the wall. Finally I left Tessa to try to talk to her, and sat down on the bottom step, my legs weak from adrenaline as the rush of fear began to fade away.

While we were busy with Sue, Dan had jumped to his feet and disappeared into the other room, and he came out a minute later with one of the hazmat suits, walking fast, already starting to shrug himself into it.

I grabbed his arm. "What are you doing?" I asked.

He spun to glare at me, breathing hard. "Going after him."

"That's a bad idea."

"It might not be too late," he said. "If I can just get to him quickly, bring him back—"

I glanced at Sue. "Not here," I said.

When we entered the bedroom, Jimmie was in the same position he'd been in before, sitting up ramrod straight in bed, head slightly cocked to one side, eyes glassy and sightless. He did not move, did not even blink. Jimmie, at least the person we knew, was not there.

"Jay was like that in the kitchen," Dan said. "And then he just suddenly snapped out of it and went nuts. Knocked us to the side and ran for the hatch. There was no warning, nothing."

I nodded. "I found him like this when I came in here. He wouldn't respond to me."

"What the hell was that noise they made?"

"I don't know."

I realized we were both whispering, as if Jimmie were sleeping and might be disturbed by our discussion. It seemed like a ridiculous thing to do, considering the circumstances. We could have invited Kiss in for a live reunion concert and he wouldn't have heard it.

"Jesus Christ," Dan said, pacing back and forth, his voice rising. "I should have stopped him, Pete. I should have, I don't know, grabbed him, kept him inside—"

"No." I shook my head. "There's no sense blaming yourself. There was nothing any of us could do."

But I wondered about that. Sue had come to me for help, and I'd failed miserably. Jay was a good friend too, and he'd needed me. I let them both down. It wasn't that I hadn't taken them seriously, but those were the facts, and now he was gone.

Maybe I'd made a mistake not telling Dan about Jay's mental condition. Maybe together, we could have done something to stop the meltdown.

But I didn't really believe it. There had been something else alive in Jay, something that none of us could have understood.

The same thing that was alive in Jimmie now.

"He was so strong." Dan looked up at me, his eyes red. "It happened so fast. When he pushed past me in the kitchen, it was like getting hit by a two-hundred-and-fifty-pound linebacker. I didn't know he had it in him."

"Adrenaline can do some crazy things," I said.

"I have to go out there," Dan said. "It's my job, to take care of everyone. I'm the leader, *I'm* the one in charge. I have to try—"

"Listen to me," I said. "He's as good as dead. There's no way he could survive out there, even if he's close enough for you to find him he'd be poisoned by now from the fallout. We have to assume he's gone for good. And we can't risk someone else to find out. We can't lose you, Dan. You're right, you are our leader, but more than that, you give everyone hope, some sense of control. We need you in here."

Dan shook his head. *"Goddamn it,"* he said. He sat down heavily on the nearest bed, punched the mattress, the hazmat suit still half draped on his shoulders. "I feel like everything is coming apart."

"I guess maybe it is, but if you think about it, we've done pretty well, considering the circumstances. I think the real question right now is, how can we take care of the people we have left? What are we going to do about Sue? She's hysterical. How are we going to keep her from following him out the hatch?"

"We'll talk to her," Dan said. "And we'll keep a close eye on her, and if she looks like she's freaking out . . ." He shrugged. "We're going to have to get more aggressive."

"You mean, like tying her up? I don't think that's the best way to handle it. We can't keep her like that forever. And we have to sleep sometime."

"We'll take shifts. That worked the last time."

I didn't know how to answer that. Had it worked, or had we just gotten lucky?

"Okay," I said. "But there's something else too." I hesitated, unsure about whether I should even bring it up. *Everything on the table*. "Those things Jay said, about Sue's grandfather knowing about the attack. She didn't exactly deny it."

"Jay was out of his mind."

"Maybe." I shrugged. "Or maybe not."

"Oh, come on," Dan said. He stood up. "You're not telling me you're buying all the conspiracy-theory bullshit, are you?"

"Jay's never been wrong before."

"You buying that crap about the engineered bugs too?"

"Regular old ants don't do something like what we saw with Jimmie's leg, Dan. Just trying to keep an open mind here. We've seen some pretty crazy stuff the past few days. I can't explain all of it with the usual theories."

"Okay, so what?" Dan said. "Sue's grandpa could have helped drop the bombs. I don't see how, but why not? Hell, he could have been the devil himself. What difference does that make for us?"

I thought about that for a moment. I could see Dan's point; we were stuck in a godforsaken hole, no matter what had happened to get us here. Figuring out whatever or whoever was responsible might not make one bit of difference.

Except it would to Sue. And maybe, just maybe, it would give us an edge too. If I could only figure out what that edge might be.

Regardless of what we wanted to do, she was in no shape to be pushed on it now. We'd have to wait.

I went over to the bed and touched Jimmie's cheek. It was like touching a plate just out of the oven. "He's burning up," I said. "Hey, Jimmie, snap out of it." I slapped him lightly on the cheek. Nothing. "You think he's okay?"

"No," Dan said. "I don't. Maybe some kind of coma?"

"If it is, it's the strangest coma anyone's ever seen. So what do we do?"

"We wait. Maybe he'll just fight it off on his own."

"And if he doesn't?"

Dan shook his head. "Let's hope it doesn't come to that."

We got Sue calmed down enough to take something from the bottle of Jack Daniel's, and then we put her to bed. Tessa was really good with her, remaining calm and continuing to speak in low, soothing tones, which seemed to help. She was always good with stuff like that. She had a gentle, soothing way about her, almost like she'd been built to care for people. She was slender, small and delicate, and her face was open, which put others at ease. Tessa could never hide her emotions, which was one of the things I loved about her. She was an open book, and you responded to that even if you didn't consciously understand it.

Sue kept saying Jay's name, over and over again, as if by saying it, she could somehow keep from losing him for good. Her face was all blotchy from Jay hitting her and the crying. It was bad enough what he'd done, but to leave her with his fist as a final, lasting memory of the two of them seemed unimaginably cruel. Eventually she fell asleep with Jay's pillow clutched to her chest, and Tessa curled up next to her.

People deal with grief in different ways, I guess. Some get angry and want to tear something apart. Others deny everything, at least for a while; and a few never get through that stage and just bury it deep. There are others who say they've accepted it but most of them really never do. Saying something doesn't always make it true. Me, I've found it's sort of like a scar: the wound heals, but the damage remains, and when the timing's right it can ache like

a ghostly memory of something sharper and more immediate.

After they were asleep Dan and I shared some more
from the bottle and played a round of cards, neither one
of us speaking much. Dan checked the radio again, more
out of habit than anything else; and for some reason I
could not explain, I started poking around the shelter,
starting with the kitchen. Something Jay had said just
before heading for the hatch had remained with me. *Find
it . . . it's in here, somewhere, the answers to everything.*

I remembered how he'd turned the place upside down
the past few nights, as if searching for something important. Maybe it was delusional, or maybe not. But I felt like
honoring his last request.

The problem was, I had no idea what I was looking for,
and after nothing interesting came to light in the kitchen,
and nothing in the bathroom or dining room, I gave up. I
was exhausted, running on fumes. I'd gotten maybe three
hours of sleep before Jay and Sue's argument had woken
me up, and now I was feeling the strain. Even my eyes
ached, my body refusing to cooperate with one more step.

Dan was still trying the different radio bands, so I
climbed into bed and almost immediately slipped into a
dream where Jay was standing in darkness. Then, as he
stepped forward into the light, his face started to peel
away. As I watched in horror and his skin began to drop
like orange peels at his feet, he turned into my mother,
only in the dream she could still walk, and she turned and
started moving away from me as if floating on air. I chased
her through darkened city streets and into an alleyway full
of people who stood like statues, their features obscured by
the shadows. I didn't know who they were, or what they
were doing there, but I knew they were waiting for me.

My mother stopped at the end of the alley and turned

back to me. I cried out for her, trying to run forward, but I could not gain any ground; the faster I ran, the farther away she appeared, until she was only a pinprick in the distance, framed by thousands of ghostly silhouettes of people frozen in place. Finally she was gone, and as the sky bloomed red and black with mushroom clouds, I sat down and cried, and black bugs started pouring out of my eye sockets and nose and mouth.

I woke up sobbing, an ache in my stomach, the feel of those bugs in my mouth still fresh in my mind, along with my mother's sad face. I didn't know how much more of this I could take. Not knowing what had happened to her was the worst, and yet I had to accept that I might never find out the truth. The chances she'd survived the attack were ridiculously slim, but I wanted to believe, and that made it all so much worse.

If you don't allow a wound to heal, you'll never have a scar.

Something brushed against my leg.

Chills ran up and down my spine as I looked up, startled. Jimmie was standing over me in the darkness.

"Jesus Christ," I said. "You scared the shit out of me."

He didn't move or speak for a moment, and the chills returned, prickling my scalp. I didn't know why, but I sensed danger. I sat up and hunched backward until I was up against the headboard, the bunk above me kissing the top of my head.

Jimmie reached out his hand to touch my arm. I could see the reflection of his eyes shining in the dark, but nothing else of his face. He blinked and swallowed, his throat making a dry clicking sound.

"Jimmie?" I said. "You okay?"

"What happened?" he said, his voice rough and weak. "My head is . . . killing me."

"You don't remember?"

"No, I . . ." He seemed to drift off again for a moment. "I don't remember anything."

He sat down near my legs and I explained what had gone on with Jay. "He left," I said. "We couldn't stop him in time."

Jimmie didn't answer. When I got to the part of describing how I'd found him, sitting up in bed and stiff as a board, he shook his head in bewilderment. "I remember someone saying my name, but it was like it was coming from really far away, and I couldn't respond. Like a dream."

"You made a . . . sound."

"A what?"

I struggled with how to describe it. "You and Jay, when you went into this state . . . you both made a sound like you were communicating with each other, but we didn't hear any words."

"I don't remember anything like that." Jimmie was sitting so still on the bed, and his voice was so flat that I started getting worried again. It wasn't like him at all. Jimmie could talk a mile a minute, and he was the most highstrung of any of us, usually with his leg bouncing or fingers tapping or fidgeting in some other way. I used to joke about him having attention deficit disorder when we were kids. Maybe part of it was what he'd been through the past few days; hell, that would have slowed any of us down. But I didn't think that was all of it.

"You're acting weird, man," I said. "You're creeping me out. You sure you're feeling all right?"

"I'm not feeling anything except this headache," Jimmie said. "My leg, the pain is almost gone, but I feel like someone cracked my skull open with a hammer."

I remembered what Jay had said, just before he went crazy and left the shelter. "You're not hearing voices, are you?"

"I . . . I'm having trouble concentrating on anything. I can't think straight. Maybe I better lie down again, okay, Peter?"

"Sure," I said. I watched him get up from my bed and go back to his own and lie down flat on his back, staring up at the bunk above him. Eventually he closed his eyes.

Maybe it was nothing. But the thing was, I was always Pete to Jimmie. He hadn't called me Peter in years.

CHAPTER TWENTY-ONE

I took a shift three hours later, sitting up in the dining room and drinking instant coffee while the rest of them slept. Sue and Tessa were still huddled together in Sue's bunk, and I let them be. The longer Sue could escape from the reality of what had happened, the better.

The coffee was bitter and it burned my throat going down. I took my time, blowing across the top of the cup, and stared at the marks on the wall that served as our rudimentary calendar. Nearly four neat sets of seven marks now, six vertical lines with a slash through them; we'd been down here almost a month. It seemed impossible to believe, the time both passing too quickly and not quickly enough. I wondered if Dan had missed a day or two, and figured he had not. If there was one thing we could count on, it was Dan's orderly mind. Got it from his father, who had served twenty years in the army and demanded the same disciplined approach from his family that he'd received in the service. But Dan's father did it with love and affection, from everything I'd seen, which was vastly different than my own father's tactics. There was discipline, there was order, and then there was cruelty. Sometimes the lines blurred together, and sometimes they didn't.

For a moment I felt a mix of panic and disorientation as

I looked at the clock on the wall: 6:30. I couldn't remember if it was morning or night. Did it matter, really? If I opened that hatch and looked out, would I even be able to tell?

Sitting there in the silence, I had plenty of time to think. I listened to the occasional grunt and creak as someone turned over in bed, and thought about Jay, all the years I'd known him, the times we'd spent together. It was mostly as part of the group because, although I liked him a lot, Jay always seemed to have this layer of reserve, this protective aura about him that kept most people at arm's length. Jay was the kind of guy you could know for years without really *knowing* him; he didn't share many secrets, he didn't break down, he didn't let you see behind the mask very often. I guess he must have with Sue, but even with that relationship he was secretive. After all, we hadn't found out they were dating at all until we were locked together down in the shelter, but from the looks of things they'd been a couple for quite a while.

That got me thinking about the others. How well did I really know any of them? Back before the bombs hit I would have described them all as my best friends, and I would have meant it. But now I wondered.

The private thoughts they don't share with anyone. The dreams they don't want to let into the world. Things that make them bleed inside.

The prevailing wisdom is that tragedy brings people together. But it can do the opposite too. It can drive a wedge between you, I think. Make you look at a person you thought you knew, and wonder if you really ever knew them at all. Tessa was the only one of the group that I really felt like I knew as well as I knew myself. But she was different. She was closer to me than anyone else in the world.

Jay wasn't coming back. It seemed so strange to think about our gang without him. But right now I was feeling alone down here in the dark, even with four sleeping bodies in the other room, and the weight of the world seemed to be pressing down on me.

I don't know why I got up to get the radio. Dan had already listened to it for nearly an hour that day, scanning every channel several times and finding nothing. Maybe I needed some noise to fill the empty space, even if it was nothing but static. In my mind I kept hearing Jay's voice, the way he strained to get the words out: *You take care of her, you p-p-promise me. I . . . can't hold them off anymore . . . hurts . . . so bad.*

I was beginning to get decidedly creeped out. I took the radio scanner off the shelf, then sat back down. It was one of those fairly high-end emergency kits that had a flashlight built in and ran off batteries, and if the batteries died it had a hand crank on the side that could generate enough power with a few turns to run the thing for five minutes or so.

We'd been lazy, up until now, running it from the large supply of batteries we'd found on the shelves. We'd only had to replace them once so far, and there were plenty left. Still, if we were going to remain down here for weeks longer, we should have been more careful.

I turned the crank for a while, the soft whirring sound rhythmic and soothing. Finally my arm started to ache, and I switched it on, turning the sound down low enough to keep from disturbing the others. There were something like a thousand channels on there, including aircraft, police, fire, ambulance, military and ham radio—from 25 MHz all the way up to 1.5 GHz. If someone were broadcasting, we would hear it.

Static up and down the traditional FM band, which wasn't surprising. I knew that FM wavelength didn't cover very long distances. Traditional AM radio offered nothing but crackles, pops and hisses. But when I switched and went down into the lower frequencies, I thought I heard something.

I turned up the volume, my heart pounding, and worked my way back through, very slowly. Was that a voice, or had it just been my imagination? Already I was doubting myself, and I couldn't find it again. Quickly I got up and grabbed the book we'd found that explained the frequencies and who broadcasted on them.

The area I was scanning, down at the lowest end of the readable spectrum, was normally used by the military.

I tried again, and this time, when I worked the dial back down, I heard, very clearly, the word *doomsday*.

Something else followed, but static filled the speaker again, the sound washing in and out. I turned up the volume. The voice was a man's, that much was certain. My scalp prickled as I bent closer, every nerve in my body alive and screaming, my muscles taut and quivering. I felt this strange sense of unreality, as if I were outside myself watching a play happen onstage, or asleep and dreaming; a voice on the radio, the same radio we had been listening to for weeks now with nothing but static, a voice from the outside world that seemed so far away, so divorced from the world we now knew, these concrete walls and floors and narrow rooms that had become our prison.

It had to be a dream. Yet there was more, and this time I heard him say something like "doomsday waltz," but that didn't make any sense.

I sat back for a minute and exhaled, trying to will myself to relax and think. There was someone still alive out there. *Someone was alive and broadcasting.*

I smiled, then chuckled, and then I gave a great whoop, all my emotions spilling out at once in a cry that would wake the dead. The others came running, first Dan, wide-awake in an instant and ready for action, carrying the battery-powered lantern like a weapon; then Sue and Tessa, both of them groggy from sleep but equal parts terrified and bewildered; and finally Jimmie, limping slightly but otherwise looking remarkably like his old self, apart from the odd bald patches on his head.

When I explained to them what had happened, they looked blankly at me at first, as if unwilling to believe it. But my enthusiasm must have convinced them, because one after another, smiles broke out across their faces, then laughs and claps and hugs. Even Sue, her dirt-smeared and tearstained face still slightly swollen from Jay's slap, seemed to light up from the inside.

They all gathered around me at the table and listened as we scanned through the frequencies again. This time the static was unbroken, and I went back through again, then again, one click at a time. Nothing. Slowly the light in them began to dim, the energy draining from the room.

I went through it yet again. Nothing.

"Doomsday," I said. "I'm telling you. Something like 'doomsday waltz.' Pretty poetic, huh?" I pictured a thousand couples slow dancing to music through mushroom clouds, as the world slowly crashed and burned around them. Some image.

Rainbows are visions, but only illusions, and rainbows have nothing to hide . . .

"It doesn't make any sense," Dan said. "Are you sure you weren't hearing things? Pops in the static that sounded like a voice? I mean, it's understandable, we're all tired, we want something badly enough—"

"I swear to God," I said. "You think I'd make this up? No, no way. I heard it loud and clear."

"What were you listening to the radio for, anyway? You know I listen to it every morning and every night—"

"Hey," I said. "Sorry. I didn't realize you were lord of the airwaves. Is there a sign-up sheet or something?"

My voice had gone up a notch. Dan sighed heavily and sat down in the chair next to me, rubbing his face with his hands. "Sorry," he said. "It's just that I'd been listening earlier and didn't hear a thing."

I knew what he really meant. *If what you're saying is true, I wanted to be the one to hear it first.* As our fearless leader, I suppose we owed him that much. But it wasn't the way it went down, and there was nothing I could do about it now.

I could sense control getting away from me, the excitement in the others fading fast. I knew I'd heard the voice. I hadn't imagined it. But I didn't know how to convince them, and I heard the urgency in my own voice when I spoke. It sounded weak, almost whiny, and I hated it.

"It's a military frequency," I said. "NORAD, actually. 10.19 through 10.45. Look it up in the book. That makes sense at least, right? If we're going to hear something, it would be down in that range."

"Sure it does," Tessa said. I looked at her gratefully, and she gave me a wide smile and a nod. I could have kissed her right then.

"NORAD, eh?" Jimmie said. "What the hell's that?"

"North American Aerospace Defense Command," I said. "It's a part of the U.S. and Canadian military that monitors missile attacks and protects the airspace over both countries. I think the main base is in Colorado, but there are others in Canada and Alaska."

"Doomsday waltz," Dan said. "Doesn't sound military to me. Just because it used to be a NORAD channel, doesn't mean it still is. Maybe they're a couple of crazy ham radio operators holed up in some abandoned shell of a building, talking to themselves."

"The Doomsday Vault," Sue said.

We all turned to stare at her. She'd sat down on the bottom step of the staircase to the hatch. She'd started crying silently again, and the tears ran down her face and dropped from her chin to the floor. Right then she looked about a hundred years old, a husk of her former self. I realized I'd mostly stopped referring to her as "Big Sue" in my own head a while ago, a nickname we never actually used in her presence, but one I suspected she probably knew about, and hated. She'd dropped at least ten pounds since we'd been trapped down here, and her normally pink, soft skin was a grayish color, her eyes red from crying.

Sue had been a pretty girl, larger than life in every way, tall and big boned and usually bubbling with energy. But not anymore.

She shook her head, letting loose one great hitch and shaky sigh, and wiped her eyes. "Jay told me about it," she said. "The Doomsday Vault. One of his conspiracy theories . . ." She took a deep breath, seemed to balance herself, and went on. "I read an article from *Time* about it a few months ago that he sent me, so I know the place exists. The official story is that it's an underground seed vault created by the United Nations and some of the wealthiest foundations in the world, along with the U.S. government and a few foreign countries. It's designed to hold millions of seeds, hundreds each of every single important crop and plant and tree in the world, and at temperatures cold enough to keep them viable for centuries. Sort of nature's safety net in case we screw up the world. Go figure, right?"

"If this is a real place," Dan said, "what's the conspiracy?"

"There were a lot of online rumors that it wasn't just a seed vault. That it was a cover for a complete underground ecosystem, a place where people high up in society could hole up with plenty of food and water and live for months, maybe years. It was built above a huge oil reservoir and they tapped into that for power. A little underground city, complete with electricity and filtered air and even growing rooms for fresh fruits and vegetables."

"The Doomsday Vault," I said. "Of course. *That's* what I heard. Not *waltz, vault.*" The excitement was back in me again. I could feel the buzzing snap of it through my veins, that feeling that I'd been right, that there *were* people still alive in the world besides us, and they were broadcasting, looking for survivors. There was hope again, after all this time, and goddamn, it felt good.

"Where, Sue?" Dan asked. He seemed to feel it too. "Where is it?"

"Alaska," she said. "Up north beyond the Gates of the Arctic Park. They tunneled down about three hundred feet into the base of a mountain, through the permafrost."

"That's gotta be five thousand miles from here," Jimmie said, his voice cracking. "Even if it's true, and there are people alive up there, there's no way for us to reach them."

We all sat quietly after that for a minute, thinking it over. Jimmie was right, of course. Knowing something about what had happened aboveground, and with all the other threats we'd already encountered in our time in the shelter probably multiplied tenfold if we tried to leave, whoever was broadcasting might as well have been broadcasting from the moon.

I didn't want to lose hope yet again. But despite my best efforts, I felt my mood sinking slowly, as if the chair I was sitting in were pulling me right down through the floor.

"Why did he have to run?" Sue said. "If he'd only held on a little while longer, we could have helped him, we could have found a way out of here, I know we could have done something . . ."

The sobs that she had been holding in so tightly burst through all at once, and she lay down on her side on the floor at the foot of the steps, digging her nails into the carpet and moaning, looking for all the world like she were dying. This was worse than she'd been right after Jay had left, much worse. This was raw and screaming and completely unhinged. I'd never seen such naked pain in my life, and the sound of her despair nearly sent me over the edge. I didn't know if she was crying just for Jay, or for herself and all of humanity too, but her grief seemed to symbolize everything we'd been through, and it made me wonder if all this was worth the fight. Maybe Jay was right after all; maybe one more glimpse of the open sky, even if it was filled with ash and gray as death, was the best way to go.

I wondered how it would happen, how it was happening with Jay right now. Would it hurt to breathe in the first few minutes, would the acid in the air start eating away at you from the inside? Or would it take much longer, days of thinking you were going to make it after all before the sores began to erupt across your limbs and your lungs filled with fluid and you drowned in your own vomit?

Or maybe the bugs would get you before anything else could . . .

I went over and crouched beside Sue. When I touched her back she jumped, but I rubbed in gentle circles.

"It's going to be okay," I said. "I promise." I flashed back to that night when I woke up to find Sue sitting on my bed, and how angry she'd gotten at my useless reassurances then. *Fuck that, Pete . . . you show me how we're fine. How are you fine? You think we're just going to wait a*

few days, then walk out of here and start rebuilding the world?
She'd been right then, but maybe not now. Maybe that
voice on the radio offered us real hope. A chance. Wasn't
that all we could ask for?

But even if we did make it out of here somehow, there
were so many tragedies we had not yet faced, and so many
things we'd never get the chance to do. The loss of family,
the loss of a chance to ever say you're sorry to those you
have hurt, or tell them how much they meant to you. The
loss of innocence, of first love. Those feelings you only
get one shot to experience; being able to park in some
deserted back road and kiss, with nothing to fear except
getting caught with your pants down. No mushroom
clouds, no fallout, no dead and dying friends and no end
of the world to take all that away.

"Everyone you have ever loved in your life becomes a
part of your soul," I said. "They never leave. They're always inside you, and you can bring them out whenever
you want."

I don't know where it came from, or why I said it. But I
felt Sue's cries begin to slow, the jerking in her limbs began to quiet down, and she took deep gulping breaths of
air. Eventually I helped her sit up again, and she hugged
me very close, and held on for a long time. I felt her wet
face against my chest, her tears and snot bleeding through
my shirt, and I didn't care at all. It felt good to be needed.

Finally she pulled away from me. "Thank you," she whispered. "You're a good guy, you know that?" Her chest
hitched and she sighed like children do after a hard cry.
She looked so lost right then, I wanted to gather her up
and hold her forever.

She touched the wet spot on my chest and smiled.
"Sorry. That's kind of gross."

"It's okay." I frowned. Something on her neck . . . I tried to pull her shirt down, but she yanked away from me.

"What?"

I touched my own neck, just above the collarbone. "You've got something here. Let me see." I reached out toward her and she looked at me suspiciously with a crease in her brow, but she let me move the collar down until I'd exposed what looked like a small but deep wound in her skin.

"Does that hurt?"

"I don't understand. Does what hurt?" Sue looked bewildered. She tried to bend her head but couldn't see it without a mirror, and she glanced around the room at everyone else as if she wanted some kind of confirmation. "I don't feel anything." She touched the wound and looked at the faint blood on her fingers with surprise.

"We must have scraped her," Dan said. "When we were trying . . . to keep her calm."

"It's a puncture wound," I said. It looked perfectly round, like something long and sharp as a needle had punched through her skin. A very large needle. "Did you fall on anything in the kitchen, or out here, the shelf maybe?" Sue shook her head.

I pressed down a little harder on the outside of the wound, and more blood welled up. It was deep, all right, and the area directly around it looked inflamed.

She flinched away from me. "Ow. *Now* it hurts." She rubbed at her shoulder. "Thanks a lot."

"Put a Band-Aid on it," Jimmie said. "Who cares? It's just a little cut. I got ten times worse in my leg, and I'm doing okay. Keep the iodine on it, keep it bandaged, you'll be fine."

I nodded, trying to look reassuring to Sue, who had

started to appear pretty worried. Maybe she'd sensed it from me. I didn't want to make a big deal out of it, not in front of everyone, but I didn't feel reassured at all. I remembered what Jay had said, that the bugs looked for cuts, breaks in the skin, so that they could get into your blood.

I didn't know exactly why, but I had a very bad feeling about that wound.

It looked to me almost like something had been sucking on her.

CHAPTER TWENTY-TWO

"If the NORAD base is in Colorado, maybe they're broadcasting from there," Jimmie said. "Maybe they're telling people about the vault, gathering as many survivors as they can before they head to Alaska. That's not as far, is it? We could make that, you know?"

Dan shook his head. "Two thousand miles, I guess. But the cars and debris on the roads—"

"But those would be main roads, highways. There would be multiple routes. We'd have a much better chance of making it alive."

Tessa had gone off with Sue to wash and dress that puncture wound, and Dan, Jimmie and I sat up discussing the possibilities, still energized by what had happened. They all seemed to accept the fact that I *had* heard something on the radio, and now it was a matter of what to do about it. Dan was in favor of waiting to see if we could hear anything more, while Jimmie felt that our best shot was in heading for Colorado. Me, I didn't know what to think. On the one hand, we couldn't stay here for the rest of our lives. But on the other hand, at least we were alive.

"We don't know what's outside that hatch," I said. "We have no idea what would happen to us if we left. Is the air poisoned? Are there other more dangerous things out there? It doesn't matter if we need to go five miles or five thousand if we choke to death as soon as we step outside."

"We have those suits," Jimmie said. "That'll give us some protection."

"But not much. And we can't wear them for days. We'll have to take them off to eat, drink, take a piss."

"So we find a building or something, some place with a basement that's safe," he said.

"It's safe here—"

"No," he said. "This place, it makes me crazy. I have these dreams . . ." He shrugged, the hair growing from below his lower lip and his chin looking even more ridiculous now that half the hair on his head was gone. "I dream about all these people talking at once, thousands of them. They need to tell me something important. Only I can't understand a word they're saying. I almost feel like I can, the words are so close, but they slip away. And then they climb all over me and smother me."

"Calling Sigmund Freud," I said. "Like *Night of the Living Dead*. You remember waking up last night and standing over my bed? That was creepy enough, without you telling me about this."

"Hold on," Dan said. He got up and went into the other room, emerging a few moments later with a book in his hands. "I saw this when we went through the whole shelter," he said. "I've been reading through it. There's a section on fallout, and when it's safe to return to the surface. Maybe it'll help us figure out whether it's possible to survive out there now."

The book was called *Surviving Nuclear Winter*. It had a silver cover with the words printed in white like snowflakes and peppered with black spots.

"Why the hell didn't you tell us about this before?" I asked.

"I thought it might freak everyone out," he said. "There's some pretty intense stuff in here, but most of it isn't going to do anything but get people upset. I figured I would share anything relevant with the group when I came to it."

I wasn't sure how I felt about that. Protecting us was one thing, but this went a little too far. We weren't children. And what if there was something in that book that he didn't think was important, but we did? What if he missed something that would save all our lives?

"You should have told us," I said.

"Look, you want me to lead this group, you gotta trust me," he said. He looked me in the eyes until I looked away. "What if Sue had read something in here and it had made her want to leave with Jay? She's fragile, Pete, you know that. Jimmie too—no offense, Jimmie."

"None taken, prick-face."

I smiled, more to keep the tension down than anything else. "So what's it say?"

Dan flipped through it until he found the right section. "Here," he said, marking a passage with his finger. "It says that fallout can be deadly almost instantly after the blast, but it loses its intensity pretty quickly. If you're far enough downwind from ground zero, you could return to the surface in a matter of days for short periods of time. After a couple of weeks, it could be possible to be aboveground all day and return to the shelter to sleep."

"What's far enough downwind, exactly?"

"That's the hard part. We don't know where the bombs hit, or how large they were. From what we saw, I'd say it was at least ten miles away, which means we'd probably be safe by now to move around aboveground. But if I'm wrong—"

"What if you're right?" I said. I tried to remember exactly how far the mushroom clouds had been when we first saw them—ten miles? Twenty? Fifty? "Or what if it was even farther away than that? Are you saying we'd have been safe leaving this shelter a week ago?"

"If you'd let me finish," Dan said slowly, staring at me, "it also says that we should wait until the authorities get a radiation reading and give the all clear. The point is, this fallout is unpredictable. It could be almost nonexistent a few miles away from the blast zone, and then dump a truck-load right on top of our hatch. It also depends on whether the warheads exploded in the air or on the ground. If it hit the ground, the blast zone is smaller, but the fallout can be a lot more deadly and spread over a wider area. You see what I'm saying?"

"No," I said. "Not really. All I know is that this is the kind of decision that should have been made as a group. We should have been talking about this stuff on day one." I wanted to be careful with how I handled this, but I felt my blood pressure rise. I was coming close to saying Dan might have made a serious mistake, and I had no idea how he might react.

"This isn't a democracy," Dan said. He got up and closed the book with a loud snap, standing over me in a way that was vaguely threatening. "That went out when the bombs hit. Decision by committee is never the best way to go when you're under fire." He looked at Jimmie, then back at me. "You guys agreed to put me in charge," he said. "What, you want me to make decisions when it's convenient for you? That's not how it works."

I leaned away from him, surprised by the sudden heat in his voice. For the first time since we'd been locked away down here, I started to question whether blindly letting Dan lead was the right thing to do. He was so rigid in his authority, so strong with his confidence in making decisions, and yet he was far from the brightest of our group, and I had often felt in the past that he acted without thinking things through. What else had he kept from us?

Finally I stood up, my heart thudding in my chest, my legs trembling with something like anger or fear, or maybe both.

"This brings up another question," I said. I was inches away from his face now, and he didn't back down. "And it's a tricky one. What if Jay *is* still alive out there? What if he needs our help? I kept you from going out there before, because I thought it was too dangerous. Maybe I wouldn't have if I'd had the chance to read this book."

It was a shitty thing to do, Monday-morning quarterbacking at its worst. But I was so angry I didn't care. Dan didn't say a word. He stared into my eyes and for a moment I thought he would take a swing at me, and my hands clenched into fists and for my own sake I almost welcomed it, the tangled energy that had emerged after hearing that radio voice coiling within me and begging for a release.

Then he just shook his head and walked a few steps away, his back to us as if gathering himself. Jimmie and I shared a glance, but I didn't say anything else at first. I could feel my heartbeat in my neck, my mouth suddenly dry. I was still burning, my emotions simmering just below the surface, threatening to burst through all at once. I didn't want to lose control; that wasn't me. I was the joker, the guy who always tried to defuse a tense situation. When things got bad enough for me to snap, it was usually time to cut and run.

"I can't answer that," Dan said. "I don't know if he's alive or not, and I don't know if we did the right thing. What I'm saying is that up until now, there were so many variables it was impossible to make an informed decision."

He turned back to us, his face set and determined. "My dad always told me, in situations like this, you must remain conservative in your approach. You don't leave a safe place unless you have a good idea of your odds, and what you'll be facing. I was acting on emotion when I wanted to go after him, and that's a mistake. I should have been thinking more rationally."

This wasn't like the Dan we knew. I wasn't quite sure how to react. "And now?" I said. "What would your dad say?"

"Things have changed. Jay left the group, put himself at risk, and we're facing some kind of threat down here, inside, which means we need to reassess our options. This shelter may no longer be the safest place for us. And if you're right about that voice, there could be help on the way. Or at least there's a place for us to try to reach."

"I heard it," I said. "Don't worry about that. It was real."

"So what are we gonna *do?*" Jimmie asked. "You guys can bitch at each other all you want, and believe me, I'm glad I'm not the one in the middle right now. But we're not getting anywhere doing that. You know?"

"You're right, for once." Dan turned again and went to the shelf, returning with the atlas of North America and opening it on the table. "Here's where we are," he said, pointing out the area on the U.S. map where Sparrow Island would be, although it wasn't large enough to be marked. "Here's Peterson Air Force Base in Colorado." He traced a path across the map to the spot, tapping it with his finger. "And up here is Alaska . . ." He paused, searching, until he found it. "Right here." He tapped a spot way up near the top of the state. "Gates of the Arctic Park. This is where Sue said the Doomsday Vault is supposed to be."

I concentrated on the map. The way to Colorado would give us a better chance. If we headed to Alaska instead, the trip would be both twice as long, and offer fewer options in the event a main highway or smaller road was impassable. But then again, that's where the vault was, and it was the most likely place to give us lasting shelter and the possibility of survival.

"If we leave, Peterson is our best shot," Jimmie said. "Anyone can see that."

"But we don't know if anyone's there," Dan said. "We have no idea where they're broadcasting from. Without some kind of clear instructions, we have to assume they're in Alaska."

We all studied the two routes in silence for a minute. It gave both Dan and me some time to cool down. I took a deep breath and tried to relax. I wasn't clear on why I had been arguing in the first place; I wasn't even remotely sure that leaving the shelter was the right thing to do. We were basing everything about the vault on a faint voice through the radio, along with Sue's recollection of the ravings of a possible lunatic and something she had read in a magazine months ago or more. And whatever threat we might face from the creatures that had attacked us down here could be ten times worse aboveground. Who knew what was lurking up there for us?

But whatever our final decision might be, it had to be made by the group, I knew that much. And we all had to have every important detail possible on which to base that decision. No more hand-holding.

"Any place that's got main roads named Hickel Highway and Winter Trail can't be all bad," I said. "Let's try the radio again. Maybe they'll say something else."

We listened for another hour, but we heard nothing more. I'd heard stories in the past about the way radio waves could travel huge distances under certain atmospheric conditions, something about the way weather patterns formed tunnels that could bounce a signal along for hundreds of miles farther than the normal strength of the broadcast for brief periods. Maybe that had happened here and I'd been in the right place at the right time. If so, we might not hear the voice again for days. Maybe never.

Finally I got up to go to the kitchen for a drink of water and a chance to be by myself for a minute. My head was pounding and I couldn't seem to think clearly. I needed space.

But I didn't have very long alone. I'd hardly poured the water when I turned to see that Jimmie had followed me in. I hadn't even heard him limping up in his socks.

"I gotta talk to you," he said quietly, glancing back once at the doorway and the faint sound of static still coming from the radio. "I can't say anything around him, you know? But we gotta do *something*. I feel like I'm going to lose it."

He was close to whining now; I could hear the urgency in his voice, and I didn't like it. Jimmie in a panic was a bad thing for everyone. We had plenty of examples of how he lost his head while under stress, and the last thing I wanted was to get him all worked up again. Ever since the rat attack he seemed to be all over the map, calm one minute and frantic the next, reminiscing about the old days, then turning around and calling me Peter instead of Pete. It was almost like he'd become two different people. I could fool myself for a while that the old Jimmie was back, and pretend that the craziness of the past few days had never happened, but the truth was, there was something wrong with him. We just didn't know yet how bad it was going to get.

"Take it easy," I said. "Let's just take our time, figure things out."

"I can't stay here much longer," he said, stepping closer. I could smell the rankness of his body, a mix of body odor and something else beneath it, something far worse. "I can't. You don't understand. What happened, those things inside my leg, and now Jay and what he did . . ." He licked his lips, flakes of white dropping from the corners of his mouth. His breath, this close, smelled like a sewer. "I wonder if maybe I *can* hear them, sometimes. Those voices."

"What do you mean?" I asked. I'd locked eyes with him, my heart beating faster in my chest again. I felt alert, on edge, as if waiting for something to snap.

"It's like a pressure, somehow, behind my eyes, and these dreams I'm having of all these people standing there like statues, watching me, and then they start whispering but I can't understand what they're saying."

"How's your leg feel now?"

He looked at me, bewildered. "It's fine, half the time I forget it's there. I've been cleaning it and keeping the bandage tight. But I don't know why it doesn't hurt more."

"Your headache gone?"

He shook his head. "No, man, no. That's the thing. It's still there, this dull throbbing, that makes it hard to think. I can't—" He grabbed his head in both hands, cradling it, and the gesture was so much like Jay's just before he left, it gave me chills. "God, I just gotta get out of here! You know? Don't you feel it? It's like there's this weight pressing down on me, all these layers of rock and dirt and concrete above our heads, we can't get away from it, we can't breathe!"

"There's someone else alive out there," I said. "Focus on that, Jimmie. There are other survivors. That means there's hope for us, even if we have to stay put for a while longer."

He stepped even closer, our bodies close to touching. He had me up against the sink. It took everything I had not to slide backward away from him.

"There's someone else in here with me," he whispered. He tapped his temple. Tears shimmered in his eyes. "I think I'm going crazy, Pete. You, you gotta help me."

"I don't *gotta* do anything," I said. I was suddenly angry and disgusted with him, tired of his complaining and his neediness, his inability to grow up with the rest of us. When I looked at him I didn't think about old sledding hills or *Star Wars* figurines, I didn't remember him waiting for me outside my window when my father was on a bender. I didn't see my old friend anymore at all. I saw some stranger who wouldn't back down and leave me alone.

I didn't have any excuse for what happened next, other than exhaustion and the remaining tension over my confrontation with Dan, but when Jimmie reached up to grab my arms, I took him by the shirt with both fists and practically lifted him off the floor.

"You stay the fuck away from me," I said, into his face, the force of my hissed words wetting him with spittle. My entire body was burning with anger, and I felt an overwhelming sense of disgust, the way you'd feel if a giant spider crawled out of the shower drain at your feet. The look of shock on his face changed quickly to fear, and I shoved him backward, his shirt making a tearing sound before I let go.

Jimmie went down and cowered in the corner as everything sort of washed away in a red-tinged cloud. I felt as if I were drifting away from my own body, watching from somewhere else and incapable of controlling myself anymore; and as I drifted I seemed to go back in time to another place that was much darker and more dangerous.

Just as I was about to go after Jimmie with both fists, Tessa appeared out of nowhere. She stepped in front of me and took hold of my wrists.

"Easy," she said. "You don't want to do this, Pete. Look at me. I'm right here. Focus."

I did, and the cloud began to clear, my heart slowing down as I snapped back to reality. I didn't want to hurt him, of course I didn't, but I couldn't always be there to prop him up either.

Tessa understood that. When I met her gaze, she smiled, and I felt the remaining tension melt away. "I swear I could feel it building inside you from the other room," she said. "It's like we're psychically linked. You remember the last time this happened? Do you?"

I shook my head. "I can't go there," I said. "Not now. I'm sorry. It's too hard."

"Okay. But I know about it, you told me everything. I wasn't with you then, but I am now, and I won't let that happen again. You're a good person, Pete, maybe too sensitive for your own good. Your father's death wasn't your fault. You can't let that rule you forever."

"I know that," I said. "I do. But this place, it's getting to me. It's getting to all of us. Bad things come to the surface, things you want to forget."

Tessa nodded. Then she hugged me close, her soft body warm against mine, her breath tickling my cheek. "I love you," she said quietly. "You know I do. I'll always be here when you need me."

When she stepped away, Jimmie was staring at me, a look on his face I didn't entirely understand. He was still sitting on the floor with his hands behind him holding him up, and now he crab-walked backward away from me and Tessa until he hit the pantry door.

"Jimmie," I said, taking a step forward, my hands out, placating him. "Look, man, I'm sorry about what happened. I don't know what came over me."

Jimmie just shook his head, fear in his eyes. "Who—who *are* you?" he cried. Then he scrambled to his feet and ran from the room.

I sighed and turned to Tessa.

"He'll be okay," she said. "Just give him time."

I nodded as if I understood. But I didn't believe her. I thought it might be too late for us both.

CHAPTER TWENTY-THREE

That moment in the kitchen was the beginning of Jimmie's final unraveling. I must have been the last thing standing between him and whatever darkness was trying to claim him, and what I'd done had broken his trust and left him alone. He mostly avoided me after that, intentionally moving to another room when I entered, sleeping on different shifts, finding any way he could to keep our paths from crossing. This couldn't have been easy in such a small space.

But even though we didn't speak, I could see the strings coming loose, one by one. During the next couple of days his restlessness increased until he was pacing the floors, his eyes darting back and forth and settling on nothing. It reminded me of Jay, just before he'd broken out of here, and that made me uneasy. I started watching him more closely while at the same time trying to keep him from noticing. I didn't want to make him even more paranoid. I heard him muttering to himself more than once, cocking his head as if listening to something, and I caught him clutching what remained of his hair and moaning low and deep in his throat once in the kitchen before he slipped out and away. Tessa tried to look at his leg wound a couple of times, but he wouldn't let her see it.

I should have known there was something terribly wrong then, I should have done something to stop it. But I didn't. I let myself believe that he would come around again, if I left him alone. Looking back, that seems to be the story of my life—ignore the warning signs and pretend everything is okay, even when the walls are crumbling around you, even where your abusive father is lying close to death in a hospital room, even when the bombs drop and you're one of the last left standing, even when your friends are peeled off from what's left of the herd and taken down, one by one.

Pretend everything is right in the world, and eventually it will be. Some philosophy.

I wanted to talk about the voice I'd heard on the radio, and what it all meant for us. I wanted to weigh our options and not hold anything back; talk about fallout and the chances of our survival if we left this place. Dan had a pretty strong opinion that we should remain in the shelter, hoping we heard some clear instructions through the radio. We sat in the dining room late one night, just the two of us, maybe trying to heal the rift that had opened up between us after the incident with the radio. Dan got out the cards and we played a couple of hands. The pack was missing the ten of diamonds, so we had to make do with a piece of cardboard, which was pretty stupid since anyone with a pair of eyes could tell it from the rest of the pack with no problem. Jimmie had drawn a picture on it; he was pretty good at that, always doodling, drawing cartoons and other stuff.

Dan held that piece of cardboard with Jimmie's picture in his hands, turning it over and over. We drank a few beers and smoked the remains of one of Jay's joints Dan had found stashed under the sink in the bathroom. We talked about opening up the hatch to take a look. But that strange buzzing sound we had both heard when Jay left, combined with what Dan had read in *Nuclear Winter*, kept us from doing anything.

It seemed that the rest of the group was split, with Sue in favor of leaving now for Alaska, and Jimmie seeming to want to head to Colorado. I was paralyzed with indecision. If we left, we couldn't be sure we were headed to the right place. Getting to the Gates of the Arctic Park seemed pretty damn near impossible, with the distance and the state of the roads up there. But the alternative meant we could drive for 2,000 miles and end up in an empty air force base, nothing but ghosts among the wreckage.

Alone for a moment in the bedroom while Dan and Tessa tried to get Sue to eat something and Jimmie locked himself in the bathroom doing God knows what, I flipped through *Surviving Nuclear Winter*. I could see what Dan meant; it was terrifying. Nearly every page was filled with diagrams, charts and lists, radiation levels, climate patterns and illustrations of the effect of different-size bomb blasts on structures and people. It was a dense technical read, and much of it centered on what the climate would be like after a nuclear war.

But the first section of the book dealt with the sheer destruction a major attack would bring. The detonation of a fraction of the number of warheads that existed in the world would kill an estimated one billion people, with another billion suffering extensive injuries and radiation poisoning. Fires would rage across cities and forests. Temperatures would drop, the sun would disappear for weeks or months, disease would overwhelm most of the survivors.

I read as much as I could take and then I closed the book. I felt an emptiness inside, a sense of time getting away from me with no clear direction on when it might end. I sat alone while the others' voices drifted through the closed door, and thought about my mother in the middle of all that death and destruction. If she had survived, she would need medical assistance. She would need someone to help her get from her wheelchair to the bathroom, to help her fix meals, to get into bed at night. I thought about her locked away down in some school or church basement filled with dusty, broken pews and tables, sitting in the corner, calling for help and getting nothing in return, having to swallow her pride and crawl. Who was helping her now?

And, God help me, as much as I tried to block them out, memories came drifting back like dusty cobwebs: my father's broken, twisted body at the foot of those stairs, the drive to the hospital behind the ambulance, the rush into emergency surgery to try to stop the bleeding and repair his collapsed lung, the sound of the life-support machines in the intensive-care unit like a call to action and his body looking so much smaller and more fragile lying in that bed and connected to so many tubes and needles.

I saw my mother sitting in the chair in the corner, her own arm in a sling, sobbing quietly, policemen waiting in the hall, and me standing there by the bed in my surgical mask, looking down at him and wondering whether she was crying for him or for the two of us left behind. Perhaps she was just relieved to have it all end. His hatred of her had grown worse over the years as his mind had continued to slip toward darkness. It had come to the point where he could not even look at her, and when she spoke he would cut her off with a wave of his hand and a grunt. Those were the good days.

Tessa was right; my anger back then swelled up and overwhelmed me, and I wished him dead.

The doctor came into the room and asked me to sit down too, and explained to us both in low, even tones that my father had suffered an intracerebral hemorrhage and was clinically brain-dead. He could no longer hear us or understand anything or even breathe on his own. The machines were the only things keeping him alive.

My mother stopped crying. I remember that. "Can he recover?" she asked.

The doctor explained how the pool of blood had killed a large portion of his brain, and he would remain a vegetable for as long as we chose to keep him alive. There was no chance of him regaining consciousness. The parts that had made him human were gone.

She looked at me. "We'll need to decide whether to take him off life support," she said.

The doctor, a short Asian man with an accent, gave us some time alone to talk, but we didn't need it. The choice was simple, really. After all, I'd wished he were dead, and now he would be. The fact that it would also end any suffering he might be going through was beside the point.

An hour later we were by his bedside when the doctor turned off the ventilator. As much as we'd been told it would be quick, my father did not go quietly into that good night. His body jerked upward, then slammed back onto the bed. He gave a deep, shuddering sigh, and then sucked air into his lungs once, twice, three times, the wait longer between each breath. His mouth opened and closed like a landed fish. I smelled shit as he soiled himself. And then his heart stopped, and he died.

We were left alone with the body, to pay our respects. After a while I went out into the hall and one of the policemen asked if he could talk to me. He wanted to know if I was the one who had found my father that night, and whether I knew if he'd been drinking. He asked me if I'd seen him fall, and I told him I had not. And then, more gently, he asked if my father was abusive to me and my mother. Maybe he had seen the bruises on my mother's face, or her arm in that sling, or the way she did not come too close to my father's bedside. Maybe he saw the bruises on me. Or maybe there were rumors floating around in the department. That day I'd soiled my bed and my mother fell down the stairs was not the last time the doctor had come to our house.

I shook my head as my mother came limping out into the hall to hold my hand. She tried to pull me away, but I resisted.

"No," I said. "Absolutely not. He was a good man."

I heard a knock on the door to the other room, and Dan stuck his head in. I'd drifted off there for a while, I wasn't sure for how long, but the knocking had brought me sharply back into myself and away from thoughts I'd blocked out for years. I felt vaguely sick.

"You okay?" he said. "We're going to play some poker, if you want to come out. Just try to blow off a little steam. Get Jimmie too."

I got up and went to the bathroom door and knocked. I heard him shuffling around in there, but he didn't answer. I put my ear to the door and thought I heard a sound like a low moan, but I wasn't sure.

"We're playing cards," I said into the door. "Dan wants you to come join us."

Something thumped inside the bathroom. "Everything all right?" I asked. "Jimmie?" I rattled the handle, but it was locked.

"I'm . . . okay," he muttered. "Bandage. Be out . . . pretty soon."

His voice sounded strange. I thought about trying to break the lock, but decided against it. If he still didn't open the door in five minutes, I'd figure something else out.

In less than half an hour, he was gone.

CHAPTER TWENTY-FOUR

I've already told most of what happened immediately after that; Jimmie did eventually come out to play cards, but when he did he was too jumpy and he wouldn't meet my eyes, and the fever was clearly back, judging by the paleness and sheen on his skin. I noticed a dark stain spreading through the new bandage he'd put on his leg, and the hives were getting worse again.

I could smell him as soon as he entered the room, and it was the smell of sickness and rot.

We should have forced him to let us help right then, but as I looked at him a chill settled in my bones, and all I wanted was to keep as far away from him as possible. There was something entirely alien about the way he acted, and I was reminded once again about how I'd felt about him and Jay a few nights back. Husks of human bodies with something else inside.

Like pilots of an airplane, Pete . . . a means to an end, an inanimate object, nothing more. Puppets getting their strings pulled.

Still, he didn't deserve what Dan or I did to him. For hours after, as those of us who remained tried to cope with what had happened, I thought about that, about Dan's punch and the blood dripping from Jimmie's chin and the way he'd looked at all of us, like a wounded animal, lost and confused and waiting to die.

I thought about when he stood up and started screaming and pulling out what remained of his hair; how much it had reminded me of Jay just before he escaped through the hatch, as if he was struggling with something terrible and could not stop himself from doing it, and so the only choice was to throw himself to the wolves or whatever else waited outside the hatch.

But mostly I thought about how I laughed at him, and what that must have meant. His best and only real friend who had already abandoned him, now ridiculing him in front of the others, my laughter like a razor blade against his throat.

Maybe that was why I tried to make Dan feel better. Maybe I was trying to make myself feel better too, pretending that it wasn't anyone's fault. Pretending to care. Because the truth was, I was numb. I didn't feel anything at all. And somehow, that was worse than everything else. All my life, I had gotten through hard times by making light of everything. The jokes and laughter and goofy looks were my way of coping, and they had served me well. Now my laughter was hollow and cold, my jokes were gone, and I was left with the echoes of my own defenses, unable to hide anymore. I felt raw and exposed and alone.

For the first time in years, Tessa's presence didn't help calm me, and that worried me the most of all. She held up better than the rest of us after Jimmie left, but then again, underneath that tiny frame she'd always been the strongest one. I'd depended on her for so long. But now, when she sat with me and held my hand, I felt my anxiety still simmering just under the surface, like the humming of high-tension wires.

Cabin fever. That's what Dan tried to convince all of us was going on; first Jay, then Jimmie, the two of them feeding off each other. "We have to be aware of it happening in all of us," he said. "It's a common reaction to being in enclosed spaces for too long. We need to recognize the signs, and help each other through it."

I didn't buy that for a second. Sure, we were all on edge, but whatever was going on, it wasn't just a psychological reaction to stress. For days now, I had felt something building, that humming sound in my mind growing louder as whatever was coming got closer to the surface.

We argued some more about whether to stay or leave. We didn't know it then, but before we could make any decision, it would be made for us.

When Jimmie went through that hatch, I thought we might have seen the worst of it. The two most high-strung people among us were gone now, and as much as I missed them and felt guilty about my role in the whole thing, I also felt a kind of relief. I thought maybe we could remain safe down here until whoever had been broadcasting through the radio would come for us.

I thought the worst was over.

But we hadn't seen anything yet.

CHAPTER TWENTY-FIVE

The night after Jimmie left I had a dream about him, but all I remembered when I woke up was that blood was everywhere, and that he started bleeding at the mouth and it got worse and worse until we were drowning in it. My dreams were getting more intense, which was probably pretty natural considering the circumstances. Usually I was glad I didn't remember much the next day. But that night I lay there trying to remember the details, as if something from my dream could help me cope with what we were going through, some clue to a way out. I found nothing, and after a few minutes I gave up.

After that I listened to Sue breathing in the other bunk. Dan was keeping watch out in the dining room, and Tessa was in the bunk above me. The bed to my left was conspicuously empty. I lay blinking into the darkness, the room illuminated only by the battery-powered lantern, and listened to the humming sound that I had been hearing off and on for a couple of days now. It got into my head like nails across a chalkboard, until I couldn't think of anything else. This time it was louder than before, and it stuttered like a fluorescent light blinking on and off.

It sounded like it was coming from Sue's bed.

I turned back in that direction, staring into the faint light. Shadows speckled the space under the top bunk.

Sue was lying on her back, and I thought I could just see the tip of one nipple above her bra where it had slipped down while she slept. She had taken to sleeping nearly naked; said she wanted to feel if anything climbed up on her. Normally I didn't think of Sue in a sexual way, but for some reason the look of her sleeping, her breasts half exposed, stirred something in me. I thought for just a brief moment about getting into bed with her. I'd slept with only one person in my life, a girl two years older named Janice Renalli, who had a bit of a reputation; we had gone out my sophomore year for a couple of weeks, and she had taken my virginity in the backseat of her father's Volvo one night after a drunken party at her friend Katy's house. We'd slept together twice more after that, but it hadn't been particularly good, and then our relationship had just petered out. I didn't have much to give her, and she was busy with other guys before long. I don't think I was anything more than a brief distraction to her. Tessa called her a slut, and said I was better off without her. I guess maybe she was right, although I didn't feel great about it then.

Of course I would never have done that to Sue. It would have been the last thing she wanted. She was still reeling from the loss of Jay, and I felt guilty even thinking about it now.

Sue stirred in her sleep, a mumbled word escaping her lips. She shifted toward me and into the light, exposing more of the soft white curve of her breast.

But that wasn't what I was staring at, not anymore.

There was something in the bed with her.

It huddled between the crook of her neck and shoulder. It looked like some kind of animal, about the size and shape of a large mouse, but I knew instinctively that a mouse was not quite right. Mice didn't have wings. I couldn't see it well, but as it moved, fluttering as it went slightly airborne before settling again, I heard the humming, buzzing noise, a whine like a high-powered engine in the distance or a power tool. And then it stopped as the thing went still again.

A chill ran down the length of my body. I could not move, cemented to the bed, a cold sweat breaking out on my skin as I watched it huddle against Sue's neck.

Feeding.

That was what it was doing, I realized, as my stomach began a slow, lazy turning, over and over again. The hole in Sue's neck, like a puncture wound. I was right: she hadn't gotten it from Dan or me wrestling her to the ground. She'd gotten it from this thing, sucking at her, like some kind of vampire.

As it lifted slightly and I heard the humming again, the spell broke, and I thrust myself up and off the mattress, a strangled shout ripping itself from my throat as I crossed the room and hit the light switch and Dan burst through the door. Sue opened her eyes in the suddenly bright light, blinked and squinted and muttered groggily at us. Then she frowned and raised her hand and waved vaguely at her neck, the movements of a girl with a tickling sensation but too sleepy to care much.

As her fingers brushed its back, the thing at her throat lifted into the air and darted out from under the top bunk.

It looked like a giant mosquito. It was about six inches long, covered with a fine brown fur, with a set of wings that buzzed and hummed as it flitted through the air. A set of multijointed legs hung down from its body as it flew. It had a long proboscis protruding from between two huge, mirrored eyes, and its engorged abdomen ended in a nasty, needlelike stinger.

When Sue saw the creature, her eyes opened wide, and she screamed. She rolled off the bed and scrambled toward us at the door in her bra and underwear, waving her arms wildly as the thing swooped and darted around her head.

The next few moments were lost to me, the utter chaos that ensued mostly missing from my mind later except for the feeling of sheer panic. I remember the terror of not knowing where the thing had gone, and the sound of Sue screaming and Dan shouting something I couldn't seem to understand. Somehow we all ended up outside the closed bedroom door, Dan leaning up against it and panting heavily, Sue still screaming and me with my hands to my head, trying to slow my breathing down and calm my hammering heart before I collapsed.

"Jesus fucking Christ," Dan said. He turned around, his back against the door. "Sue, are you okay? Did it hurt you?"

Sue's screams had settled into a nearly constant moan, and she kept brushing at her nearly naked body frantically with both hands, as if trying to wipe the memory of the creature off her. I caught a glimpse of her neck as she moved; the area where it had been sucking at her was bloody and inflamed and slick with some kind of shiny substance.

Slowly I regained control of myself. We were outside and the door was closed, so we were safe for now. But we were missing someone.

Tessa was still in there.

I knew that I wasn't thinking clearly, but I didn't have time to figure it all out. Once again filled with panic, I ran into the kitchen and came back with the fire extinguisher. I'd washed it in the sink after the fight with the rats, but as I held it I could imagine the bits of gore still stuck to the handle, and I had to struggle to keep from tossing it away from me. This time I'd make sure to pull the pin. I just hoped there was enough foam left inside to do the trick.

As I approached the closed door, Dan held up his hands. "Hold on," he said, "what do you think—"

"Get out of the way," I said. "Now." I held up the extinguisher like a club. There must have been something in my eyes because he backed away, hands still up.

"Easy," he said. "Take it easy, Pete."

"Close the door after me," I said. And then I turned the handle, pulled open the door and slipped inside.

The room was empty.

I stood just inside the door and shot the lock through, holding the extinguisher in front of me, so scared I was shaking. I didn't want anyone else opening that door and letting the thing out. But I was no hero and never had been, this much I knew. I was terrified of needles, I hated confrontation, and I refused to be dared into doing anything I didn't like. I was the only person in my sixth-grade group never to jump off the high rock into Black Pond, even when the eight-year-old sister of one of the boys did it and the others laughed at me and called me a pussy, and the story dogged me for years. That was one example, but there were many others.

But once forced into action, I tended to strike quickly and hard. I'd only been in two fights in my life, both of them started by someone else. Both fights had been over pretty quick, with the other guy getting the worst of it. I gained a reputation after that and people generally stopped messing with me.

Some might have thought I was brave. Only I knew the truth; when backed into a corner, my fear became so overwhelming that I fought with a kind of animal instinct, my body taking over as my mind shut down.

There was no choice now. I had to act.

I scanned the room, left, right, up, down, looking for any movement. Tessa wasn't in her bunk, and I couldn't see the creature anywhere.

I crouched down, looking under the beds. For a moment I thought I saw something hanging from the far corner of the one nearest the closet, but I blinked and it was gone.

I stood up again, on full alert, every nerve in my body screaming at me, breathing fast and hard. The bathroom, maybe? The door was closed, and I couldn't see any light coming from underneath it. The feeling that I wasn't thinking this through correctly remained, that something was wrong.

"Tessa?" I said. Then, a little louder: "Tessa!" No answer. I took a step into the room, then one more. I felt a kind of doubling, as if seeing everything through two sets of eyes from two different locations. It made me light-headed and dizzy, and I had to steady myself for a moment before continuing.

The thing, when it attacked, was incredibly fast. It came out of nowhere. I heard the buzzing from somewhere to my right, and a split second later I saw it darting at my head. I raised the extinguisher hose and let loose with a shot of foam, but the creature swerved neatly around it and hummed right by my ear, close enough for me to feel the air from its wings.

I swung the extinguisher in a wild arc, but only served to excite the thing even more. It increased its speed, swerving around and dive-bombing me again. It was moving so fast now I could barely track it with my eyes. I shot a blast of foam that splattered across the right bunk and the wall, missing again by a good three feet.

As it came around again, I tried to anticipate its flight

pattern, but it darted sharply left and avoided the spray easily before buzzing by me again even closer than before, so close its wings brushed my face. I thought of summers in our home with the windows open to the breeze, when hornets would sneak into rooms and buzz around bumping into ceilings, then land in a corner lying in wait for someone to disturb them. I remembered how my father seemed to look forward to those moments, entering the room with a rolled-up magazine or newspaper in one hand, and closing the door on us while we waited in the hallway. Then he would come out a minute or two later, oddly defeated, with the crushed body of the hornet cupped in his palm. Perhaps it hadn't offered enough of a challenge, but I always had the feeling he wanted to get stung, excited by the hunt but let down by the end of it.

This was no hornet. I glanced up as the creature passed. It turned and hovered for a moment about five feet away, its abdomen engorged and pulsing, stinger dripping a clear fluid.

Panic rose up in me. This wasn't working. I had to outsmart it somehow. Otherwise it would sting me, and for all I knew that might be a death sentence.

I could hear Dan shouting through the door at me, but didn't have time to answer him. As the thing came at me again, I shot high, intentionally driving it downward, and then let loose with a horizontal sweep of foam directly into its flight path.

This time the creature dove directly into the foam and was driven backward, into the wall, where it hit with a wet thud and slid to the floor, wings twitching.

I crossed the room in three quick strides and slammed the metal bottom of the extinguisher directly down onto it with a satisfying crunch.

The thing's abdomen popped and dark, clotted blood splattered across the wall. Its legs twitched twice and it was still.

I stood in the silence, breathing hard, a thrill running through me as I stifled the urge to shout in triumph. I lifted the extinguisher and stared down at the crushed body. Christ, the thing was ugly. It was very much like a giant mosquito, and it had clearly been sucking at Sue; the blood that spurted from its belly was much more than it would have held otherwise. It had a proboscis like a mosquito, but the stinger on its rear end was not like any mosquito I'd ever seen. It was close to half an inch long and still oozed a clear fluid. I didn't know for sure, but I could bet that it would hurt like a son of a bitch if you got hit with something like that.

The bullet ant . . . an inch long with the most powerful stinger on earth . . . they say it feels like getting shot.

Jay's words came drifting back to me, sounding more and more prophetic. The thrill I'd felt in crushing the creature was dying fast. I'd beaten one of these things in here, sure, but what about the larger picture? Had Jay been right all along, was this some kind of engineered killer insect? What was it like aboveground, were they all over the place?

Or were there worse things than giant mosquitoes out there?

Dan was hammering on the door with his fists. "It's okay," I shouted. "It's dead. Hold on." I opened the closet, looking for Tessa. Nothing but tangled sheets and shelves full of boxes. I tried the bathroom, nothing there either.

Dan and Sue were both calling to me now. When I finally unlocked the door and swung it open, Dan barreled in holding a wooden mop handle in one hand, his finger in my face. "Are you fucking crazy?" he said, glancing around the room at the foamy mess. "We don't need that cowboy bullshit in here."

Then his gaze found the mangled body of the insect against the wall. "I'll be damned. You did kill it," he said.

"What, you think I didn't have it in me?"

"Maybe. I guess you proved me wrong. Crazy son of a bitch." He walked over and nudged the remains with his foot in grudging admiration. "Nice work. But Jesus. Why'd you lock the door? I was about to break it down."

I didn't answer him. I was too busy staring at Tessa, who stood just behind Sue in the open doorway. She smiled slightly and shrugged. How the hell she'd gotten behind me and out that door, I didn't know. I was just glad she was okay.

"Pete," Dan said. His voice had gone quiet, but tense.

I realized Sue and Tessa's gaze had shifted. They were staring at something back in the room, and their expressions had changed. I turned. Dan was standing there, absolutely still, looking down at what had been Jimmie's bunk.

Long, many-jointed legs had appeared from underneath the bed and wrapped themselves around the mattress. As we all stood and watched, another giant mosquito pulled itself up, clung to the edge and fluttered its wings. This one was even bigger than the last. The humming noise started and stopped as it cleaned itself with its front legs, cocking its head and rubbing along the length of its antennae with a soft rasping sound. Then it turned to look at us, its alien eyes gleaming in the light.

"Now," Dan said. "*Do it.*"

I let loose with a spray from the extinguisher, hitting it dead-on and knocking it to the floor. The thing's wings buzzed angrily as it landed on its back, stuck for just a moment in the foam.

That was long enough. Dan swung the wooden handle down like a lumberjack splitting wood, the shock of the impact vibrating up his arms with such force I could hear his teeth snap together. The blow nearly cut the creature in half and sent body parts flying everywhere. Greenish fluid spattered Dan's arms and face. Two amputated legs continued to twitch where they landed two feet away.

Dan made a strangled, coughing sound, rubbing at his face with a shirt already damp with bug guts. Some of it had gotten into his mouth, and he kept spitting onto the floor, grimacing and spitting again. I wondered how it tasted, but didn't ask. Not exactly filet mignon, that much was clear.

I crouched down and peered under the bed. In the far corner of the mattress, the same place I thought I'd seen something when I first entered the room, was a hole about two inches across.

I saw a hairy leg poke out of the hole, then disappear back inside.

"They're in the mattress," I said. "Those fuckers ate a hole into the bottom of it and hollowed it out and made a nest."

How long had they been there? What were they waiting for all this time? Had they been sucking at the rest of us during the night, undetected? I remembered reading about how regular mosquitoes had something in their saliva that made the blood keep running and kept you from feeling their bite. Christ, they could have been sucking at Jimmie right through the mattress as he slept, and we would have never known it.

I felt my own neck and shoulders, looking for a wound, but there was nothing. I couldn't see or feel my own back, of course. We would have to check each other over from head to foot to be sure.

I shook my head, unable to think clearly. There was another possibility, some other reason they might have been holed up in there, sneaking out to feed. Something that hovered just out of my reach. But for the life of me, I couldn't seem to grasp it.

Without waiting another second, afraid of giving them the chance to get at us again, I set the extinguisher down and grabbed Jimmie's mattress with both hands, yanking it out of its frame and onto the floor, covering the hole and trapping them inside. I jumped up on it and stomped as hard as I could on the area where I'd seen that leg poking out.

Crunch.

Dan climbed up and started stomping with me, and we began at the head of the mattress and moved down together, section by section, covering every square inch. I could feel the crunch and pop of their bodies as we landed on them; there must have been half a dozen more in there.

It went on and on. Dark, wet stains began to appear in the mattress's surface as blood and bug guts bled through the fabric. Sue and Tessa watched us from the doorway, their eyes wide. I saw Sue's hand going to her neck again, rubbing at the place where she'd been bitten. We kept stomping long after they would have all been dead, getting out our own anger and frustration, until my legs started to burn with fatigue and the mattress looked like a crime scene.

Finally I stepped down, breathing hard, goose bumps running across my arms and legs. I felt sick to my stomach and vaguely light-headed again.

"We need to check the other beds," Dan said. "And anywhere else they might be holed up too. Every inch of this place—"

At that moment, a hollow, booming sound echoed

through the shelter. Once, twice, three times. The sound sent fresh chills down my spine. It sounded like the clanging bells of doom, a symbol of death, of destruction, of hopelessness, bringing with it the Grim Reaper, come to carry us home.

We all stared at each other, nobody willing or able to move, the significance of that sound registering on four faces at once. Nobody spoke; nobody could say a word in the awkwardly normal brightness of that room. I couldn't tell if the expressions were of hope or fear.

Someone was knocking on the hatch.

CHAPTER TWENTY-SIX

"Check the other mattresses," Dan said. He was already shrugging into a hazmat suit. "Make sure they're clean. I want you all locked away in here, safe. You hear me? I'll go open the hatch and see what that is."

"Bad idea," I said. "We don't know what you'll be facing. And that suit won't protect you from much."

"That's not up to you," he said. "It's my call. It could be the military, some kind of help."

"Or a band of thieves and murderers." *Or worse.*

"We can't just ignore it, Pete."

"At least try to talk to them, see if they can hear you before you open it up."

Dan hesitated, the hazmat hood still unzipped and hanging down his back, mask around his neck by its strap. "Fine," he said. "But if I have to act fast, I don't want any argument from you. They don't answer, you and Sue get in that room and lock the door and don't come out until you hear me call the all clear. Understood?"

I nodded, swallowing my frustration, and we followed him out to the foot of the steps, where he climbed halfway up the ladder to the hatch, listening. I could feel Tessa's warm hand on my back, and it felt good. The energy in the room had skyrocketed; I think the rest of us were desperately hoping for good news, but nobody wanted to say anything out loud for fear of jinxing it. My own adrenaline was pumping and I was both exhilarated and terrified. We'd been attacked by creatures we couldn't have imagined existed just a few short weeks ago, so it wasn't difficult to see some pretty terrible possibilities if that hatch came open.

"Hello?" Dan called out from the ladder. "Identify yourself, please."

Silence. "Maybe they can't hear you," Sue said. "The walls are pretty thick."

"Hey!" Dan shouted, cords standing out in his neck. "Who's out there?" The sound echoed off the concrete and wood paneling, ringing in my ears and sounding somehow obscene before dying away into silence.

Nothing for thirty seconds, a minute, two minutes, as we stood and waited.

And then: *boom . . . boom . . . boom.*

It was so much louder out here, directly below the hatch. We should have been thrilled; someone was alive out there, and they had found us. They were going to get us out.

But nobody said a word. I don't know why, but I didn't like that sound. I didn't like it at all. And apparently I wasn't alone.

"Get back in the bedroom," Dan said. He still gripped the wooden handle in one hand, the muscles of his forearm standing out as he squeezed it tightly.

As we turned to go, Dan grabbed my arm. "Hang back a second," he said quietly.

I waited until the girls had entered the bedroom, then turned back to him.

"I don't know if whoever's out there is friendly or not," he said. "I don't know if it's even human. We're going to need to be careful and use any advantage we have."

He stood the mop handle against the wall, secured the mask over his mouth and nose and pulled the hood over his head. He looked like an astronaut with the hood and mask over his face.

When he spoke again, his voice was slightly muffled by the suit, but I could hear it clearly enough.

"Get the gun," he said. "Right now. Quickly."

I opened the closet door and reached up to the top shelf to push the blankets out of the way, my arms trembling so badly I could barely grasp the box where the gun was kept. It was pretty far back there, and as I stood up on tiptoes I hit the box and knocked it into the back panel of the closet. I heard a click and felt something give.

I stepped up onto the bed frame for a better look. There, at the back of the shelf, a panel had opened up a crack. Blackness loomed from inside.

"What are you doing?" Sue said. She was standing with Tessa in the middle of the room, arms crossed over her chest, still in her bra and underwear. She was shivering from cold or fear, or maybe both. Tessa rubbed her shoulders as if to try to warm them.

I tossed her a blanket. "I'll be right back," I said, hopping down and holding the box in my hands, trying to appear as calm as possible. Everything seemed to have speeded up; my voice, the movement in the room, the way my eyes ticked over every detail and back again, even the flickering of the light. I set the box on the bed frame, grabbed a hazmat suit off the garment rack and began to step into it, just in case.

"Pete," Sue said, her voice breaking, "what if it's—"

"Stay here," I said as I pulled up the suit and zipped the front, then grabbed the box with the gun. "Check the mattresses, lock the door and wait for me to knock."

I didn't have time to explain anything more, and she didn't say anything, just wrapped the blanket around her shoulders and watched me leave.

I pulled the door shut and heard the lock click. Dan was waiting for me at the foot of the steps in full hazmat gear. "What do you think you're doing with that suit?" he said.

"I lied before. I'm going with you."

"No," he said, unzipping the hood, pulling the mask off again and shaking his head. "No way."

In response, I set the box on the floor, pulled out the .38 and casually checked the chamber. Then I slipped in the bullets, one by one. "Ever fired one of these?" I asked.

"No," he said, watching me. "You?"

"My mother taught me," I said. "Thought I might need to know how one day. Pretty smart, huh?" I didn't tell him the real reason why, just slapped the chamber shut and looked at him. "You ready?"

"Aw, hell." He shrugged. "I guess I do need you. Let's do it."

I tried to smile at him, slipped the mask over my face and pulled up the hood. It was hot and smelled like rubber. I might have been putting on a brave front, but inside, I was terrified. I knew that the suit wouldn't stop one of those bug stingers for a second. I kept imagining what kind of creatures we might encounter out there, what the earth might look like after such a devastating attack. Most importantly, who was knocking on that hatch. I began to be aware of that familiar feeling, my back against the wall and fighting for my life, and the red-tinged cloud started to descend across my vision as the blood-thump increased in my ears.

It was time, the situation had its own momentum, the seconds were continuing to march along, and the decision to act had been made for us. Whatever was outside had to be met and dealt with, whether we were ready or not.

Come and get me, I thought, gripping that gun. *Give it your best shot.*

We were going to open up the hatch, after all this time, finally open it and see what was waiting for us.

CHAPTER TWENTY-SEVEN

When I realized there was no turning back, a strange sort of hyperfocus consumed me. I felt reenergized, wildly confident and reckless. The red-tinged cloud disappeared as Dan settled the hood and mask over his own head and climbed back up the ladder.

I heard him start cranking the wheel, and the alarm began to sound and the red light came on. Dan punched the code into the keypad, and the alarm stopped. Then he reached up and kept turning the wheel on the hatch until the seal broke with a soft hiss.

As he lifted the hatch up and away and it clanged open against its supports, I heard the humming noise I'd heard before when Jay and Jimmie broke out, and this time it held a deeper and more sinister meaning. I stood directly below Dan in my insulated suit, gun up, legs planted firmly. I was waiting for more of those bugs to dart inside.

But nothing happened. I could just see a glimpse of the sky from where I stood. It was low and mean, silvery gray, and I could hear the wind whipping across the hatch opening. Bits of gray slush drifted down toward my upturned face and settled on the clear plastic shield of my hood. I wiped them away.

"Hello?" Dan shouted. He was still standing on the ladder, his head about two feet below the hatch. His muffled voice seemed to be immediately diminished and then disappear entirely, swallowed by the angry wind.

I felt my skin prickle. I could hear my own breathing through the mask, a whistled sucking in and a pop and hiss as the valve released on exhale.

I didn't know why whoever was out there hadn't appeared by now. Something felt very wrong.

Dan tilted his head back toward me, the shiny expanse of his plastic hood catching the light from below, so I couldn't see his eyes. "I'm going up," he said.

"Dan, don't," I said. "You know those dumb movies where you're shouting at the screen, telling them not to leave the room? We're there. I don't like this."

He reached down. "Give me the gun," he said. "It'll be okay."

"You don't know how to shoot," I said. "It's not like you see on TV. It's not something you just pick up and do. There's the right grip, and remembering not to jerk the trigger, and recoil, and wind shear—"

"Just give it to me," he said.

When the hand appeared through the hatch opening, Dan was still looking down at me, and didn't see it at first. But I did. I shouted a warning as it snaked down toward him, moving fast, an entire arm exposed now, bare to the shoulder and covered with blisters like a third-degree burn.

I could see the silhouette of a head, black against the sky. Someone was kneeling outside and reaching into the shelter, trying to get at us.

Dan turned as the hand grabbed hold of his suit and yanked. Whoever it was, he was strong; I could see Dan's weight begin to shift upward before he tightened his grip on the rungs of the ladder. Then he reached up with his free hand, grabbed the person's arm and yanked back.

All this happened in the blink of an eye. I was still raising the gun, debating whether I had a clean shot, when Dan's grip slipped, his fingers sliding through skin that came loose in twin furrows of blood. Still the arm pulled at him, the suit now stretching and dangerously close to tearing a hole. Dan grabbed the arm again, around the wrist this time, and he used his weight to pull the attacker headfirst over the edge of the hatch opening.

I jumped out of the way as the attacker's body slammed into Dan's shoulders, knocking him free, and the two of them tumbled down the ladder and hit the floor hard. I heard a grunt as the air was driven from Dan's lungs, and he lay there gasping, his mask half off his face behind his hood.

The attacker was completely naked. His skin was blistered and raw from head to foot. He lay motionless across Dan's body for a long moment, facedown, and a glint of recognition made me step back and shake my head, as if an act of simple denial would make it all go away.

Oh my God.

Jay raised his head, his movements stiff, strangely robotic. His trademark glasses were missing, the white of his right eye so filled with blood that I could barely make out the pupil. His hair was mostly gone, showing blistered scalp and patches of skull.

He climbed off Dan, who was still writhing in pain, and stood up.

He was an abomination. His bony torso and limbs were covered with sores the size of saucers, his shriveled penis hanging limply in a nest of pubic hair. His entire body vibrated like a dog trembling with cold.

His skin rippled everywhere, a seething, moving carpet of raw flesh, things moving underneath the surface.

And yet he was still there, still inside. I could see this

in his face, or what was left of him. I could still see something of Jay in the way he looked at me, the way he raised an arm toward me, as if pleading for help.

The sight of Jay was horrible. I gagged, stumbled backward down the steps and then pointed the gun at him, my hands trembling so much I couldn't line up the barrel with his chest.

"R-r-uu-unnnnn," he said, straining for every syllable, his neck rigid, his mouth a raw, weeping hole. "I c-c-c-aann't—"

Then his expression changed, his face losing all emotion. Jay was gone, even as his body remained standing. He looked at Dan between his feet, reached down in a jerking, awkward way and grasped him by the front of his suit. Dan must have weighed at least 200 pounds, but Jay lifted him as if he were a rag doll. I heard a tearing sound as Dan's feet left the ground and one of the arms of his suit came loose. Then he grabbed the hood and mask and ripped them off Dan's head.

Jay brought his face close, as if waiting for a gentle kiss.

"Let him go," I said through the mask.

Jay didn't appear to hear me. He went rigid, his mouth opening wide, wider, until I heard the tendons crack. Then something began to spill out of him.

I could not register what was happening with reality. I knew what I'd seen the past few weeks, knew that we were not only dealing with nuclear devastation but with something far worse and more inhuman, something that crept damn close to insanity. And yet my mind had refused to acknowledge that fact deep down in the places where these things really mattered, the places that allowed you to act without thinking, to accept something as truth and common natural law.

I saw, and yet I did not; my mind erased the fringe

elements from my memory as soon as they appeared, and I was left with the futile hope that maybe I'd seen things wrong; maybe there was a reasonable explanation; maybe we would find out that this was all an elaborate practical joke. Jay was badly injured and mentally unstable, but soon help would come. Soon we would be rescued, and the government would explain to us what had really happened, and how they were going to rebuild and make the world right again. My mother would be found at a local shelter, tired and worn and hungry, but alive. Our home would be damaged, but repairable. We would begin to put our lives back together piece by piece, transformed by the experience but alive and able to hope for a better future.

What I was seeing now did not conform to that vision. The thin black cloud that swirled from Jay's mouth, a cloud that was *alive*, that moved and seethed and changed direction with purpose, did not fit into any neat, natural pattern. It was an aberration of nature, a man-made virulent monster. It was insatiable, a single-minded entity with endless segments, impossible to stop, impossible to destroy.

And it wanted us all dead.

The gun shook in my gloved hand, and I slapped my other hand on it in a shooter's grip, trying to steady myself. Even seeing what was happening, I could not pull the trigger. I could not fire at Jay, even in this state, even knowing that whatever had control of his body was trying to kill Dan. My mind returned to a familiar mantra, repeated again and again, a prayer for the faithful: *Someone will come. Someone will help us. It's not too late. Someone will come.*

The black cloud hovered for a moment between them, pulsing and bulging with thousands of tiny specks of dust all spinning at once. I was reminded of the swarms of black flies in the woods back home in spring, the boyhood memory of emerging from a trail into a clearing and running into them and getting bugs in my mouth and ears and eyes, ducking under and through, waving my arms and watching them swirl apart and then back together again, some unknown communication enabling them to regroup in a way that was both fascinating and strangely unsettling.

Watching this now, I knew why. It was the implication of group intelligence in such an act, the idea that these things had a purpose, a goal, and knew exactly what they were doing.

Dan saw the cloud too. His dazed look vanished, and I saw fear wash across his features. He clenched his mouth shut and tried to lean his face away from it. Still dangling a foot off the ground, his left arm hanging useless at his side, he swept his right arm up, trying to dislodge Jay's grip.

It looked like he'd hit a stone wall, for all the good it did. I remembered how Dan had described the impact of Jay barreling into him in the kitchen as he tried for his escape.

Like getting hit by a 250-pound linebacker.

Whatever had hold of Jay now, it was inhumanly strong.

Dan redoubled his efforts, throwing his knees up against Jay's stomach and clawing at his fingers as the black cloud enveloped his face. He twisted away in panic, turning his shoulders, and this time Jay's hands slipped, the skin sliding away from muscle and bone and leaving him with bloody, raw mitts of flesh.

Dan's suit tore loose and he fell heavily to the floor, rolling backward down the steps with a brief cry until he stopped at my feet.

He stood up coughing and choking, holding his left arm tightly against his side. I knew immediately that whatever he'd done to himself when he landed on the floor, it was bad; the grimace of pain and the look in his eyes were enough. His shoulder was either dislocated or shattered, and any normal person would probably have been screaming by now.

He wiped black flecks from his eyes and nose with his right hand. I could still see the remnants of the cloud whirling around his head. I didn't know what they might do to him, but I could guess. I shivered at the idea of those things swarming down my throat, entering my lungs and bowels, opening me up to something else none of us could understand. Not yet.

Swarms of black flies . . .

"Shoot him," Dan said, gritting his teeth. "Pull the fucking trigger, Pete, damn it! Do it now!"

I turned back to Jay. He was tottering down the steps at us, raw, skinless fingers dripping blood, his mouth still stretched impossibly wide, his nakedness only serving to magnify the threat of him. Being nude can make someone appear more vulnerable, but that was not the case here. He looked like an escaped homicidal mental patient, like he wanted to eat us alive, and I suppose that was close to the truth. Mental illness or not, shooting him would clearly be self-defense, and I wanted to be strong enough to pull that trigger, put a bullet into his brain and end it all right now.

Life ain't civilized. That's a human creation, rules and order and compassion. Nature doesn't care about any of that. Things kill . . . or they die.

The red tinge began to descend over me as the hiss-pop of my breathing through the mask intensified. It was impossibly hot inside my suit. Sounds grew fainter as the world retreated into a fun house–mirrored version of itself, shrinking into a pinpoint focused on the strange human-like creature before us.

I don't remember actually squeezing the trigger, or the pop the gun must have made when it fired. I don't remember the smell of the smoke or the sound of a bullet smacking muscle and bone. I remember only the way Jay's forward momentum suddenly stopped no more than five feet away from us, and the red flower that bloomed in the center of his chest, as if his flesh had opened up and begun to weep.

I sensed, rather than saw, a ripple pass across his skin, beginning at his feet and moving in a wave up his legs and torso to his face.

The second bullet hit him in the neck. I had closed my eyes by then, and the barrel must have begun to float upward before I fired, because when I opened them again a glistening red fountain was pumping from this second wound, and he was looking at me, bewildered, the real Jay back again, if only for a few precious moments. It broke my heart, that look, probing my face for an answer I could not provide: *why?*

Looking back on it later, I thought that might not have been the question at all, that perhaps the look was more one of forgiveness, or even relief. I chose to believe that he was thanking me for his release, the firing of the gun a gift I'd given him to end his pain.

But at that moment, I thought only of the fawn in a clearing from my distant memory, running in circles and crying for its mama, who lay dead at its feet.

My father's voice: *this one's yours.*

The rippling in Jay's flesh grew faster, more agitated, until his entire body seemed to be vibrating at a high frequency. A chattering sound came from his teeth clicking together. His eyes overflowed with blood-tinged tears, and blood dripped from his nose and mouth and ears. The hives that covered his body began to weep a yellowish brown fluid and his skin took on a flush of heat.

I could not tear my gaze away from the insanity standing before me, as desperately as I wanted to, as badly as I wanted to run and hide in a corner somewhere as far away from this place as I could get. I had to see it to try to understand the truth. What I was watching was real, and there was no avoiding it, no way of erasing this from my mind.

He let out another strange sound, similar to the one he'd made days before in the kitchen, but this time the answering sound from directly behind us was very human, and full of undisguised pain.

I turned to find Sue, framed in the open doorway to the bedroom, an expression of despair and terrible agony on her face as she looked from the gun in my gloved hands to Jay's ravaged body, and screamed his name. The sound of the shots must have brought her out. Tessa tried to pull her back into the room, but she wouldn't move.

There was nothing we could do to stop her seeing everything. She did not try to run to him this time, just stood there screaming.

When I turned back I understood why. Jay had begun to come apart. Fissures appeared across the flesh of his naked chest, quickly spreading and swallowing more and more of his unbroken skin. The largest of the hives burst open and seething black waves of insects poured out of the wounds, chewing in ever-widening circles and exposing yellow pockets of fat, strips of muscle and white bone.

He was being eaten from the inside out, the flesh of his face falling away as more ants swarmed from his nose and mouth and ears. Already half his jaw was exposed, giving him a lopsided rictus grin, and the blood on his teeth shone in the light as he continued to dissolve.

As his eyes went with a soft, liquid pop, I heard Sue fall to her knees, begging for it to just please stop, praying to a god who was not there and never would be. I thought of my own mother and what might have happened to her alone in our home, and the rest of my friends and neighbors, children and dogs and occupants of nursing homes and hospitals, all taken this way. I wondered what kind of god would allow such a thing.

The end happened incredibly fast; Jay's skin was gone in moments, and shortly after that he was little more than a skeleton held together with strips of flesh. Still they swarmed over him, chewing until what was left of him collapsed to the floor in a pile of white bone.

And then there was nothing but the sound of Sue's anguish, the whipping of the wind from above, and the emptiness we were left with in the aftermath of his passing.

CHAPTER TWENTY-EIGHT

The ants were everywhere. They spread out in coordinated patterns across the floor, as if intent on searching every square inch of open space. They looked for all the world like a miniature army marching in perfect formation, and I supposed that was exactly what they were. Killing machines, built from the cellular level and engineered to do what they were doing right now. No conscience, no hesitation. Total and complete annihilation.

Somehow we all made it back into the bedroom and locked it, and I took off my mask and hood and breathed gulps of cool air while Dan grabbed blankets and sheets from the closet with his good arm and stuffed them up against the cracks around the door. I didn't have the heart to tell him how futile it all was; if those things wanted to get in here, they would. It seemed like the end game to me, and now all that was left was for us to wait until we were consumed like Jay had been.

But nothing happened for several minutes. We all sat huddled together in the middle of the room, rocking, watching for signs of attack, all of us deathly silent and so paralyzed with shock and fear we would have given in without a fight. There were no more tears, no more hysterics or begging for mercy from some god who did not listen.

Maybe it was because we'd already let Jay go when he first escaped up that ladder, and the fact that he'd returned did not change the uncoupling of emotion that we had all gone through over the past few days. He had returned, yes, but it wasn't really him; his body had no longer been his. Or so we told ourselves, even as we waited for the same thing to happen to us.

"The hatch," Dan said finally. "It's still open."

Sue made a moaning sound like a trapped animal. I pictured the open hatch, dark, menacing clouds racing by far above, icy ash flakes drifting down to cover the concrete steps with a gray film. I imagined things climbing into the shelter, one at a time, creatures that walked upright but were no longer human, moving with purpose to search and destroy.

I shivered, and Tessa snuggled closer to me, the warmth of her body bringing an ache deeper and more profound. If I died, she would surely die with me. I could not let that happen.

"I can't climb the ladder," Dan whispered, gritting his teeth. He turned to me, the look in his eyes a far cry from what it had been the past few weeks. "My arm . . . you'll have to do it, Pete."

I stared at him. I saw fear and uncertainty and a lack of conviction. What I saw angered me, as if he'd let us all down, selling us a bill of goods he could not deliver. I felt like Toto had exposed the man behind the curtain, the real Dan, wracked by the same insecurities and weaknesses as everyone else. Maybe I was being unfair, and the damage to his shoulder was far more painful than he was letting on, and he simply could not act. But whatever the reason, our fearless leader was scared to death, and maybe, I thought, that explained everything. Maybe that was his secret, that he chose us as a peer group simply because we were easily led, easily dominated, and it offered him a way to continue the illusion of control.

"Sue and I will check the mattresses in here, make sure it's safe," he said. "We can barricade the door and hold them off if we have to, if that's what it takes."

He blinked, once, twice. Tiny black flecks floated in the corners of his eyes and had settled in the cracks of his lips. I did not want to think about what that meant.

I nodded. Tessa held my arm, pulled me close. I thought she might ask me not to go. But she kissed me gently on the cheek. "I'll come with you," she said.

I didn't argue the point. If we were going to die, I'd rather she be there with me. We left the room together holding hands, and it felt like walking toward an execution.

The dining room was empty, the ants gone. Jay's bones remained, a stark reminder that what we'd seen was no nightmare. I thought about sweeping them up into some kind of container and hiding them away to spare Sue more agony, and then realized how silly that thought was; we could be attacked at any moment, and I was thinking about cleaning up the mess.

The ash flakes had continued to drift in, and the steps were now nearly covered with them. It was cold in here, the temperature dropping maybe twenty degrees since we'd opened the hatch. I steeled myself, motioned for Tessa to stay back, and brought the gun up as I walked quickly across the open space and climbed the steps to the ladder.

I looked up and squinted into drifting flakes, suppressing the bizarre urge to stick out my tongue like I used to do in winter at the first snow. The sky was even darker than before, and I thought it might be dusk or night now, but I wasn't sure.

The opening was unbroken by shadows or shapes, and I scaled the ladder quickly before I lost my nerve, the gun clanking against the rungs as I ascended.

At the top and just before the opening I hesitated, holding my breath and wondering whether I should put my hood and mask back on. I wasn't thinking clearly. But I wanted to be able to see, and the hood obscured my view too much. I kept them off.

As the wind died down above for a moment and a longer calm settled around me, I climbed the last two rungs and stuck my head through the hatch opening.

The landscape around me was too dark to see very well, but what light existed held an eerie purplish quality, sort of like how the world looked through an expensive pair of sunglasses. I sensed a vast plateau of singed dirt and ash, and from somewhere in the distance I heard the angry crash and hiss of waves breaking against the craggy cliffs of Sparrow Island. Directly in front of me rose the gigantic, sleeping form of Sparrow Rock, and I had the strangest feeling that it leaned toward me, ready to topple at any moment and crush me back into the shelter like one of those whack-a-mole games at the carnival.

The wind came up and whipped my hair, sending dirt flying and dust swarming into my eyes and nose and mouth. I squinted into the assault, my heart pounding in my throat, holding the gun out and sweeping the area. I sensed emptiness within the darkness. I saw nothing at all—no people, no trees, no grass or shrubs, no insects, nothing.

The world appeared, for all intents and purposes, to be dead and gone.

"Pete?" Tessa called from below. "You okay?"

I nodded, wiping tears from my eyes. I blamed them on the wind.

Then I reached up, grabbed the hatch and slammed it shut, twisting the wheel and cutting off everything else.

Chapter Twenty-nine

Back in the bedroom, Dan had pulled the rest of the mattresses off the bunks and pushed the frames against the walls. He was shiny with sweat, and he looked too pale, dark circles ringing his eyes. He held his left arm close to his body. His hazmat suit had been badly torn, the hood gone and one arm of it almost completely separated from the shoulder. It would be useless now, and I tried to remember how many we had left. I would have to check.

Sue was sitting on one of the mattresses with the blanket, staring into space and rocking, clutching herself.

"Is it done?" Dan asked.

I nodded. "I don't think anything else got in."

"I checked everything in this room and the bathroom. It's clear." Dan sat down heavily on the nearest mattress, wincing and holding his injured arm. "Can't be sure about the rest of the place."

"We can push the bed frames against the door," I said. "That might help us sleep."

"Maybe," he said. "But we don't know where those ants went, the ones that came from . . ." He trailed off into silence, glancing at Sue, who didn't appear to have heard him. "They're in here somewhere."

"I know."

"We can't stay here much longer. They know we're here. I can feel it. They'll be coming for us."

I hesitated. *They'll be coming for us.* "Do you . . . feel okay?"

"My arm, I think the shoulder's separated—"

"Not your arm. I don't mean your arm." I couldn't say it out loud, couldn't give voice to the memory of that swarming black cloud that had enveloped his face. I did not want to think about what that meant, and yet I had to try to understand it.

They get into the blood . . . they get inside and they start chewing, and they don't stop until they're in control.

"If we can find help, maybe they'll have a treatment," I said. "I mean, if you're . . . infected."

"I'll be fine," Dan said. But his voice was dead, and when I looked at him, I saw a beaten-down, broken teenager. I'd always seen Dan as a little larger than life, in many ways a hero or at least someone to look up to, a man among boys. Jay's attack had exposed the weaknesses that he'd tried to hide for so long. He would fold under pressure, or in the face of any real challenge to his authority. We might not say it out loud, but we both knew the truth: I was in charge now.

I glanced around the room, wondering where they would come from when they attacked. And that was when I saw them. I'd never really noticed before; the builders had done a nice job making them blend in with the walls, painting it all the same color and making them so that they were almost invisible.

"The ventilation system," I said. I pointed at a fine mesh square about six inches across, set up high near the ceiling. The swarm had been made up of such small specks, and whatever they were, surely they would be able to find a way through whatever filters had been set up through the system. "That's how they'll get in here."

Dan didn't even look up, just nodded. I realized he'd already seen them, had already come to that conclusion. Maybe that was why he seemed so defeated, but I doubted it. There was another possibility, one that I hardly dared contemplate, but one that we'd all have to face, sooner or later: that they'd already been in here, in the night, and we were all infected.

I walked toward the nearest one, climbed up onto the frame for one of the bunk beds and put my hand to the grate. I could feel a slight wash of cool air. I thought about a black cloud of tiny insects swirling through the ducts and pouring out through the mesh, covering our bodies, taking control. What were they after? The death of everyone left on the planet, as Jay had said? And if so, what were they waiting for? Why weren't we dead already?

I turned to study the group. Dan, still seeming oddly broken, grimacing and holding his arm tightly to his side; Sue, still in her bra and underwear under the blanket, rocking and staring at nothing; and Tessa, the only one looking back at me, watching my face, a half smile touching her lips. She nodded as if in encouragement.

I realized I'd already made up my mind. The only thing left was to say it out loud.

"We'll leave tomorrow," I said. "We're going to the Doomsday Vault."

PART FOUR:
HIVE MIND

"N-nothing important. That is, I heard a good deal about a ring, and a dark lord, and something about the end of the world, but please, Mr. Gandalf, sir, don't hurt me. Don't turn me into anything . . . unnatural."
—J.R.R. Tolkien, *Lord of the Rings: The Fellowship of the Ring*

CHAPTER THIRTY

"I don't get it."

Tessa and I were sitting up on a mattress, our backs against the wall, keeping watch. We'd all agreed to try to get some rest, and then gather up as much as we could carry before we left the shelter. I'd volunteered for the first shift, and Tessa said she couldn't sleep either, so she stayed up with me. Dan and Sue were snoring softly, both of them worn out from the events of the day before.

The plan was to leave through the tunnel to Sue's grandfather's house, the hope being that he would have more supplies there as well, including weapons and his black Jeep Cherokee with a tankful of gas still sitting in the garage. Sue mumbled something about the house being built like a fortress and the garage being screened from the EMP set off by the bombs, so the Jeep would probably run. We would have to siphon gas from other cars along the way, but this could be done. It was the access to food, clean water and shelter that concerned me the most. We'd bring as much as we could with us, but eventually we would have to rely on finding clean basements or other intact structures that had a fresh supply.

In the back of my mind I knew that this was, for all intents and purposes, a suicide mission. Even if we somehow found enough food and shelter to survive, even if the fallout wasn't radioactive enough to kill us, there would be dangers we could not even comprehend right now. But we couldn't just sit here waiting for the end either.

Of course, I had other plans that I hadn't shared with the others yet. A detour along the way. But now that other little thing that had been nudging at my mind since the earlier attack just wouldn't go away. Something didn't make sense, but I'd be damned if I could figure it out.

"What don't you get?" Tessa asked. She was sitting up straight, alert and well rested, looking for all the world like she were relaxing with a group of friends at the local watering hole, rather than stuck in a bomb shelter at the end of the world. She never changed, my Tessa, no matter what happened. She was the only constant thing in my life, and right now I was so thankful I had her with me.

"Why those things haven't come for us by now. Why they used Jay that way, instead of just slipping in through the vents or finding cracks in the floors or something."

"Maybe they need to move between hosts."

"But *why*?" I shook my head. "We've seen the damn things survive outside a body, we've seen those mosquitoes attack us. What's holding them back now?"

Tessa didn't answer, but I wasn't expecting her to anyway. The reason was there, in the back of my head, floating debris from some old high school science textbook or website article that I'd filed away long ago. I just couldn't bring it to the surface.

The cold.

It snapped into focus, all at once, like I'd flipped a light switch. I remembered wasps gathering on our windowsills in late fall, unable to fly, barely able to move. Insects were cold-blooded. What was the proper word? *Ectothermic.* I retained very little about them from my high school biology lectures, other than that. When Jay left and the mosquitoes had gotten inside, it had been daytime, and probably warmer outside; but even then, the particles in the atmosphere had almost certainly dropped the surface temperature enough to make them sluggish, which was probably why they had nested and hadn't come after us immediately. And when I'd gone out to close the hatch, it had been night, and even colder, and there had been no sign of them at all.

I thought of the fire extinguisher I'd used on the rats and the mosquitoes, how they slowed down, avoided the spray. That kind of model worked through carbon dioxide, which was like spraying dry ice. It was cold, cold enough to cause frostbite if you weren't careful.

"You've got something, don't you?" Tessa said.

I nodded. "Maybe."

I explained my theory, and the more I spoke, the more her eyes lit up. "That's it," she said. "That's our way out. We're going north, and it'll get colder the farther we go. Oh, Pete, you're brilliant!" And she hugged me close, the warmth of her body warming my own until I almost believed her. I didn't have the heart to mention that it would be colder up there for us too. Maybe cold enough to kill us.

And then I remembered something else; that clicking sound like a latch popping open, and a slit of darkness. In the craziness of what had ensued, it had completely slipped my mind. "Hold on a minute," I said. I stood up and went to the closet, using the nearby bunk to boost myself up.

It was still there, at the back of the highest shelf, a crack in the panel. I pulled the shelf off its brackets for better access, got my fingers around the panel and pulled. It swung forward on silent hinges, revealing a secret compartment.

I remembered Jay's voice, just before he broke out: *it's in here, somewhere, the answers to everything.*

My scalp tingled as I reached in and pulled out several thick black binders. I carried them back down to the mattress next to Tessa, glancing at Sue, who was still sleeping with her back to us. Something told me this was going to involve her, and that it wouldn't be easy to read. I wanted to make sure I handled it correctly, if I could.

"What is it?" Tessa said. I plopped down next to her and showed her the binders. They were made of some kind of pebbled material, the metal three-ring kind with the extra-large hoops that snapped together. And they were old, the covers flaking at the edges.

I flipped open the first one. Inside were hundreds of laminated newspaper clippings, some of them in foreign languages. The first dated back to the 1940s. The ones I could read were accounts of the Nuremberg trials, attempts to track war criminals across South America and the Middle East, and the fall of Adolf Hitler. There were stories about networks called ODESSA that had helped Nazis through secret escape routes called ratlines, and more about a U.S. effort called Operation Paperclip that provided Nazi scientists refuge in exchange for their expertise in rocket engines, medicine and engineering. Others were investigations into rumors of vast stolen treasures being smuggled out of Germany near the end of the war and hidden in the Austrian mountains, buried in abandoned salt mines and tossed into deep glacial lakes.

As I flipped through more of them, I saw accounts of Nazis still at large. Others were feature articles on various fascist movements in the U.S. and foreign countries in the 1960s and '70s, new generations trying to bring Nazi ideals back to prominence; the FPO and NDP, extreme right-wing demonstrations on college campuses. There were dozens of them. Belgium, Croatia, France, Germany and

Russia all had active movements, many continuing to the present day.

The final article was a recent, very long feature in the *Times* by an investigative journalist who had attempted to track the dizzying web of rumor and innuendo to form a cohesive whole, and had written a book about it; the writer claimed, with some authority and citing extensive research, that as Nazi Germany collapsed near the end of World War II, Hitler and his advisors had devised a plan to scatter Nazi leadership and go underground, hiding a fortune in gold and other treasures, and creating pockets of Nazi survivors across the globe. This effort was led by a group called Die Spinne. Their goal, the writer argued, was to build a vast web, creating wealth and influence and eventually mass panic and destruction through the financing of various terrorist organizations, which would result in the rise of a new golden age of Aryan power. They called it the Fourth Reich. The writer even claimed to have discovered evidence that this movement had financed the World Trade Center attacks, and was planning a much larger one that would kill millions.

The strings behind al-Qaeda. The tingling in my scalp deepened. I put the binder aside and picked up the next one. There were a series of maps inside, with lines drawn in complex patterns, and red dots marking locations in South America, Austria, Russia and the Middle East, followed by a large number of documents and reports in German. I saw what appeared to be scientific articles and diagrams, charts and timelines. I saw bank statements with staggering sums of money listed. There were expense reports and withdrawals and payments to hundreds of what I assumed were legitimate businesses, some of which I recognized.

I turned to the third binder. This one was far more

personal. It contained handwritten letters and other correspondence, a number of grainy photos, a few more newspaper articles, and diary entries, as well as genealogy reports.

I scanned the lines of the last part several times, trying to get my head around what it meant. According to this, Sue's great-grandfather, a man named Joseph Grase, had been a high officer of Hitler's elite guard. He had never been caught.

"What are you doing?"

I looked up to find Sue staring at me. I slammed the binder closed, my face reddening. I felt like someone who'd been caught looking at a pornographic magazine, and even as I felt this, I was bewildered. Why should I feel ashamed? I'd done nothing wrong. And yet the way she kept staring at me, and the look on her face, made me want to brush it off and pretend it was nothing.

"I . . . found these," I said. "Hidden in the closet. I think they belonged to your grandfather."

Her reaction was nothing like what I'd expected. She didn't scream at me, berate me for snooping around her business or even ask questions. She simply rolled away from me, onto her back, and stared at the ceiling.

We all stayed like that for what seemed like a very long time, Dan's slow, even snores somehow rhythmic and soothing in the silence. I had a million questions myself, but I kept my mouth shut. Tessa too, thank God. Whatever Sue needed to say, she would have to find her own voice for it.

"He was supposed to meet us here," Sue whispered finally. "He and my mom. Something must have happened to them before they could get to the tunnel. Maybe it came more quickly than he'd expected."

"You knew," I said. Sudden anger flushed through me,

surprising me with its heat and intensity. "All this time, you *knew* what we were facing? What was going to happen?"

"No, not everything. It's not what you think." Abruptly Sue sat up, the blanket falling away from her shoulders. She seemed oblivious to her near nakedness, wiping a hand across her nose and sniffling. "I didn't *know*. He, he told me I had to get to the shelter that night. He *saved* us. But he's not part of this." She shook her head vigorously, and I wondered how much of it was trying to convince herself. "My grandfather was never a part of it. His father, yes. But not Grandpa."

My God. I sat there stunned, trying to comprehend what she was saying. *His father.* Not *my great-grandfather.* Distancing herself.

"You don't understand," she said. "You think you do, but you don't."

I thought of the looks I'd seen passing between her and Jay, the increasing levels of paranoia he'd shown, his obsession near the end with searching through the shelter for something he wouldn't talk about with us.

Tell them, Sue . . . they deserve to know the truth.

I felt dizzy with what this meant, almost drunk with it. "Jay was right," I said. "About all of it. The conspiracies, who was behind the attacks and why, the engineered insects. He tried to tell us, but we wouldn't listen."

She nodded, still sniffling. "You know how he was with that stuff, always digging into everything, always wanting to believe the worst. But his logical side kept him honest, you know? He was just too smart, too driven. Once we started dating, once we slept together, things changed, he looked up my family history online, you see, for fun. It didn't take him long before . . ." Her voice trailed off, and she glanced at me, then quickly away. I realized with a shock that she was embarrassed. Of course she would be; what person in her right mind would ever want to admit she was a direct descendant of a Nazi war criminal? But this went far deeper than that. By association, if nothing else, she was part of some gigantic twisted web that had done nothing less than destroy the world.

"He linked our name to Joseph Grase, and then he found him in a report on the trials," she said. "He started reading more articles, piecing things together. He started believing it all. I didn't know any of it at first, nothing. But my grandpa did. He hated his father, and I never knew why until Jay started asking questions. Where did our money really come from? Why was my grandfather so secretive? Why didn't any of us know about this link to Die Spinne?" She shook her head, crying again, fighting against it. "He wouldn't stop, and at first I thought he was crazy. It all seemed so ridiculous. I made him swear not to talk about it. I made him swear it. He loved me. He would have done anything for me."

"So he kept your secret, and he died for it." As soon as the words were out of my mouth, I regretted them. It was a terrible, hurtful thing to say. After all, was it really Sue's fault? The authorities certainly wouldn't have listened to a couple of crazy teenagers, even if they'd tried to tell. Did it really matter now, knowing who was responsible for what happened, and why? The bombs had dropped, there was a plague upon the earth, and we were all in danger. Those were the relevant points here, not whether Sue's family had a connection to the people who caused it all to happen.

Dan's voice came back to me: *Sue's grandpa could have helped drop the bombs. I don't see how, but why not? Hell, he could have been the devil himself. What difference does that make for us?*

Sue stopped sniffling. When she spoke again, her voice

was cold, and she stared at the wall, refusing to look at me. "My grandfather spent his life gathering evidence of what was happening. He wanted to stop it, but he was in terrible danger if he ever spoke up. We all were. Die Spinne has connections to everything, every government, every huge corporation, even the military."

"Sue," I said. "I'm sorry. I didn't mean—"

"I know," she said. "It's okay."

But it wasn't, and I knew it. She should have told us, but I understood why she didn't. I understood the power of secrets. I glanced at Tessa, and she just shook her head and looked away. The sick feeling in my stomach deepened into a bitter ache.

We all sat without speaking for several minutes. Dan's snores had quieted, and he lay still, his back to us. I didn't know if he was awake and had heard any of this. But that didn't really matter either.

"We can't stay here forever," I said. "We need to leave the shelter and try to find help. The Doomsday Vault is still our best shot. Do you know anything that will make a difference for us now? Why we're being attacked this way, what their end game is, whether the vault even exists?"

Sue shrugged. She still wouldn't look my way. "Jay figured they wanted to start the world over again. Create a new Aryan race, or something, the way Hitler never could. They've built a special bunker in the Austrian mountains to ride out the storm. The nuclear attack was meant to disrupt any government response, to keep them from being able to function while the second wave took care of what was left. Jay figured they'd engineered the plague carriers to have a short life span and be unable to reproduce after a certain point. Then they'd begin to rebuild."

"This bunker in the mountains, it's like the Doomsday Vault?"

She nodded. "Even bigger. Miles and miles of it, carved out of a natural cavern system and old mines and turned into an underground city. It was meant to hold the only survivors. But there were others like Jay who saw this coming, some with a lot more money, and they built shelters like this one and like the vault in Alaska to keep themselves safe if the worst happened."

I opened the third binder again, and stared down into grainy faces, men standing close together, smiling out at the camera in full uniform, people laughing together, looking the same as any other group getting a few photos taken on a sunny day. They had to be insane to drop the bombs. What kind of world was left to rebuild? And yet they'd done it, murdered billions of people in search of some twisted truth.

I strained to see the monsters underneath, but I could not. I thought of my own father, how so many in our community had ignored the warning signs and welcomed him into their own lives in some small way, helped pump his gas and cleaned his furnace and delivered his mail and let him handle their money at the bank where he'd worked for twenty years, while deeper among the shadows and away from prying eyes he was hitting my mother until she bled.

My father, as close to a monster as anyone I'd ever known. Evil so often had a human face.

I closed the binder again. I struggled to grab and hold on to something hopeful, something real. If Jay were right, the plague would not last forever; there was some kind of biological kill switch built in, and, of course, that made sense, if you could make sense of anything at all in this. We just had to find a safe place to ride it out, and a place that could protect us when those responsible for the attacks came looking for any remaining survivors. Because if all that Sue had told us were true, this was only the beginning. I remembered the emergency beacon Sue had told us about when we were first trapped down in the shelter. It would lead them right to us.

The Doomsday Vault was our best chance; we just had to find a way to reach it.

We had to move now, before it was too late.

CHAPTER THIRTY-ONE

It was still the middle of the night, and if I were right about the cold affecting the insects' ability to function, we had to move quickly. We would gather our supplies, maps, the radio, first-aid kit, as much food and water as we could carry. We would travel at night, when the insects were dormant, and find places to hole up during the day. We would find a way to make it all the way to Alaska, come hell or high water.

But first we had to take care of Dan's shoulder. He wouldn't admit it when I woke him up, but it had gotten much worse as he slept, stiffening up and demanding attention. He grimaced in pain as he rolled over and sat up, clutching at himself. Tessa found the medical kit and I made him swallow three ibuprofen. We should have had him take them earlier, but I hadn't been thinking clearly. I couldn't afford to make mistakes, not anymore. I had to do a better job.

We all washed up in the bathroom, not knowing how long it would be before we found fresh water again, and then set about making packs out of the bedsheets. We bound up the corners so that we could carry our supplies to the house and tied them together in twos with more strips of sheet so we could loop them around our necks, and we piled everything we thought we might need into them from the bathroom and closet. We found the Geiger counter, a small yellow box with a handle and a black tube on a coiled cord, and set that aside to carry with us too. We could use it to test the air as we went along.

Sue worked alongside us without speaking. She had put on an oversize white men's T-shirt from the closet and the same pair of jeans she'd come here with, washed in the bathroom sink the week before. She'd taken off her bra, which was dirty and becoming ragged with constant wear, and her heavy breasts hung loose inside the shirt. I could see the wound from the mosquitoes on her neck, and it looked puffy and red.

She looked like someone who was beginning to fray around the edges. Come to think of it, we all did. All of us except Tessa, of course, who still looked just as cool and put together as she had when we first arrived.

There were enough hazmat suits in the closet to go around, and Sue helped Dan into a new one before using a torn sheet to bind his arm as tightly as she could to his side. Finally we were all zipped up and ready. The only thing left was to open the bedroom door and see what might be waiting for us in the rest of the shelter.

I went first with the gun, keeping the suit's hood off and the mask hanging around my neck so I could see more clearly. The dining room was empty except for the pile of bones, and the steps to the ladder held nothing but that gray ash that had drifted in from outside.

I tried not to focus on those bones, how picked clean they were, how perfectly white, as if they had been sitting out in the sun and rain and wind for months. I saw a row of teeth scattered like little polished pebbles across the floor, and I thought of Jay's lopsided grin as his jaw was exposed to me, looking for all the world like a happy smile, before I turned away.

I walked through the kitchen, checking the pantry, inside the cabinets, even the fridge and oven. Everything was clean and neat and orderly. It was almost, I thought, like the events of the past few hours had never happened.

Except for Jay's remains.

I went back into the kitchen and found a plastic trash bag, and scooped up the bones as quickly as possible, hating the slippery dry smoothness in my gloved hands. We should have been having some kind of ceremony for him, something to mark the moment, instead of stuffing what was left of him into a plastic bag. It seemed so terribly wrong. But what choice did we have?

I tied the top of the bag and stuck it in the back of one of the kitchen cabinets, as far away from anything else as I could. It would have to do. Then I went and got the others.

I put Sue in charge of the shelves in the dining room. We packed the rest of our supplies as quickly as we could, throwing ready-to-eat meals, energy bars, powdered milk and water into the makeshift packs, enough to last us several days. We took the radio, maps, flashlights and as many batteries as we could carry.

Even with our makeshift packs weighed down to the breaking point, I felt like it wasn't enough, that we could never have enough. My thoughts were racing, wondering if we were insane to leave the relative safety of the shelter. At least here we had plenty of food and water and fuel. But from what Sue had told us, help would never come. Nobody was looking for us, at least not now, and when someone did come, it was likely to be people we didn't want to see. We had to take our fates into our own hands.

Time went by too quickly, and it wasn't long before we were all standing in the dining room, packs ready. It was just past two A.M.

Looking around, I felt a strange sense of nostalgia for the place where we had spent so many hours together. I stared at the slashes marching down the wall in sets of seven, Dan's calendar marking off our days in hell. There were a lot of lines. It seemed hard to believe we'd been here that long. I thought I probably should come up with some kind of speech, a rousing call to battle the way leaders did in the movies. *Braveheart* for a new generation, inspiring everyone to stay strong and focused and purposeful.

"Let's go then," I said. It was all I could do, and it would have to be enough.

We all looped our strips of cloth over our necks and hoisted our packs. Dan grabbed the mop handle again as a weapon, Tessa and Sue took large carving knives. Sue also held the Geiger counter, which was ticking steadily. I already had the gun. I led the way back to the kitchen.

The steel door gave a slight hiss when I turned the handle, then swung open without a sound. A puff of dry, foul-smelling air wafted in from the tunnel; rotten meat that had gone far beyond the spoiling point and was now a separate entity entirely. I put my hand up to cover my nose and breathed through my mouth, which wasn't much better, but I didn't want to put on my hood yet.

It was cold and black as pitch inside.

I hadn't expected this, and already I was fumbling to keep up. I started digging through my packs for a flashlight as my hands trembled more violently with the seconds ticking by. The rats must have chewed through the wires for the lights, or else there was some other source of power from the house that had since gone out. Another example of my inability to anticipate, to prepare.

We're making mistakes. We should shut off the generator in the shelter before we go. We should make sure everything is

locked down, just in case we have to return. We should leave
a note in case someone comes here, letting them know where
we're headed . . .

I felt woefully unprepared for this leadership role that
had been thrust upon me, one that seemed far more difficult than I'd thought it would be. My mind continued to
babble until I found the flashlight and switched it on. I
held it up, sweeping side to side with the gun as my heart
hammered inside my chest.

The beam washed over the empty tunnel, across the
ruined carcasses of the rats we'd crushed, illuminating the
broken ceiling and blood-spattered walls.

Sue's grandfather's body was gone.

I didn't want to think about what this meant. She must
have noticed it at the same time I did, because I heard an
abrupt intake of breath. I didn't take my eyes from that
tunnel, worried about the way the darkness swallowed up
the flashlight beam and made the walls seem to fade away,
so that it looked like a walkway on the edge of an abyss.
Maybe that was exactly what it was; the entrance to hell.

I took a trembling step out into the hall, avoiding the
rats' remains. I wondered why the insects hadn't eaten
these away like they had Jay's body, and if there could possibly be any method to what they'd done to Jay. A warning, a show of strength, an attempt to weaken our resolve?
This is what we can do, once we get inside?

But that was too terrible to contemplate, the idea of
intent in their actions. I felt like the gazelle in one of those
nature videos, head up, sniffing the wind, while a few feet
away a lion crouched, waiting to pounce.

I waited for another long beat, listening and watching,
sweeping the beam from the hallway to the hole in the
ceiling. Nothing moved except the dust I'd stirred up in

my passage. It was cold enough to see my breath. I waved a hand, and we all shuffled out into the tunnel, but before I'd gone more than a few feet I heard the sound of the door closing on us.

I whirled around, pinning Sue in the beam of the flashlight. She blinked, held up the hand with the knife in it to her eyes, and I let the light play over the steel door and the keypad set into the wall on the right.

Locked out.

"You let the door shut," I said.

"I . . . I thought it would be good to keep things from getting inside," she said.

"Do you know the combination?"

She shook her head. "I'm not sure," she said. "If it's the same as the hatch, yes."

"Try it."

She turned to the keypad and I let the light shine on her fingers as she punched some numbers and hit ENTER. The light remained red.

I let that sink in for a moment. Let them all understand it. We couldn't go back now, even if we tried.

We were trapped inside a blackness so deep it was almost a physical presence.

I could feel the others' anxiety ratcheting up. "It's okay," I said, as calmly as I could, while inside I felt the panic rising in me too. "This doesn't change a thing. We're going forward, not backward."

Tessa touched my arm with her free hand and squeezed, a familiar, comforting pressure. I could feel her heat even through the glove and the suit's slippery fabric.

The Geiger counter ticked softly, steadily in Sue's hands. At least the radiation levels were remaining low. We could leave our masks and hoods off, for now.

It wasn't much, but I would take what I could get.

Sue pulled a lantern from one of her sacks and switched it on, bathing the tunnel in a cool, blue-tinged light. She and Dan brought up the rear as we began to move again, a small, glowing beacon swallowed up by the arrow-straight blackness ahead.

The tunnel seemed to go on forever, even though it was probably only a couple hundred feet long. As we continued, the smell got stronger, an acrid, biting stench that seemed to seep into everything, invading my nose, settling in my hair and coating my skin. I breathed shallowly and through my mouth.

Eventually the slope of the tunnel began to rise, and the beam of the light picked out the bottom of a set of concrete steps leading up. The door at the top was open about a foot.

I'd seen the Myers house from the outside many times, of course, and it was a giant concrete-and-steel fortress. But I'd never been inside before, and I had no idea what to expect. I assumed the door would lead to some kind of garage or storage room, and beyond that would be the entrance to the rest of the house.

"We'll go up one at a time," I said. "I'll clear the other room first. Dan, you watch the tunnel and make sure nothing got behind us."

He nodded, and I started up the steps, gun out, flashlight aimed at the crack in the door.

I paused at the top, glanced down at the group huddled below me, then pushed open the door, blood thumping in my ears. The flashlight beam revealed a large, windowless mudroom, wire shelving against the walls, jackets hung on hooks, shoes and boots lined up neatly under a white wooden bench. I stepped quickly inside and swept the entire room. It was empty, one door directly across from me, another to my right, both of them closed tight.

I let out the air I'd been holding in a long, slow hiss, and set my sacks down on the floor. The smell was overpowering up here, but I began to wonder if it might be spoiled food from the kitchen. I saw none of that ash anywhere, no evidence of a struggle or other damage. It was possible the house was intact, which seemed to be more than we could have hoped for; I'd wondered if we would find anything left standing at all, even with Sue's assurances that her grandfather had built the house to withstand the full force of a hurricane.

I went back to the top of the steps leading to the tunnel. "This room's clear," I said, and a moment later Tessa appeared, followed by Sue and then Dan, who closed the door with a soft click. Once shut, it was cleverly disguised with paneling and flush with the rest of the wall. I never would have noticed it if I hadn't known it was there.

They put their sacks down and all of us stood in the center of the room, the lantern's light allowing us to see everything clearly. It was an entirely mundane mudroom, some garden tools hanging from a rack on one wall, more shelves and covered cabinets full of paper towels, leaf bags, some canned goods and other supplies.

The Geiger counter's ticking went up a notch, then settled again.

"That's the garage," Sue said, pointing to the door on the right. "The other one leads into the kitchen."

"Check for the car first," Dan said. He was standing a bit straighter than before and looked a little less pale. Maybe the ibuprofen was working. "That's our way out of here."

I nodded, kept the gun up with the flashlight as Sue opened the door, and then I stepped through. The garage had more than enough room for three cars, but there was only one inside now. The black Cherokee sat in the middle bay, dark and silent. It looked clean and in top shape. I smelled oil and tire rubber on top of the deeper stench that still lingered.

There were no windows in the garage either. I let the light play around and saw nothing out of the ordinary: more tools, a snowblower and riding mower, lawn chemicals, a bicycle. All three doors were closed. They didn't appear to be cracked or damaged in any way.

A perfectly normal garage in a perfectly normal house, everything neat and in its place, like a million homes in a thousand different cities and towns. *While outside, Rome burns.*

"The keys," I said, turning back to Sue. "Where are they?"

"He'd have them on him," she said. "Or they'd be on his dresser upstairs."

I didn't mention the obvious; where was Grandpa Myers now? I'm sure we were all thinking the same thing. "Okay," I said. "Am I right in assuming your grandfather would have a backup generator for this place, just like the shelter?"

She nodded. "It's all hardwired."

"The switch will probably be around here someplace," I said. "What about his guns?"

"In the study, in a locked cabinet."

"Good. I say we get some lights going, get fully armed, then sweep the house, room by room. Gather what we can and bring it to the Jeep. Let's be ready to move—"

We all heard it at the same time; a muffled thud and crash, like dishes falling to the floor, coming from somewhere beyond the mudroom. I put my finger to my lips as Sue switched off the lantern and I pointed the flashlight down, to keep its beam from being seen under the door.

My heart was pounding again. The darkness closed in on us as I made my way across the mudroom to the door that led to the rest of the house.

CHAPTER THIRTY-TWO

I swung the door open onto a vast, echoing space, sweeping the light over a family room with vaulted ceilings, hardwood floors and a line of square, blank windows looking out into the night. The windows all appeared to be intact, thank God—made of safety glass, maybe. The family room was open to a large kitchen on our right, a six-foot-long granite-topped island with five bar stools separating the two spaces.

A woman was standing behind the kitchen island.

She held what looked like a piece of shattered china, obviously shocked to see us, her jaw hanging open. I pinned her with the light, brought the gun up and centered it on her chest. The trigger was halfway down before I took a breath, blood thundering in my ears. I had become capable of shooting someone in the blink of an eye. As hard as it would have been to believe just a few short weeks ago, now it hardly surprised me at all.

"Don't move," I said. I swallowed, my throat clicking in the silence. I suddenly felt so dry I could barely speak.

The woman put the piece of dinner plate down on the counter, then raised her hands in the air, squinting at me. "This your house?" she said. "Sorry about the dishes. I just needed something to eat. Come a long way and I'm hungry."

"How'd you get in here?"

"Front door." She motioned vaguely over her shoulder. "Mind if I put my hands down now?"

I shook my head. "Not yet," I said.

"Okay, fine, fine. How about lowering that light a bit? It's in my eyes, and I've been operating in the dark long enough for it to hurt."

"That's the point." But I dropped the flashlight beam away from her face a bit, and she sighed. She wore a knitted gray cap and several layers of grimy clothing, a type of army jacket over long gray pants that looked a size or two too large. She was probably in her fifties, just leaving middle age, not old enough to be frail. She had a kind face, lightly freckled, crow's-feet around the eyes, and her dark blonde hair was cut short under her cap and starting to gray at the temples.

She looked enough like my mother to make my stomach churn. For just a moment there, I'd thought . . .

I heard a shuffling and a click as Sue switched the lantern back on behind me, and the room was bathed in a soft, cool light. I lowered the flashlight beam to the ground, but kept the gun up and pointed at her.

"Karin Claus," she said. "But most people call me Grease Pot." She tried to smile, but when I didn't react, the smile died away. Her gaze went from my face to the others behind me, and back again. "What's with the suits? You guys going on a moonwalk or something?"

Nobody answered her, and we all stood in awkward silence for a minute. I had no idea what to do next. The woman was jumpy, clearly on edge, her hands trembling, fidgeting on her feet, but that could have been from being caught in a stranger's house with a gun in her face more than anything else. Still, I didn't like the situation at all. I should have been feeling euphoria over finding another person alive after all this time, but instead I felt danger thrumming around my head.

"I'm going to put my hands down now," the woman said. "Can't keep 'em up there forever. Car accident a few years back gives me bad pains, and with the walking I've been doing I feel like someone shoved a hot iron up my shorts." She smiled again, lowering her arms very slowly until they rested on the counter. "Bikram Yoga helps, just so you know." She squinted at me again. "Why, you're just kids. Where are your parents?"

"Gone," I said. "Is the house safe?"

"I . . . I don't know," she said. "Why, don't you live here? I just got here an hour ago myself. Nice place."

"We were holed up downstairs," I said. "You haven't looked around?"

"Not much, just poked through the first floor a bit. Too hungry to care. I made it this far, I figure I'm damn lucky. If something's going to kill me, it'll come whether I like it or not."

"Must be more than luck, Karin."

She nodded. "Told you, it's Grease Pot to my friends. I'm a trail rat, that's where I got my nickname. Been hiking ever since I was young, I know how to survive out there. Through-hiked the Pacific Trail ten years back. I can live on bark, not that there's any left, but you know what I mean. Right now you move at night, when things are quiet, hole up during the day."

I felt Tessa's hand on my back. "I think she's okay," she whispered against my ear. "You can put the gun down."

I lowered the barrel slowly and held the gun at my side. I trusted Tessa's instincts, but I was still not entirely convinced.

The others came forward to stand next to me. "Where'd you come from?" Sue asked. She'd turned off the Geiger counter and set it down near the door, and now she held nothing but the lantern and the kitchen knife she'd taken from the shelter.

"South." Karin shrugged. "Lived in Colorado for years, came east a few months back to hike the Appalachian. First time I ever hiked alone. My husband Andrew, he thought he was too old to make it, his knees were bad, so I flew to Georgia myself. Got all the way to Maine before . . . well, you know." She glanced toward the family room and the windows that looked out over the water. "I was in my tent when the bombs hit. I could hear it, see the sky change. I didn't know what had happened for sure though, not until I got down from the trail and saw . . ."

"Saw what?" I said.

She looked from face to face, as if searching for something. Her mouth moved in a chewing motion and then stopped. "Everyone was dead."

Everyone was dead. I nodded, feeling ridiculous acknowledging such a thing, like it were a commonly understood fact. As if, just by nodding, I'd made it true. And yet, we'd expected that, hadn't we? It shouldn't have felt like such a shock.

"You didn't see anyone alive at all," Sue said, her voice flat and quiet.

"Oh, here and there," Karin said. "I mean, one or two since I've been on the move, but they were either crazy, or . . . real sick." She scratched the back of her neck. "When the ash started to fall I found an abandoned cellar and holed up for a bit. There was some bottled water there and cans of food, enough to keep me alive. When it ran out I started hiking the roads. Nobody much left. Saw one man outside of Camden, he lasted a whole day before he went. That was the longest."

"But you're okay," Dan said. He'd been quiet until now, and I could tell by the tone of his voice he didn't quite buy Karin Claus's story. "Why is that?"

"Lucky, I guess, like I said. I come from hardy stock." She smiled again quickly, flashing slightly yellowed teeth. Nervous energy was coming off her in waves. "Grew up in the woods of Minnesota, my folks lived off the land, they taught me to be tough. Spare the rod, spoil the child, you know? I learned how to survive."

"You see anything else unusual?" I said. "Anything not quite . . . human?"

Karin stared at me. "You mean the bugs," she said. "Sure I did. They're smart little bastards. Bugs never liked me much though. I was always the one who never got bit on the trail, while others were eaten alive. Sour blood, I guess."

"Is that right," Dan said. "Why don't you take off your clothes."

Karin took a step back. "What'd you say?"

"Take your clothes off," Dan said again. "I want to see your skin."

"Dan," Sue said. "I don't think that's necessary, is it? She's harmless."

"We need to be sure."

"Not gonna do that," Karin said, her gaze jumping back and forth between us. I saw her face change as she began to digest what Dan had said, the indignity in it. Shock turning to outrage; or was it something else? She'd started twisting her hands together, picking at herself. "Not fair to ask me that. What kind of kids are you, anyway? Take advantage of an old woman just looking to get by."

I glanced at Dan. Sue had her hand on his good arm, but he wasn't looking at her. He didn't take his eyes off Karin Claus.

His hand crept to his throat and scratched. I noticed a small red spot on the side of his neck, just above the hazmat suit's collar, and a chill ran down the length of my body.

"I survived a lot more than you," Karin was saying, her voice rising. "I'll survive long after you're gone. I've seen more than you can imagine, done things I didn't want to do, but I did them. But I won't do this. How dare you ask me?"

"I think my friend just wants to make sure you're not infected," I said. I wanted to calm her down, calm everyone down. "You understand? Just trying to be safe." I kept the gun down, but my finger remained on the trigger. I didn't like the way this was going at all, the way Dan looked, the feeling in the room of mounting tension, events getting away from us. For all we'd been through, and for all we'd changed, we were still just teenagers, and confronting an adult like this felt like blasphemy. What would we do, now that she'd refused? Force her to strip at gunpoint?

Dan took a single step forward. He held the mop handle out like a weapon. "I can hear you," he said. "Inside my head."

Oh, shit. I raised the gun, not exactly sure what to do with it. "What do you mean," I said. My voice shook and I was powerless to stop it.

Dan glanced at me. "They're inside her. I can hear the voices." He took another step, and Karin Claus shrank back away from him, her long shadow cast by the lantern on the move, her entire body beginning to tremble.

"Not fair," she said again. "I didn't ask for this, don't want it."

For a moment Dan's body blocked my line of sight, and I caught a flash of something off to the side. I turned to the family room, sweeping the flashlight beam across hulking, oversize furniture, a buttoned leather couch and loveseat and two chairs, end tables and lamps and a dark rug. Whatever I thought I'd seen was gone; maybe more shadows dancing in the soft light.

When I turned back Dan had taken another step and Karin was standing rigid behind the counter, her body vibrating like a tuning fork struck against a hard surface.

Only a few feet separated them now. She opened her mouth very wide, gagged like a choking bird trying to force a bone out of its gullet.

"Sorry," she croaked. "Sorry. It . . . made me. I didn't want to . . ."

A tear trickled down her cheek before her eyes went dead.

Moments later, they came for us.

CHAPTER THIRTY-THREE

The sound was next, that earsplitting screech torn from her throat like a piece of machinery coming apart. I remembered the same noise Jay had made in the shelter's kitchen. I remembered the way he grew frantic just before the end, and the sound of his hand slapping Sue's face, and with that came the memory of his smell, a rank body odor that was more inhuman than it rightly should have been. I smelled it again, only worse.

This time, the sound Karin made was answered by three more.

It seemed to surround us, echoing from all sides. At first I thought it came from my friends, but that wasn't right. It snaked its way into my skull, whispering things I could not understand. It was a horrible sound, alien and wrong, and yet I was drawn to it in a way I could not explain. I sensed myself drifting through a self-induced fog, the world tilting under my feet.

I hear the voices too . . . Sometimes they soothe me. Sometimes they try to give me advice. And sometimes they don't make any sense at all.

Sue's scream snapped me out of my trance. Dan swung the wooden handle at Karin Claus's head as the black cloud began to swirl from her mouth, and I heard the crack of the wood hitting bone and a spray of blood splattering the wooden cabinets, and then I sensed movement again to my left.

I whirled as a woman with a swollen, bloodied face came at me with her arms up, fingers hooked into claws.

"Momma!" Sue shouted, lunging past me, the jiggling of the lantern in her hands turning everything into a strobe-lit freak show.

I raised the gun and pulled the trigger, the bullet hitting the woman in the chest and driving her over the back of the couch.

"What did you do!" Sue put the lantern on the floor and turned to me, chest heaving and frantic, spittle on her lips. *"What did you just do?"*

"She was coming after us," I said. "They set us up—it was an ambush, she—she was infected."

"No." Sue shook her head, staring at me, a mixture of horror, rage and anguish in her eyes. "Oh my God. No." She moaned deep in her throat, raised her fist as if to attack me herself, as behind her I watched her mother stand up, climbing back over the couch, blood still pumping in a thick spray from the front of her shirt where her heart would be.

Her mother's face betrayed nothing, no emotion, no pain or fear. A machine that had been programmed to kill.

I remembered my own mother taking me out to the backyard when my father had gone from the house, tacking up a hand-drawn paper sign and showing me how to load and stand with my feet firmly planted, how to exhale before squeezing the trigger gently until the pop. I never knew where she learned to shoot, had never asked, but I knew why she taught me. Knowing how to handle a gun was supposed to make me feel safer, but it had done just the opposite; it had made the possibility of needing to use it more real.

I pushed Sue roughly to the ground as her mother's mouth opened wide, spilling its black contents toward us, and I raised the gun and pulled the trigger.

The bullet caught the top of her skull and took a part of it off, exposing a wet gray furrow of brain, and still she kept coming. I fired again, hitting her in the stomach, aware of what I'd done to Sue, taking not just what remained of her boyfriend from her, but now her mother too, a one-man executioner.

I heard Dan grunt from somewhere but dared not look away as Sue's mother stopped less than five feet from me, shaking as if she were having a seizure. The black cloud kept pouring from her mouth, and I shouted about our masks, *put on your masks*, before clamping my own to my face with trembling fingers, yanking the straps into place over my head.

Sue was on her knees a few feet away when her mother began to shake more violently and the hives opened up across her skin like delicate, blooming flowers, the insects swarming to the surface and then quickly across her flesh, consuming her as they had with Jay. But I did not have time to watch the end, or even make sure Sue had put on her mask, because Dan was shouting frantically now to me for help.

I spun to find Karin Claus had vanished, probably reduced to bones somewhere behind the kitchen island now that she had spilled her seed, the insects that had eaten her escaping into the cracks in the walls. But Dan and Tessa had been joined by two others, and they were closing in quickly.

Tessa had put on her mask, but Dan had not. He was bleeding from his right ear. He kept swinging the handle around, trying to keep them at bay, but he was nearly useless with only one good arm.

We should have cleared the house first, I thought. *Wasted precious time talking when we should have been making sure it was safe.* I felt useless and stupid and furious with myself. There might be more of them; the house might be full of them, for all we knew, a buzzing hive of the infected, and we'd just stepped right into the middle of it.

The smell was almost unbearable now. The lantern cast huge, misshapen shadows across the walls. One of the new arrivals was Sue's dead grandfather. I could tell by the clothes he wore, but that was the only way I knew; the rest of him was unrecognizable. He moved more slowly than the others, a broken-down machine still driven to perform its function until the very end. His shirt and pants were darkly stained and wet with fluids. The damage to his face had become much worse as the rot had set in. His head was little more than a grinning skull, and what remained of his flesh was covered in a mosslike, fuzzy growth.

As he turned to me, I shot him twice in the chest, and he went down easily, the insects already starting to boil out of him.

The second figure was Jimmie. He was covered in sores, but from the look of him, he was still alive, at least in some form. There was nothing human about him though, not in the way he moved, or the blank stare on his face, or how his mouth was opening wider now, looking like a snake unhinging its jaw.

The longer something's dead, the harder it is for them to control.

I wanted to feel some kind of satisfaction in figuring that out, but I did not. I listened to the hiss and pop of the valve in my mask and tried to settle myself. It didn't matter. None of it mattered. I had just shot and killed my friend's mother, faced the walking, infected corpse of her grandfather, and already I was moving on, rejoining the fight, feeling nothing but a numbness that had seemed to spread from my scalp down the length of my body, turning me to stone.

What had I become? Some sort of monster? My best friend, here in front of me, who had begged for my help, and whom I had denied, not once, but twice, and all I could do was prepare to kill him like I'd killed the others.

Like father, like son.

Murder was nothing new to me. I thought of the jokes I used to tell, how clever I thought I'd been back then, how sophisticated and mature. I thought I knew loss, thought I had looked death in the face, had survived, and was stronger for it. I had known nothing.

But there was no time for this, not now, not one spare second to question anything more. As Jimmie closed in on Dan and Tessa and the cloud appeared like a sinewy black tendril of smoke wafting from his mouth, I stepped forward and shot him in the head.

The bullet entered just below Jimmie's left ear, making a neat, round and nearly bloodless hole.

Its exit, however, was considerably messier. Blood and bits of pink flesh splattered across the counter and cabinets, splashed and pooled on the floor.

Jimmie's head snapped sideways. He moaned, stumbled and slipped, and then fell with a loose-limbed crash, his skull cracking hard on the tile.

I watched his legs tremble and twitch, making bloody snow angels. I shot him again in the spine, watching his body jerk and writhe.

"Jesus," Dan said. "Pete—"

"Shut up," I said. "Just shut the fuck up and put on your fucking mask." My guts were churning, the numbness washed away all at once. Tessa was staring at me with a look I did not recognize. Was it a new respect, or was it disgust? I couldn't bear the thought of her feeling that way about me. It was something like that red cloud that she spotted just now, the way fear could paint me into a corner and make me into a hero on the outside, while on the inside I was shaking like a little boy.

Tessa saw through that, and it had never bothered her. She could see the weakness at my core. She knew the worst of everything, and she'd remained at my side all these years. But maybe something had finally changed. Maybe her eyes had been opened, while I felt like I were drowning, my head going under, and I had nothing to cling to and save myself.

The pop-hiss of the valve in my mask had speeded up alarmingly. I broke her stare and looked down. Jimmie was shaking, his head tapping a violent staccato against the floor, his eyes squeezed shut tight and his mouth yawning open.

I could see the hives opening up under his clothes, bursts of red soaking through the cloth as the insects began to chew their way out.

Dan shouted a warning and I instinctively flinched left as something hit me hard from behind. I felt a biting pain and sudden warmth in my right arm. The weight slammed right through my kidneys and I went down, hitting the floor hard, a clattering sound near my head. As I lay there facedown and stunned, I felt a body on top of me, fists glancing off the sides of my skull, my mask wrenched free by the blows. I bucked and rolled, my ears ringing, got myself turned over and tried to grab and hold the arms that kept swinging at me.

It was Sue, sitting on my chest and shouting at me as she tried to claw and punch her way through my body. I grabbed her as hard as I could and held her to me in an effort to protect myself and keep her arms pinned at the same time.

"You killed her!" she screamed. *"I hate you I hate you I hate you—"*

Her weight was lifted up and away from me all at once, and I lay there, gasping, my eyes watering, the pain in my arm sharper, a tightness and pressure like teeth clamping down. I glanced at the tear in my suit just above the elbow, blood seeping through.

I pulled the fabric away from a long, thin slice through my skin, not deep enough to hit bone, but bleeding steadily. She had tried to stab me, and it was probably only the fact that she had lost the knife in the process that had kept her from finishing the job.

"Stop it," Dan was saying, as Sue struggled against his one good arm. He'd wrapped it around her waist, trying to hold her back, and I could see him wincing from the pain in his bad shoulder as he was jostled around. "It's not his *fault*, don't you understand that? He saved our lives."

I settled my mask back into place. I'd lost the flashlight and gun somewhere, and I sat up and looked for them, finally locating the gun against the kick plate of the counter near what was left of Jimmie's head. He lay about five feet away, his entire body barely recognizable through the swarm of black insects.

I picked up the gun, looked away quickly and climbed to my feet. "I'm sorry, Sue," I said.

She didn't seem to hear me. She was clinging to Dan's chest now, sobbing, while he held her in his good arm and stared at me over her head.

I looked at him, and I knew, and he knew it too. I

hadn't saved him at all. He was sweating, and it wasn't just from the suit. There were red spots across his neck, and I was willing to bet they were scattered across his body as well.

It was true. Dan was infected.

CHAPTER THIRTY-FOUR

"How long, do you think?"

Dan's voice held a strangely flat, emotionless quality, as if he'd already given in to the idea that he was going to die. He still wasn't wearing his mask. The blood from his torn ear had dried now, but it looked bad.

We were sitting on the floor in the downstairs den, our backs against the richly paneled wall, a beautiful handwoven Oriental rug under our feet. There were no windows in here, and it felt about as safe as we could get right now.

"I don't know," I said. "It could take a long time. Maybe even long enough for us to get you to someone who could help."

I didn't really believe this myself, and Dan just shook his head. "You can still make it," he said. "I want you to promise me that you'll do everything you can to survive. I don't want it to all end for nothing."

"Look," I said. "Stop the bullshit. We're all going, we'll get as far as we can, we'll fight. We'll—"

"I'll have to act long before that," he said. "I can't take the chance of . . . hurting someone."

I didn't push him to elaborate. I knew what he meant. I stared at the elegant surroundings, the mahogany desk and leather chair and shelves lined with leather books, gold-leaf mirror and huge, colorful painting of a ship and white-capped sea that hung over the slate fireplace, statues on display that must have cost a fortune. All of it useless now. I thought about how I'd first seen Dan as a hero, and how I'd changed my mind somewhere along the way. I wondered if maybe I'd been a little too harsh in that assessment. He was still willing to die to protect us. If it came to it, I wasn't sure that I could do the same.

It was about three thirty in the morning. I found it hard to believe less than two hours had passed since we left the shelter, but a battery-powered clock on the wall confirmed it.

After the fight in the kitchen we had retrieved our sacks quickly, and I had found some duct tape that I'd used to patch the hole in my suit. My arm had stopped bleeding, and I didn't think I would need any stitches. I didn't know if patching the hole would matter at this point. Whatever might have gotten to me in the past hour had probably had the chance to do its work. But I had to try.

We'd done a quick sweep of the first floor and found nobody else lurking around, but we didn't want to risk going upstairs. There weren't enough of us to make that safe anymore. Sue was useless; she'd gotten into the scotch in her grandfather's liquor cabinet and downed a third of the bottle before we could stop her.

So we retreated to the study where the weapons cabinet and liquor were kept, and barricaded the door. We needed a little time to think and regroup, and this might be the last chance we got.

"I'm going to my house first," I said.

My little surprise detour. I'd expected resistance, arguments, even shouting. But Dan just shrugged. "I figured you might," he said. "It's crazy, but it's what I would do." He glanced at me and then away. "You do know she's dead?"

I didn't answer him. Of course I knew he was probably right, had to be. My mother was alone and damn near helpless, and it had been weeks since the strike. But I had to be sure.

"It's a dangerous road," he said. "You'd be better off taking Route 1 to 95, head down towards Boston and then out 90."

"I was thinking up through Montreal. Stay north, where it's colder. Better chance of losing the bugs that way."

"Either way," he said, "going to your place in White Falls is a suicide mission. You might not even make it over the bridge. But I'm not going to stop you."

"I'll need your help."

"You got it, for as long as I can hang on."

I hesitated. "You can really hear them? In your head?"

He nodded. "It's like a thousand voices whispering, but it's not a language you can understand. It's white noise. When you get closer to one who's infected, they get louder. I think they can communicate with each other. I think that sound they make, it's like a signal to join together. It . . . itches."

Hive mind. I shivered. "Are there others nearby? Can you hear them now?"

He shook his head. "I don't know."

Tessa was with Sue in the adjoining bathroom, using the water from the toilet tank to wash her face with a cool cloth, and the door was closed. I wondered if they were okay, and decided to let them be for now.

"We shouldn't have left," I said. "I made a mistake. We should have stayed down there, where it was safe—"

"No." Dan shook his head again. "You're wrong. We had to take a chance. You can't second-guess yourself like that."

The house was too quiet. I never realized before how

much noise a house made normally, the hum of a refrigerator kicking on, the soft tick of a clock, a furnace rumbling faintly from somewhere down below. Now there was nothing. Even the lantern we'd put on the desk made no sound at all.

"You'll have to take the lead," Dan said. "Hell, maybe you should have from the start. I let you down."

"You're injured," I said. "Worse than any of us know, I think."

He waved away my comment with his good hand. "That's not it," he said. "You know, my father, he was a leader since the day he was born. He was made for it, and he figured I was too. The military was perfect for him, and I think he wanted me to follow in his footsteps. But the idea of it . . . that scared the shit out of me."

"Nobody wants to die."

"It's not the battle. I'm not scared of that. It's the idea of a whole troop of soldiers depending on me to make the right decisions. How can I lead them when I don't even believe in myself?" He glanced at me. "With you guys, it was easy. Nobody challenged me, nobody saw through me and called my bullshit."

"You *were* a leader, Dan. We always thought of you as the strong one. You were the same way on the football field."

"That was different too. That's a game, not life and death."

We sat in silence for a minute, listening to the noise of splashing water from the bathroom.

"I always liked you," Dan said. "Right from the first day we met. You were a little twitchy, you know? But there was something there, something harder than most of the other kids . . . something different. I admired it."

"You looking to get lucky or something?" I said.

Dan just sat and stared into space. "You still don't know much of anything, do you?" he said. "Clueless bastard." He stood up and moved away, going toward the liquor kept behind glass doors.

"Hey," I said. "I'm sorry. I didn't mean to come on so strong. We can slow dance first, if you want."

I regretted it, my old jokes feeling hollow and out of place now, even to me. But I could not change my own nature, any more than a river could stop running downstream. Dan stood absolutely still for a long moment, and I thought he was still angry, but when he turned back, he was smiling.

"Good old Pete," he said, shaking his head and chuckling, and for a single minute it felt like the old days between us, and I half expected him to come over and give me a punch in the shoulder or a nipple twister or something equally painful.

Instead, he poured me a drink, and I risked pulling the mask aside to take a long swallow. We toasted to life, love and happiness. If he thought it ironic, he didn't let it show, and for that I was grateful.

Somehow we drank more than we should have, and fell asleep. I woke up on the floor in the dark, with something brushing my face. My mask was off, but I couldn't muster up the strength to care. I sat up.

"Shhh," Sue said. I felt her try to unzip the front of my suit, her fingers clumsy and shaking.

My head was buzzing and throbbing softly, and the light from the lantern had been turned down so far I could see nothing but vague shapes.

"I'm sorry about what I did," she said. "I'm sorry I hurt you. I want to see your arm."

"Sue, you're drunk."

I sensed her nodding in the slow, exaggerated way drunks do. She kept tugging at the zipper, getting it half-way down. "I am, it's true. Aren't you?"

"You should sleep."

"I don't want to sleep. I'll sleep when I'm dead." She giggled, put her fingers to her mouth in the dark. "Oops, did I just say that?"

I put a hand over hers. Her skin was hot and sweaty and trembling. "You don't want to do this."

She slipped to her knees in front of me, and I could barely make out the outline of her face, her hair and the slope of her shoulders. She didn't move, or speak, and it took me a few moments to realize she had started crying again. I reached up and touched the tears on her cheeks, rubbed them away gently with my fingertips.

"Remember when you asked me about those first few weeks after my father's death?" I said softly.

"You said you went to Florida with your mom."

"I lied," I said. "I told that story enough times, even I started to believe it. But it's not true." I didn't know why I was telling her this, but it just came spilling out. Maybe it was the drink, making my head fuzzy, or maybe I was just tired of holding it all in. Maybe it was time to finally let it all go.

"I went to a facility. They said I had a . . . break. I don't know. I don't remember much of it."

"Shhh . . ." she said. "It's okay."

"It's not okay," I said, alarmed to find myself close to tears too. "I should have told Jay about it. I should have tried harder to let him know that I understood how he felt, before—"

"Don't," she said, a hitch in her voice.

"I'm sorry, Sue. I'm so sorry."

"Stop it. Just be quiet." She pulled at my zipper again, and I squeezed her hand.

"You don't want this," I said again. But she shook her head.

"Please, Pete. I . . . I do want to. I need to. I feel like I *am* dying. *Please.*"

This time, when she pulled the zipper, I let her unzip me to the groin, and she helped me pull my arms out of the sleeves. Then she stood up slowly, weaving slightly in the shadows, unzipped her own suit and stepped out of it. The room seemed to rotate slowly around me as I felt my heartbeat thumping in my ears, watching Sue's shadowy figure as she pulled the T-shirt up over her head, her soft, naked breasts catching the faint light for a moment before fading again into the rest of her as she moved closer.

I wanted to stop her, wanted to hold her, make her feel safe and warm. I didn't know what I wanted. As she pulled off her jeans and straddled my legs, reaching down and pulling me free, I thought about saying something important, something that would make her understand how I felt. She was drunk and in mourning, she didn't know what she was doing. If this was her way of making something up to me, it wasn't right. But I said nothing as her hand began to stroke me softly, and then nothing again as she lowered herself, opening her soft folds as I slid up and into her.

She leaned forward and put her head on my shoulder, her breath shaky in my ear, and began to move up and down in my lap, slowly at first, and then faster, her warmth and slipperiness and friction building against me.

I smelled her sex mixed with the sweat on our skin as her breathing began to speed up, and I held her tightly, my hands against her hot, slick back, her heavy breasts pushed against my chest. I thought about rain falling outside, not that dirty gray slush but a cleansing rain that washed the air clean, beating down the dust and broken glass and concrete. I imagined Jimmie and Jay, still alive out there, and that rain washing away their sores.

As my hands roamed Sue's back and up near her shoulder blades, I felt something under her skin, something I didn't want to acknowledge.

I opened my eyes and looked over her shoulder, and thought I saw a smaller, lonely figure watching us from the deeper shadows across the room.

And then I closed my eyes again, and release washed over me, drowning out the sound of Sue's breathing and burying everything else.

CHAPTER THIRTY-FIVE

I was driving past a broken and burned-out husk of a Volvo station wagon, nearly upended in the scorched brush, watching for movement behind shattered tree trunks and the drunken, leaning remains of a neighbor's fence. The world sat silent and still like the leftovers from some gigantic end-of-days celebration, the remains of trees and houses strewn like party favors across the ground, and I was the last guest to leave.

The sky was the color of bruised fruit, and the air smelled like a wood fire after the embers had died. I was alone in the car, and as I approached our quarter-mile-long dirt driveway I felt my anxiety increase, a rush of emotions making my head thud dully and my skin grow clammy. I felt like I'd been here already, but I didn't know how it ended. Strangely, the woods that lined our drive were untouched and bright green with foliage. I took the potholes and washboards as fast as I dared, and before long I was turning up the final slope, and my childhood house was in view, sitting on the edge of our small field, woods hulking behind. It was whole too, unmarked, windows intact, the shingles looking fresh and new.

By the time I left the car, the sky had descended over my head and turned black. As I ran to the screened porch, the rain began. I could hear it pounding on the roof; it sounded like a thousand tiny fists knocking on a door.

I didn't have my gun with me, but had picked up a short piece of split firewood from somewhere on the ground, and I gripped it like a club as I swung open the heavy front door and entered the house.

It was dark inside, and smelled of home, a slight mustiness that had always seeped up from the basement and persisted no matter how much or how thoroughly my mother cleaned. It felt familiar, but there was danger here, I felt that too, prickling my scalp and making me tighten my grip on the wood until my fingers ached.

I heard the sound of someone weeping.

I crept through the dark. I knew what I was searching for was at the bottom of those basement steps.

As I walked through the front hall and past the small, neat kitchen, shadows reached out and tried to pull me in. I was aware of a strange sense of doubling, that déjà vu I'd felt in the car, as if I were seeing the same scene twice, from slightly different perspectives. I did not want to know what was down there, and yet I did; and I felt a trembling knot loosen somewhere deep inside my chest, one loop at a time and with each step, but it was a painful uncoiling.

At the door to the basement I stopped, studying the old, paneled wood, the scars and marks of a lifetime of carrying furniture and boxes and equipment up and down, into storage and out again. I saw the scratch marks made by our short-lived kitten back when I was ten, before he'd run off and disappeared; there was the deep dent from the time my father had hit the lower left panel with the edge of a miter saw he was lugging downstairs for a project; the groove I'd made with a pocketknife near the hinges for some reason I'd since forgotten, and for which I'd received a terrible beating.

I heard the sound of someone weeping again, a woman. I stared at those reminders of a past life I had tried so hard to forget, and I felt smaller, reduced in some fundamental way. I did not want to open that door.

But I did, reaching out and twisting the handle, watching from some point outside myself as the door swung open and revealed a narrow wooden staircase with a rough, handmade railing. The smell was stronger here, and as I stepped forward to peer down into the darkness, I felt like I were stepping to the edge of a cliff with the urge to jump. With that came the rush of panic, my heart accelerating in my chest, my palms growing clammy, my chest tightening until I was nearly hyperventilating.

Down at the bottom of those steps, barely visible in the gloom, was a body.

I flipped on the light switch. He was crumpled on the concrete floor, one leg and arm bent underneath him at unnatural angles, his head twisted to the left. His sightless eyes looked back at me. I saw the inch-deep depression in his temple where his skull had shattered and driven shards of bone into his brain.

My father, the monster. Dead and gone, or so I thought.

The weeping was coming from the living room. I peered into the darkness and saw my mother huddled there, holding her broken arm, faceless in the dark, rocking. The familiar rage welled up in me with the force and power of a tsunami.

When I glanced down at myself, I was no longer wearing the hazmat suit. My hands were gloveless, and the piece of firewood they held was marred by the blood and hair that clung to its end.

I woke up gasping for breath, momentarily disoriented. The room seemed slightly lighter now, and I knew it was daytime, although without windows I was not sure *how* I knew. My fingers still ached from gripping the ghostly piece of wood, and my heart beat like a runaway train in my chest. I had been crying in the way people did when they wanted to get something huge and swollen out of themselves, and I felt weak and drained and helpless.

I remembered the sound of the rain from my dream, like fists knocking.

There was someone sitting over me in the dark. For a moment I thought it was Sue, and what had happened the night before came rushing back to me, along with a mixture of guilt and a flood of emotion I couldn't begin to understand.

But as my vision focused in the dimness I realized it was Tessa. She just sat on her knees and looked down at me, not moving. I couldn't make out her eyes.

"I—I killed him," I gasped out, another huge sob wracking my chest with a sharp intake of breath. "I found her that way, bloody and beaten and almost dead, and I was so angry. I took that piece of wood and I—"

"I know," Tessa said. "Shhh, Petey. Easy." She reached out with her delicate fingers and stroked the hair from my forehead, just the way my mom used to do it when I was a boy. She looked something like my mom, I thought, the way I would have imagined her as a girl.

And then I wondered what she must think of me, because it had surely been her in the shadows last night, watching me and Sue. "I'm sorry," I whispered. I didn't know what else to say.

But Tessa just smiled and leaned down and kissed my forehead. "You know I love you," she said. "I always will. You're my brother. You're family. Nothing you do can change that."

* * *

For most of a person's short stretch on this earth, it's impossible to mark the exact moment when something life changing happens. Frost wrote about standing at the crossroads of two paths in a wood, stepping down the rougher one and saying it made all the difference, but it's not often like that, at least not at the time. We make lots of little decisions every day, some right, some wrong, and some turn out to be more important than others. But how can you judge them at the moment they happen? I mean, even Frost was looking back. It's only after the fact, usually long after, that the truth becomes obvious.

Tragedy changes us too, shapes us with its little cuts into the person we'll become, but we're too numb at that moment to see this either; it's all about getting through, and our thoughts are consumed with the most mundane details and basic tasks. *Breathe in, breathe out.* Life is reduced to function, nothing more. It's not until the welts have faded when you really start to realize what it's done to you.

Before my father was rushed to the hospital, already brain-dead, there was no hesitation, no question of what to do. My mother helped me burn the piece of wood I'd been holding in the fire pit out back, and she made sure it would look like he'd hit his head on the stairs on the way down. Then she set about making calls. Even in that moment, having done such a thing, I did not feel the weight of Frost's crossroads bearing down on me; there was no time. Before I knew it the ambulance was there, EMTs were carrying my father strapped to a board up the basement steps and treating me for shock, and the event had its own momentum that carried me along with it.

Everyone assumed the breakdown that followed was because of what I'd witnessed, rather than what I'd done. It wasn't long before I began believing that it was an accident myself. He had been drinking, and he'd taken a nasty tumble. I'd had the misfortune of finding him. And that was all. The decision to take him off life support was an easy one, in the end.

But at *this* moment, right here in the study with Dan and Sue still sleeping on the rug and me sitting up with my back against the wooden paneling, tears not even dried on my cheeks and Tessa stroking my head, I realized something fundamental had changed, or was about to— something about myself and my life that I could not get back.

It probably sounds silly to say that now, considering the devastation that we'd already gone through. After all, we had spent the past few weeks buried in a hole, having to deal with the impossible, our loved ones surely dead, our lives one heartbeat away from ending too, and we had gone on living, suffering those nicks and cuts, *breathe in*, *breathe out*, life reduced to function, for the most part. We knew on some level what was happening, but we didn't really understand it, not at that deep-brain spot where something becomes a part of who you are.

A good chunk of that, I think, was the fact that we had each other. Jay leaving cut us deep, and Jimmie too, but the rest of us were still there, still together.

Now Dan was infected, and I was pretty sure Sue was too. It was only a matter of time before they were gone. That left me and Tessa, and I wasn't feeling too good about what was about to happen to us when we left this place. I'd confronted a memory I'd refused to acknowledge for years now, and it had dislodged something else in me. Maybe it was the coils of that knot coming undone, but I recognized what Tessa had meant to me all this time, and what a crutch she'd been in my life. There were things I had to face alone, things she could not help me with as much as I might want her to, and that thought was terrifying to me.

It seemed like my whole life I'd been playing a game, and only now had realized it was the wrong one. Choosing to move on, to shove the things that cut me into a small box and hide it away had felt like the smart thing to do. I was strong enough to survive, and making light of everything sharp in my life made it seem less important. If you were laughing, how bad could it be?

Only now did I realize how I'd been damaging myself. I was on the edge of adulthood, the years where most people would consider a boy becomes a man, and I still did not know whether I was capable of change.

Movement in the room roused me from my thoughts. Dan had gotten up from the rug and turned up the lantern, bathing the room with light. His hair was crusty with blood, his face too flushed with heat, tiny capillaries tracing red lines across the whites of his eyes. He looked pretty sick, and for a moment I wondered if he would start to tremble and go rigid like the others, his mouth opening wide to disgorge the foul contents that were surely gathering in his lungs.

I fumbled for my mask and my gun. But then he scratched his face and sighed, and I knew it was still Dan, at least for now.

I glanced at Sue. She'd put her suit back on in the night, but her own mask was still off, and she lay on her back, blinking up at the ceiling. She did not look at me, and I had no idea what she might be feeling. I searched for signs of sickness in her as well, but couldn't see any. I wondered how that puncture wound of hers looked now, but her neck was covered by the suit collar.

That's why they hid in the bed and fed on her the way they did. They were opening up a wound for the others to get in.

I shivered. It made enough sense for me to want to push it away from me like someone had handed me a piece of fruit with a fat hairy spider on it. It was an ugly thought, because it meant something similar to what had unnerved me about the idea of these things sending a message in the way they'd destroyed Jay in front of us: it was the idea of intent in their actions, which was dangerously close to intelligence.

"We need to go," Dan said. "Right now." He walked across the room to the gun cabinet and rattled the locked doors.

"What's happening?" I asked.

He looked around, grabbed a heavy book off the shelf, smashed the glass with it and reached in to unlock the cabinet. Then he reached in and pulled out a shotgun, two more handguns and some boxes of ammunition from a smaller drawer set into the bottom.

"They're coming," he said. He tossed me the shotgun and two boxes of shells. "I can hear them. Can you handle this?"

I nodded. "Pump, aim, pull the trigger. It's not hard." I'd never fired a shotgun before, but I knew the basic premise. Twelve gauge, pump action, devastating at close range, spreads out quickly. Moral of the story: don't fire until you see the whites of their eyes.

"What do you mean?" Sue said. She sat up. "Who's coming?"

"That noise Karin made, there were others who heard it too. It took them a while, but they're close now. They know where we are, how many of us are here, what we're doing. I . . . I think I'm helping with that somehow." Dan glanced at me, but his face gave nothing away about how he was feeling, only a determination that set his mouth into a hard, thin line. "They move during the day, mostly, and they stay in their hosts for the warmth. You're right about that part, Pete. And it's daylight now."

I glanced at the wall clock. Almost noon. We'd slept far longer than I'd thought. The fear that had been hibernating quietly inside me woke up and started to gnaw again. "Maybe we should stay put, at least until night falls," I said. "Hole up in here and wait it out."

Dan shook his head. "I'm telling you, it won't *be* safe in another few minutes. The bridge to the mainland, we have to get across it. Now."

Oh, Jesus. I was torn with indecision. Even the choice of trusting Dan was no longer so black-and-white. I thought he was still on our side, but how did I know for sure?

I slid shells into the shotgun chamber, seven rounds before I would have to reload, while Dan loaded the two handguns. He handed one to Sue, and then we all got into our full gear, masks on, hoods up and zipped.

We pushed the heavy furniture away from the door and opened it, guns up and ready, me in the lead, Dan at my back. Everything was muffled inside the hood and I felt strangely detached from what was happening as I peered out through the face mask. *Hiss, pop.*

It was brighter out here with the windows in the family room letting in some weak gray light. The kitchen was empty, piles of white bones and bloodstains the only sign that any of last night had ever happened.

I saw something glint in the light where Sue's grandfather had fallen.

The keys . . . where are they?
He'd have them on him . . .

In between the bones, right about where his pants pocket would have been, if there had been one left, was a metal zipper. Next to that was a set of keys. I scooped them up in my gloved hand, held them for the others to see. Finally, something was going our way.

"Let's blow this popsicle joint," I said.

CHAPTER THIRTY-SIX

Our sacks were still sitting on the floor of the mudroom. Sue had picked up the Geiger counter from the kitchen and flicked it on, and the tick, tick, tick of the reader started up again as we opened the door to the garage, weapons up.

It was darker inside. My heart rate kicked up a notch. Sue handed me the lantern, and I held it out with one hand, shotgun in the other. The Jeep was still sitting there, silent and still. I swept the gun from side to side, took a few steps into the garage, listening. I crouched to look under the chassis and stood up again. There was nowhere else for them to hide.

"It's clear," I said. "Let's load up."

Five minutes later, we had everything crammed into the Jeep: our sacks, plus more cans and packages of food from the mudroom, jugs of water and other supplies. Tessa found a plastic funnel and some tubing in a drawer in the workbench and I stuck that under the front seat. We had a full tank of gas, and more in a five-gallon plastic container we found next to the lawn mower, but that wouldn't get us anywhere near far enough. We'd have to depend on siphoning out the tanks of other cars.

I took a few deep breaths, trying to steady myself. My

head was throbbing dully from the drink, and I wished I had thought to take a couple of ibuprofen from the first-aid kit. Other than the glimpse I'd gotten when I went to close the hatch a few days back, this would be the first time any of us had seen the outside world since we'd been trapped down in the shelter. I didn't know whether to feel hopeful or scared to death.

We all piled in except for Dan. Since the power was off, he would have to raise the garage door manually. I started the engine and waited for his signal. He nodded at me and I switched on the lights, pinning him with their glare. He waved a gloved hand, then turned, gripped the garage door handle with his good arm, and rolled it up.

The open door revealed a scene straight out of a surreal nightmare. A ribbon of black driveway wound through a landscape that was too dark and bleak and cold to be any part of the Sparrow Island I knew. Watery gray light bled from a purple sky that had lowered itself to kiss the tops of the withered, leafless trees. The earth looked previously scorched, the brush and grass around the house all brown and dead, and everything was coated with that gray ash, as if the entire world had been cremated and tossed to the wind.

I sensed, rather than saw, the hulking form of Sparrow Rock looming over it all somewhere on the other side of the house, casting a shadow that used to feel out of place among the greenery and sunlight that often kissed the backs of the island cliffs, but seemed to fit right into the place now; granite was rough and hard and barren of all life.

Looking out at that scene, I felt completely alone and helpless, and I wondered how we had ever thought we could make our way through this.

Nobody spoke. The Geiger counter on Sue's lap began to tick faster. I glanced at her in the passenger seat, and she shook her head. Not in the danger zone yet. Of course, *danger zone* was a relative term, wasn't it? You might not start glowing green, at least not at first, but did that really make one bit of difference if you had a boiling tube of bioengineered insects hollowing out your insides?

A moment later the rear door opened and Dan climbed inside, cold air following him in. I could hear the angry ocean in the distance, throwing itself against the rocks, an ominous sound, before he slammed the door shut.

"I'd recommend you step on it," he said. I could see the fear on his face through the hood's shield. "Right now."

I dropped the Jeep into gear and hit the gas.

We exploded out through the open garage door, headlights cutting a path through the murky, permanent dusk. I had only a split second to register movement on our right before I felt the SUV shudder with the impact of something large and heavy. I glanced in the rearview mirror long enough to see a gigantic naked woman tumbling across the asphalt behind us, her pendulous breasts swinging as she got to her feet again and started limping after the car, blood on her face, her mouth opening wide as she let out one of those tortured, alien screams.

"Pete," Sue said, her voice tight.

"I see them." I gripped the wheel tightly, peering out through the windshield in disbelief. Two more people were standing in the middle of the driveway as we approached, a man and woman, lit up by our headlights. They looked to be in their thirties, well dressed, but there was something oddly familiar about their posture, too upright and stiff.

They did not move a muscle as I barreled toward them.

Why the hell were they standing in the middle of the road? If these things were intelligent like I thought, they couldn't possibly think they could stop the Jeep that way.

I looked at Sue and her eyes were closed, her hood resting back against the headrest as if she were sleeping, only her rapid breathing and her death grip on the Geiger counter in her lap giving her away. I wanted to close my eyes too and drift away from this place, but I did not have the luxury of taking that path. I had been chosen, for better or worse, to be the executioner.

I told myself that what I was about to do was self-defense; or was it murder? These people were still alive, at least in some form. I wondered if the infected felt pain, and just as quickly decided that if Jay and Jimmie's behavior inside the shelter was any indication, they did.

I honked the horn, lay my hand on it, blaring. They would not move. I had no choice.

"Hang on to something," I said to no one in particular.

We hit the man and woman going close to forty miles an hour. The Jeep's bumper clipped them hard at the waist so that they snapped forward and smashed their faces into the hood, and then flipped headfirst into the windshield, their arms pinwheeling, the impact making spiderweb cracks like two broken soup bowls before they tumbled up and over the roof.

As we hit them I *heard* them cry out, inside my head; felt something of the impact as a faint, ghostlike pain in my hips. Dan shouted something from the backseat, but I couldn't understand him, didn't have time to think before the voices drifted away. I shuddered with the memory of them, like something foul and black had bled through my pores and into my brain.

In the rearview mirror I saw them hit the pavement

behind us like rag dolls, flopping hands over feet and coming to rest in a tangled heap about thirty feet in front of the fat naked lady, who was still running after us but dropping back quickly.

The driveway took a sharp right-hand curve and descended down toward the ocean. I swung the wheel, tires squealing slightly under the strain, and as we straightened out again the bridge came into view.

I almost stood on the brakes, but managed to resist the urge in time. There was no stopping now, come hell or high water, but the bridge itself looked like it were alive, pulsing and swirling, and it took me a moment to realize that it was blanketed by thousands and thousands of the giant mosquitolike creatures that had attacked Sue. There were people on there too, but I couldn't see more than vague shapes through the swarm.

"We're going to need some industrial-strength bug spray," I muttered.

"What are they *doing?*" Sue said.

"They're attacking the supports, trying to weaken it," Dan said. He hitched forward in his seat so his head was close to us. "Those things back there weren't trying to stop us. They were just trying to slow us down, buy some time." He reached out a gloved hand and squeezed my shoulder. "We have to hurry, Pete. They're going to find a way to take it down, do you understand me? And then we're trapped here."

I nodded and put the pedal to the floor, feeling that familiar red tinge of panic beginning to creep over me.

We accelerated hard down the gentle slope toward the bridge. A gust of wind buffeted the SUV and picked up the ash from the road, obscuring the view for one heart-stopping moment before I blew through it, the Jeep lurched upward, and we entered a buzzing, snarling tornado of hell.

As soon as we hit the swarm I knew I'd badly miscalculated. Bugs slapped the sides of the SUV, bounced off the hood and crunched under the tires as we shuddered nearly sideways onto the bridge. We were going way too fast.

As the cloud engulfed us I was suddenly driving blind, and more huge mosquitoes burst against us like hailstones, smearing their guts across the glass and lengthening the cracks until the entire windshield threatened to fall into our laps.

Sue screamed, the sound shockingly loud in the confines of the car. I swung the wheel to the left, felt the Jeep fishtail through the cloud, swung it right again, trying to regain control as the rear end slid out behind us and we went into a full skid. I lost all sense of direction, holding on to the steering wheel with both hands and clamping my foot down on the brakes as we spun, terror washing over me in a paralyzing wave.

A jarring thud shook us as a human shape materialized out of the cloud beyond my driver's-side window and went down under the tires. I wondered how close we were to the guardrail and a drop of at least fifty feet to the rocky ocean below, and I thought of the moment of weightlessness that would come as we crashed through, the plunge downward and the impact with the icy sea; how it would blow out the windshield into our faces, water rushing rapidly in to strangle us, forcing itself into our mouths and down our throats and filling our lungs with salt. Ending us, once and for all, in the most merciful way.

All this flew through my mind in a split second, before we slid to a stop not three feet from the rail. The engine had stalled, and my hands ached from clutching the wheel, my legs trembling, brake pedal still pushed hard to the floor.

Everything was silent, except for the dull buzz of the mosquitoes outside, the *hiss-pop* of my mask, and Sue's Geiger counter, which was ticking fast enough now to sound like static, and I thought of that first night down in the hole, listening to the emptiness from the radio, concentrating so hard I imagined my mother's voice bleeding through it.

I could hear her again now.

Pete . . . hurts . . .

The voice sounded real enough. I lifted my gloved hands and found them shaking, and I could not seem to catch my breath. It was still cold in the car, but I was sweating hard. It occurred to me that I might be dangerously unstable, that what had happened back at Sue's grandfather's house and the dream of my father had been the last crack in the dam holding back something huge and irrevocable.

Then the cloud of insects lifted slightly, and I peered out the streaked and shattered windshield at a tightly knit group of people in the center of the bridge about twenty feet away. Somehow we had spun completely around and were facing the mainland again.

The group began to advance together, something odd about the way they moved. I realized that their steps were all perfectly synchronized; *right, left, right . . .*

"Go," Sue said, in a strangled, shaky voice. *"Hurry."*

I managed to turn the key and the engine roared to life. I stomped on the gas and the Jeep leaped forward, gaining speed quickly. We plowed right through the middle of them, sending several tumbling over the rail and pulling others down under the wheels with a thump-thud and a sickening crunch of breaking bones.

I kept going, plunging into another cloud of angry,

humming insects, hitting the gas again and roaring ahead to where I thought the bridge's exit lay. Sweat poured off me inside the suit, dripping down between my shoulder blades and running into my eyes. I could hardly see anything through the cracks and bug guts. I flipped on the windshield wipers, trying to clear the gunk from the glass, but the wipers just smeared it into a thick brown paste and caught at the bodies of more insects as they hit and spun away.

It was over in an instant. Almost as quickly as it had begun, the cloud lifted.

We left the bridge with a thump and squeal of tires and entered the mainland.

Breathe in, breathe out. I swallowed hard past the lump in my throat as we accelerated up the slope on the other side of the bridge. I sprayed blue windshield cleaner and the wipers flopped back and forth again, and I could see enough through the gunk and the spiderweb of cracks to remain on the road.

"We made it," I said, more to myself than to anyone inside the SUV. "We're okay."

Sue was crying next to me, huddled against the door, knees up and clutching the Geiger counter around her middle like a protective mother with a child. I considered trying to hold her hand, and thought better of it. I didn't know what she thought of me anymore, or whether she even remembered what had happened last night. My own mind seemed to be slowing down, rather than speeding up; I caught bits and pieces of the road before me like old sepia-colored snapshots. That throbbing ache between my eyes had intensified into dual nails being driven into my brain.

I could see more human shapes through the dim light

ahead, some of them already near us, others like shadows marching in a single-file line from the dead trees and across the flat, barren fields, the wasteland. A line of ants from their burrows. I couldn't tell how many of them were still alive, and how many might be like Sue's grandfather, but I knew that I would run down every single one of them, if that was what it took. The time for mercy was gone, if it had ever been here at all.

I looked in the mirror behind us and saw a dark cloud of mosquitoes lifting off the bridge, swarming our way. But they were falling behind as I sped up.

"They're tracking us," Dan said. "I can hear them. God-damn it! Get out of my fucking head!" I caught him clutching at his hood with his good arm, and my entire body went cold with the memory of Jay and Jimmie doing the same thing in the shelter as things got worse for them. If he lost it now, I had no idea what I'd do.

"Dan," I said. "*Dan*." I met his eyes in the mirror. "Stay with us, here. Please. Please stay with us."

He held my gaze, let out a deep, shaky breath and nodded. I saw Tessa touch his shoulder, but he didn't seem to feel it through his suit. She didn't speak, and as I blinked through the sweat I thought I saw her image shiver and blur in the mirror. I squeezed my eyes shut, shook my head, and when I opened them she was staring back at me in concern.

"Okay," Dan said, in a shaky voice, dropping his arm. "Okay."

The Geiger counter kicked up another notch. Sue uncurled herself from around it. "We're almost in the red," she said. She tapped the screen with her finger and shook the device, as if that might change the reading. When she looked at me I noticed how bloodshot her eyes were, how panicked she was behind her mask, how close to unhinged.

"Sing something," I said. I had no idea where that came from, but as soon as it left my mouth, I knew it was the right thing. She had always had a pretty voice, singing in the choir in her mother's church and in a badly directed version of *Oklahoma* our school theater department had put on during our sophomore year. We had all pitched in to help with that one, Jay working the lines with her, Dan playing a bit part onstage, me and Tessa painting the sets. Overall it had been a train wreck, but Sue had been really good, far better than any of the others.

"I . . . no," she said. "That's crazy. I can't."

"Come on. Sing something from the play. Hey, Dan, pull some beef jerky out of one of those sacks. We'll have dinner and a show."

We were still human, weren't we? After all that had happened, we had kept our dignity, and that, more than anything else, spurred me on. I wanted to see my house again, and find my mother, dead or alive. I wanted to prove to myself that I was worthy of the trust and faith she had put in me all these years, that my father had been wrong about me.

You're spineless, boy, always have been.

If I was going out, I wanted to do it the right way.

Sue gave me a shaky smile, and my heart warmed at the sight. "Come on," I said again.

"I know a way to prove what they say is quite untrue," she began softly, the melody faint and muffled through her mask and hood, her voice gaining strength and conviction as she went along. "Here is the gist, a practical list of 'don'ts' for you . . ."

Don't throw bouquets at me
Don't please my folks too much
Don't laugh at my jokes too much
People will say we're in looooove!

We drove on as the infected fell far behind, Sue's voice drifting through our heads like a sorrowful memory of something long past, through miles of empty, dead fields and shattered trees, silent houses and abandoned cars, deeper into the dark and unknown.

Closer to home, and whatever waited for me there.

CHAPTER THIRTY-SEVEN

We drove through that deserted, broken landscape, and eventually Sue's voice began to falter and died away, and nobody said anything else. We were all too horrified by what lay before us.

I turned from Ocean Road onto Route 1. As we moved inland the destruction seemed to get worse, the sky darker and more threatening. We passed the occasional abandoned cars, left on the side of the road or sometimes right in the middle of it, doors still open, ash coating everything. Frozen in time like fossil remains. The people who had driven them, those who had laughed, and cried, and made love, fought and slept and lived their own individual lives a billion times over, had disappeared, and now the world lay silent like a candy wrapper that had been discarded on the curb.

We saw no one moving at all.

Route 1 swept down past brown inlets crusted with ice, burned marshes and seedy motels, car dealerships and convenience stores, all deserted and dead under that flat, gunmetal sky, some windows shattered, others still intact and dull with ash and dust. I thought about drawing a message in them, something really clever like *Petey Wuz Here* or *Meet Me in Alaska* with a smiley face, but, of course, I didn't stop. We were like sharks in open water, keep moving or die.

Just outside the bridge to Wiscasset, the headlights picked up a nasty accident in front of us, maybe twenty cars and trucks all bunched up and busted, glass and plastic scattered across the road. At first I didn't think we could get through, but I found a way to skirt it on the shoulder, the Jeep's tires halfway into the drainage ditch.

"It's Mike Giles," Dan said from the back.

I looked, and he was right. Giles's car, anyway, one of those new Dodge Challengers with racing stripes and a Patriots sticker in the rear window, sitting in the middle of the pileup, front end smashed up enough for the engine to be half into the driver's seat. He was a football player too, a muscled offensive lineman with a plump face and a buzz cut, and Dan got along with him but he'd never been friendly with the rest of us. He'd gotten the car a couple of months ago from his father, who owned the dealership in Brunswick, and he loved tooling through the high school parking lot, showing it off.

Giles had never been one to wear his seat belt either. As we crept past, I could see the hole in the windshield where he'd flown through on impact, the edges smeared with dried blood.

"Where'd he go?" I said, and regretted it as soon as the words were out of my mouth. Nobody spoke. We all knew where he went. He was probably somewhere out in those dead weeds beyond the bridge, waiting for us to stop and take a look around.

I wondered how many of our classmates were out there somewhere, neither alive nor truly dead. How many of our neighbors and coworkers, teachers and distant cousins. Part of the hive mind now.

I glanced in the rearview at Dan, who was sweating profusely inside his suit and breathing too fast. "Can you hear them?" I said.

"No," he said. "I can't. I can't hear anything."

I nodded. But I wasn't sure I believed him. I gripped the shotgun tucked at my side. It would be hard to maneuver in this small space.

I'll have to act long before that . . . I can't take the chance of . . . hurting someone.

I wondered if that time was getting close, and whether he'd have the strength to act when it came. I met his eyes in the mirror, and he nodded slightly at me, as if he understood.

It was tight enough as I passed by for metal to scrape the side of the Jeep with a teeth-clenching squeal, and then we were free and on the bridge, leaving Mr. Mike Giles, God save him, somewhere in the rearview mirror.

Wiscasset was a tourist town with a postcard-pretty main street sloping down toward the water, and normally it would have been bright and bustling with life, but now the road was empty, the shops dark and deserted. We left the bridge and drove slowly past Red's Eats, the tiny food shack that had been an icon for so long, and the sight of the empty, ash-covered counter just about made my heart break. Jimmie had worked there part-time and we'd spent many summer evenings lined up before closing, waiting for one of Red's burgers and fries before heading to the movies or someone's house to hang out. Now it was just another memory of something we would never get back.

"Look," Sue said, tapping the glass on her side. I hit the brakes and stopped halfway up the hill, pretty little village shops on either side. In one of the unbroken store windows, someone had written THEY'RE COMING on the dusty glass.

"Should we check it out?" she said. "What if someone's alive in there?" Her leg was jiggling up and down, and I wanted to reach out and stop it with my hand. I could feel the nervous energy pouring off her, and it made me uneasy.

I stared at the glass, and what looked like a fine spray of dried blood next to the letters. "We can't help them, Sue," I said. "Besides, it could be a trap. We have to keep moving."

"Sure," she said. "Okay." But her leg kept jiggling, and she kept her gloved hand against the passenger window, as if waving good-bye.

CHAPTER THIRTY-EIGHT

I put the Jeep back into gear and started creeping up the hill, a sour feeling in my stomach. The Geiger counter kept ticking, slightly faster, then dropping back, and I resisted glancing at the screen every thirty seconds.

Past the center of town, I turned right on Route 27 toward White Falls. The fire station on the corner had all its doors up, the interior pitch-black, a ladder truck parked sideways across the entrance, but there was no sign of anyone alive. The hose was uncoiled and lay on the ground like a fat gray snake.

There was another accident near Wiscasset High School, and I had to take the Jeep up onto the grass, bumping over rocks and skirting the trees. Sue let out a little shriek as something scraped the side of the SUV, and for a moment I thought of skeletal hands reaching out from the shadows.

"It's just a tree branch," Tessa said from somewhere in the back. Of course she was right, but it was my father I imagined just then reaching up from the grave, even in death trying to keep me from getting back home again.

As we neared White Falls a few minutes later the sky grew even darker, and I remembered my dream of the night before, the clouds opening up as I ran for the shelter of the porch, the rain on the roof like fists knocking.

We reached the bridge and swept through the deserted town center as we followed the river past the church and restored graveyard and toward the old Mill Inn. I couldn't help but think of the events that had torn White Falls apart years ago and what it had meant to my family. I was only three and couldn't remember any of it myself, but the repercussions had reverberated through my life like ripples in a pond. I was feeling them even now.

My mother wouldn't speak of it until after my father died, but I'd heard plenty about what happened from others in town, the storm and destruction of the flood from the dam's collapse, the missing bodies and the violence, and the wilder rumors that nobody who had lived through it would talk about anymore: stories told second- and thirdhand around campfires about the ground down near Black Bog being diseased, a gathering place for evil. As a younger boy, I'd always thought that the people who believed those stories were crazy, but now I thought about Sue's grandfather in his kitchen, and I shivered.

Maybe it wasn't so crazy after all.

"It looks . . . like . . ." Sue said. "Pete—"

"Don't," I said. I felt the final coil of that knot inside my chest loosen, and the world tilted dangerously around me. I clenched the steering wheel so hard my fingers ached. Sue's family was originally from Boothbay, and she and her mother had moved to White Falls when she was ten. She knew about the town's history, but she hadn't been here back then. She couldn't possibly understand what my parents had been through.

How it had torn them apart, and led to everything that happened after.

I can't face that, I thought. *Not now, not here.*

And yet wasn't that exactly why I had come this far? I had been ignoring the truth for too long, and if I had any chance of surviving, I had to stand before my own demons and see things through to the end.

I turned left at the inn and we wound up the hill past the old high school, then past the elementary school and the historical society. Beyond that, open farmland stretched for half a mile before the woods began again, and we came to my driveway.

This was nothing like my dream. There was no Volvo upended in the ditch, and the woods along the driveway weren't green, but brown and dead. The road itself was smooth too; it had been grated just a month ago, and the washboard gravel and potholes that tended to form after weeks of spring rain had not yet come to the surface.

The driveway made several twists and turns, all of them as familiar to me as the back of my hand. I remembered walking down this drive as a child to catch the school bus at some ungodly hour of the morning, how frightened I would get with the woods closing in on either side, and me alone in the early dawn mist. It had seemed like it went on forever back then, like I would never reach the end, and the prospect of getting my father's belt if I missed the bus made it even more terrifying.

I made the final turn and there was my house overlooking the field, looking small and hunchbacked under the threatening sky, shingles aged and gray, everything covered with the now-familiar ash. Two windows on the second floor were broken, but it looked otherwise intact.

I pulled the Jeep up near the steps and stopped. It seemed impossible to believe that I was finally here, after all this time. Now that I was, I wasn't sure what to do.

"I'm coming with you," Dan said.

"No." I shook my head. "I need to go in alone." My heart was thundering in my chest so hard I thought it might burst. My mother was probably inside there somewhere, but there were no signs of life, nothing that would indicate she had made it through the attack. I remembered how we had left things that night, the terrible argument and how I'd treated her, after all she had done for me. It seemed impossibly cruel that she would have died without hearing me say I was sorry, and telling her what she meant to me. And yet it seemed like too much to hope that this could end in anything but a bad way.

Before I could lose my nerve, I grabbed the shotgun, opened the door and got out.

It was colder out in the open air, but there was no wind. I took two steps and Dan was out of the backseat and slamming the door behind him, grabbing hold of my arm and spinning me around. "Listen," he said, "okay? Just listen." He was shaking, sweat dripping from his hair inside the hood, his eyes bloodshot over the mask. "I want to help."

"I can't," I said. "You don't understand. It has to be me. Only me. Please."

He blinked twice, hard. "I'm—I'm not going to be here when you get back."

"What do you mean?" I said. But I knew, of course I did.

"I . . . I can't—fight them anymore." His fingers dug into my arm hard enough to make me wince. "They've gotten hold of me and they're not going to let go. God, it *itches*, so bad, you—you can't imagine . . . Pete, you . . . you don't give up, you hear? You keep going. For me."

He glanced over his shoulder at the Jeep, and lowered his shaky voice. There was a tinge of desperation in it that I didn't like. "And you watch out for Sue," he said. "I can hear them inside her. It won't be much longer."

"Oh Jesus." I looked at her through the glass, hunched over that Geiger counter again, her legs and arms still jittering like a hyperactive kid in math class, and I felt sick to my stomach. I'd touched the hives on her back last night, and I'd known what they were, God save me. I just hadn't wanted to say it out loud. She'd gotten it from that bug sucking at her, and the black cloud whirling out of Jay's diseased mouth, and I'd made love to her, and goddamn if the entire world wasn't falling down all around me without a way for me to catch my balance.

"I'll take care of myself," Dan said. "Don't you worry about that. But I don't think Sue's strong enough to do the same when the time comes. And I think there are others around here . . . I can hear *something*. It might be cold, but it's still daylight, and they're awake. So you watch your own ass."

I nodded. "Okay. I will."

"Good luck." Dan reached out with his good arm and hugged me. He clutched me tight, as if clinging to a buoy in rough seas. He was burning up even with the temperature dropping outside and it came at me right through the suit, his body slippery with sweat under the nylon and trembling so violently I could barely hang on. I held him anyway, wondering if this would be the last time we saw each other, and when I stood back again and looked at him I thought it would be appropriate to end this way; Dan standing upright like a good soldier through all that pain and gritting his teeth, staying strong for me, for all of us.

I felt like a little boy playing men's games, and the idea of Dan not being there to lean on left me dry-mouthed and weak. The real tragedy of life was that people took each other for granted far too often.

"Your dad would be proud," I said, and as much as I tried to keep them inside, the tears spilled out on my cheeks. With my gloves and hood on, I couldn't wipe them away, and so I let them fall.

I left him standing there, outside the Jeep, and went

inside the house, and after the door slammed shut behind me I thought I heard a single gunshot, but I couldn't be sure.

Inside, I nearly lost my nerve, my legs going weak and my heart stuttering in my chest. I felt a panic attack coming on hard, and I swallowed and tried to push it down, calm my breathing and remain alert.

The smell trickled through the gloom of the front hall-way, drifting to me even with my mask and hood on. A sour, spoiled stench like food gone bad. It reminded me of Sue's grandfather's house, and what we had found there. I didn't want to think about what that meant.

"Mom?" I said. I stood still and listened to my own voice die away into silence. I felt stupid saying anything out loud. It was wrong, like yelling in church, and I thought of bottomless canyons dropping away into darkness, and the depths of my own heart, black at its center like a withered apple core.

As I passed the entrance to the kitchen, I heard a noise behind me, and I whirled around. Tessa was standing inside the front door.

"I wanted you to stay in the car," I said, surprising my-self with my own vehemence. "You're not welcome here."

"But you need me."

"I don't need anyone."

"You know that's not true, Pete," Tessa said. She took a step forward, and then another. "It's nothing to be ashamed of, needing support. As long as I'm here, you're never alone. Stop trying to fight it. Stop pushing me away."

I shrugged. I'd depended on Tessa for so damn long, I didn't know where I ended and she began. I felt so tired, so small and helpless, just a little boy who needed his mother. My head felt like it were going to split right down the middle, the sharp-as-nails headache boring through my skull. I wanted to scream, but I was shaking so hard I couldn't get a decent breath.

Tessa took my hand, just like she always did, and when I felt her touch me it was like a key turning in a smoothly oiled lock.

"Come on," she said. "Let's get this done."

She led me to the basement door. It was closed, and when she reached out to open it, I drifted back in time, my sight doubling, then tripling, the echo of years past pulling me down.

The door yawned open to reveal a black hole. The steps were darker than I remembered, but, of course, they would be, without any lights to burn and the sky outside the windows so gray and thick. I hadn't thought to bring a flashlight, and as I stood on the edge of that abyss I cursed my own stupidity. The world seemed to hitch and speed up until I was dizzy with the spinning, a topsy-turvy carnival ride, and I teetered there, dangerously close to losing my balance.

Like father, like son. I was confused at the chunk of wood in my hand, until I realized with a start that it was the shotgun. I blinked down into the shadows.

There was something at the foot of the basement steps.

For a moment I saw the body of my father again, and I stifled a scream. But the shape dissolved into the outlines of a wheelchair, on its side and looking badly misshapen, as if it had taken a nasty tumble.

Like a machine on autopilot (*good old Pete, ignore the problem, it'll go away*), I reached out and flicked the light switch on the wall up and down. Nothing happened, of course, the power had been out for weeks and we didn't have a backup generator hooked up to the house like many families in White Falls.

"Momma," I said, but this time my voice was a cracked whisper. I stood there in a moment of terrible indecision, as the smell of something stronger wafted upward and found its way through my mask.

Hiss, pop. Suddenly I couldn't breathe, the hood closing in on me and cutting off my oxygen, my lungs burning. I dropped Tessa's hand and pulled off the hood, yanking the mask off my face.

"What are you doing?" Tessa cried, but I ignored her as I gulped the cold, stinking air, the sweat drying quickly on my skin. This was good, this was much better. The smell was sharp, thick and foul enough to bring tears to my eyes. But I could see more clearly without that damned hood in the way.

I ignored Tessa's protests and hurried down the steps, watching my footing in the treacherous darkness, and at the bottom I picked up the empty wheelchair and set it upright. One of the wheels was too badly bent to function, and the whole thing leaned drunkenly to the right, as if ready to collapse upon itself.

I turned to face the deeper shadows.

Our basement had been my father's domain. He built things as a hobby, chairs and cabinets and little wooden boxes, but he was drunk most of the time down here and none of them had ever been particularly good. His work area dominated one entire wall, everything still the way he'd left it the day he died, floor-to-ceiling shelves bookending a sturdy bench with a corkboard above for hanging tools, and drawers underneath. The floor was painted cement, easy to sweep up when the wood shavings fell. There were a few old gardening tools leaning in the corner.

On the opposite side, crammed into a smaller space, were my mother's canned goods, homemade pickled green beans and jellies, soups and other supplies, and scattered throughout the basement were wooden support columns as thick around as my thigh. Windows were set high in the concrete walls, but they let in very little light.

As I stood looking around, all these once-familiar things became threatening, indistinct shapes lurking in the dark. Any one of them could have been my mother's body, but I moved toward the food-storage area, knowing instinctively that she would have crawled as far away from my father's creations as possible.

In the left-hand corner, crammed into the space between the wall and the shelving unit, I found her.

CHAPTER THIRTY-NINE

She had lived for a while that way. Empty bottles of jelly and beans and soup were scattered across the floor. She died upright, her back against the concrete, head slumped to her chest, wearing her favorite nightgown that was now black with decay.

There weren't enough shadows to cover her. I stumbled away from the terrible sight, reeling, my hand fluttering to my own throat. I felt a final, irrevocable shattering inside, a crumbling to dust.

You were always my little baby. You're fragile, Pete . . . Sometimes I need to save you from yourself.

I made a noise like a dog with a bone in its throat, and was horrified to realize that the old laughter was there, close to the surface.

The sound of footsteps on the stairs and a beam of dancing light made me whirl around.

Sue was coming down the steps fast in her hazmat suit, flashlight in her hand. She reached the bottom and pinned me with the beam, flicking it to my mother's body, then back at me again.

"Oh, no," she said through the hood. "Pete—your mask—"

"What did you do with Tessa?" I said. I took a step toward her. I couldn't see very well with the light in my eyes, and I didn't realize I'd raised the shotgun until she used the flashlight beam to point at it.

"Tessa?" she said. "What? I—I don't understand. You're acting crazy. Please, put the gun down. I want to help."

I advanced on her, an unreasoning fury overwhelming me. "Everyone wants to help," I said. "What the fuck do I look like, some kind of charity case? You think I can't take care of myself, that I'm fundamentally weak, or broken, a goddamned psycho, is that it?"

"No." She shook her head. "I—I don't—"

What did you do with Tessa! My spittle speckled her face mask as I reached out with my free hand and grabbed the front of her suit. She was crying now, her face a bright cherry red under the mask, shaking her head back and forth. She pushed at the gun with her hands, trying to direct the barrel away from her midsection, but I kept it rammed in place.

"I don't know what you're talking about!" she screamed. "Stop it stop it stopitstopit—"

I shoved her away from me, and she stumbled and fell onto her back, the flashlight tumbling to the floor and rolling away, *tick, tick, tick,* the beam of light washing across the artifacts of my past and making them bulge and fade and shiver before it came to rest against the wall.

I stood over her, pumped a shell into the shotgun's chamber and pointed it at her face. "You're infected," I said. "I felt it when we were making love last night. How long, Sue? Were you ever going to tell me? Or were you just going to let them infect me too?"

She was sobbing uncontrollably, her gloved hands going to her hood, clawing at the zipper. She pulled it off, then her mask. "Oh, God," she said. "Oh my God. I can't . . . breathe." She sat up, moaning, clutching her knees to her stomach, rocking, her body trembling like a tuning fork that had been struck hard, and as her head fell forward I could see the hives on the skin of her neck. "Dan's dead, he killed himself out there and I saw him do it. He put the gun in his mouth and blew his head off. And then they . . . they *ate* him."

She looked up at me, the whites of her eyes filling with bright red blood, tendons standing out in her neck, her body trembling more violently. "Like Jimmie, and . . . Jay. We're all alone now. I don't want to die. *Help* me."

I lowered the gun and stepped back, sickened by myself, the anger that had consumed me draining away all at once and leaving me feeling hollowed out and cold.

Sue managed to get to her feet. She pulled the zipper down on her suit and shrugged her arms free, and peeled the T-shirt over her head, naked from the waist up.

Her entire torso was covered with hives the size of quarters, their centers pulsing slowly in and out.

A line of insects appeared like a fat snake under her skin, writhing upward, then sank again out of sight.

"Oh, Sue," I said.

"It itches, so bad, please, cut them out of me, *please*." Her hands were squeezed into fists and she clenched her jaw tightly together, making an *nnnn, nnnn* sound as blood-tinged tears ran down her face.

"No." I shook my head. "I won't do that. I can't."

"Then kill me . . . kill . . . me . . ."

Her body went rigid, mouth stretching open wide, her eyes losing focus, and finally, she was gone.

When the alien scream began, I raised the gun, tears blurring my sight.

I'm sorry, Sue. I'm so sorry.

I pulled the trigger.

The shotgun kicked back hard into my shoulder as the pellets ripped through her chest at close range, shoving her backward against the wall. She did not fall, and when she came back lurching at me I shot her again, this time in the stomach, and the high, keening noise I kept hearing in my head was coming from me as I watched her body hit the ground and the black insects started boiling out of her ravaged torso and I remembered the sound I'd made as the bombs approached so many weeks ago, that high, terrible screaming into the teeth of insanity.

Behind me I heard a sound like something large shuffling across the room and as I whirled around the gun was knocked from my hands and I was staring into the bloated, slimy face of my mother, or what had been my mother, and her cheeks were sliding down her skull and the bone was showing through as the insects writhed and squirmed and I fell back across Sue's quivering legs, screaming, screaming.

I shoved myself backward on my hands until I hit the wall in a panic and scrambled to my feet, the flashlight spinning away and the basement flashing light, then dark, then light again, and somewhere to my right was a shovel leaning within reach, but my mother was coming at me with her ruined hands outstretched, and I closed my eyes and waited but nothing came, and when I opened them again my mother had fallen to her knees and the shovel was buried deep in her throat, and Tessa was there, holding her up with the other end until her body fell sideways, headless and still.

I sat there wheezing in the sudden emptiness, listening to the buzzing and ticking of insect feet across the concrete as they cleaned the bones like good little soldiers, and I knew it was wrong, it was all wrong, and I was terrified that I was still far too weak at heart to face the truth of who I was, and what I had become.

"I told you to leave me alone!" I shouted at Tessa, tears

streaming down my cheeks, snot running from my nose. "I don't need you. You were never here, you understand me?"

I blinked and looked down at myself as the world snapped back into place. I was holding the shovel with my mother's head in my own gloved hands.

My Tessa was gone, this time for good.

CHAPTER FORTY

I climbed the stairs out of that basement, and I felt like I was rising up out of the depths of my own private hell. Maybe I was doing exactly that, and strangely enough, I felt lighter and calmer than I had felt in years.

If there had been any infected in that house, they would have had me without a fight, and I would have gone willingly.

But I was finally, truly alone.

I guess you know by now that Tessa wasn't the girl next door, at least, not in the traditional sense. I didn't meet her in her backyard. Hell, we didn't even have neighbors within half a mile of our house. The thing was, somewhere deep down I knew that all along. I just needed to believe otherwise, and for several years her presence was the only thing that pushed away the terror and the red-tinged cloud and kept me from a return trip to the psychiatric facility where I'd spent the first few weeks after my father's death.

So there's the irony. After murdering my own father in what some would say was self-defense, to remain sane I had to invent a sister who had died many years ago to be my best friend and companion. And she had served as the better part of me ever since.

* * *

A week or so after my father's death, my mother came to see me in the institution where I'd been committed for observation. The doctors had decided that the best thing for me was to have her keep her distance for a while, since every time I caught a glimpse of her puffy, swollen face, I started screaming.

But after a week she'd had enough, and she showed up at the front gate and insisted on seeing me. The building was an old stone behemoth, Gothic and cold and intimidating, but she stood her ground. I didn't know any of this until she told me about it later, but apparently she made quite a scene, and the director of the place had to come out and personally escort her inside.

They had me sedated enough that I didn't recognize her at first. We sat in a private meeting area, white walls and furniture bolted to the floor. There was a television mounted to the wall, and it flickered soundlessly at me. I remember that much. That television was always on, and the sound was always muted, and I remember thinking that the people on-screen had an important message for me, if only I could hear what they were saying. But they never spoke out loud.

From what she told me later, I imagine it this way: my mother sitting uncomfortably in a chair opposite me, her back aching, cradling her broken arm. The swelling in her face had gone down by then, with only the ghost of a bruise around her right eye to mar her normally perfect skin, but she looked hollowed out and defeated.

I was restrained, and I'm sure that cut her like a knife. But she didn't reach out to touch me, or try to loosen the straps. I had been violent, and had tried to hurt myself, and the staff was still being overly cautious. An orderly was watching through an observation window, and any contact would have surely brought him running and ended the session before she could express what she had come to say.

"Your father," she said. And then she stopped for a bit, because this was difficult for her. I wasn't in any shape to protest, and that probably made it easier, because when she began again, she didn't stop until the entire thing was out.

"You asked me once why he hated us so much," she said. "Our family wasn't always in such a terrible place. When you were just a baby, things were different. Your father still had his moods, but there was kindness inside him too, and a lot of that was reserved for your older sister, Tessa. She had him wrapped around her finger from birth. She liked the smell of wood shavings and would sit with him for hours in his workshop, watching him put together his projects, and he made things for her like dollhouses and carved wooden birds they would paint in bright colors and use to attract other birds to the feeder in the yard.

"And then hell came to White Falls. You understand me? I can't explain it any better than that. Whatever evil thing rose up was never clear to any of us, but it left dozens dead, the dam shattered and the town flooded and in pieces in the aftermath of that terrible storm. And in the middle of that darkness, your sister Tessa lost her life.

"The official cause of death was drowning in the creek that had overrun its banks in our backyard. She was only five years old and I . . . I was with her at the time. But I couldn't save her. It was dark and she was screaming and something just reached up out of that water and it took her down. Maybe it was just a dead tree branch, but it looked like it was moving, like it grabbed hold of her. And I couldn't find her again until it was too late.

"After that, your father retreated from us. The town was rebuilt and our lives went on, but he never came back. Maybe he blamed me for Tessa's death, or maybe he blamed himself. He started drinking more heavily, and the occasional shouting match turned into slaps, and that progressed to worse things. There was something in both of our faces that set him off: maybe we looked too much like her. But when he got to drinking and we were in his way, we suffered for it."

Telling me all this must have been difficult for my mother to do. They never spoke of Tessa in our home; all photos of her had been removed. I never knew I had a sister at all. For years she'd kept this secret from me, and the entire town was complicit in it, because I'd never heard mention of her name from anyone.

But she was unburdening herself because she thought it might help me to understand my father better, and to know that it was possible to go on, even with such a devastating wound as the death of a child.

Grief is sort of like a scar; the wound heals, but the damage remains, and when the timing's right it can ache like a ghostly memory of something sharper and more immediate.

Yes, something like that.

"I want you to understand that it's not your fault," she said. "That you're not to blame for any of it, and that your father wasn't the monster he seemed to be, at least, not at first. But that kind of pain damages a person permanently, Petey, and now we've all tasted it. We're all damaged in that sense. I only hope you can find a way to live your life without letting it bring you down the way it did your father. If you have to blame anyone, blame me."

I don't remember much of that conversation, but that's the way I imagine it. And something must have gotten through to me, because that night, after my mother left the hospital, I saw Tessa for the first time.

It was much like I've already described it, except, of course, it wasn't in her own backyard or anywhere near my home. I was unusually calm and lucid and the orderlies had left me free in a common room to stare out at the rain. I stood at the reinforced glass door and I saw my Tessa dancing out there in the mud, her hands outstretched and her face up and open to the raindrops.

She was as real to me as anyone else I'd ever seen. You have to understand this, if you're going to understand why I've told this story the way I have; somewhere in my own mind, I guess I knew she wasn't really there. But to keep my own sanity, I had to find a way out, and she gave it to me. I pushed what had happened to my father way down deep, along with what my mother had told me. And before long, Tessa was as familiar to me as my own skin, and there didn't seem to be any way back.

I tried the door that night and found it unlocked, and I went out there with her in the rain.

From that moment on, she was always with me, and I was never alone.

They called it a miraculous recovery. The director of the facility, when he sat me down to do his own version of an exit interview a couple of weeks later, said that he'd never seen anything like it.

"I'm still a bit skeptical," he said, leaning back behind his large polished desk and crossing his arms behind his head. "I was worried about you, young as you are, coming in here the way you did. You required serious corrective medication. Neuroleptics are nasty things. They make you sleepy, put your mind in a fog, make you hallucinate. Weight gain, agranulocytosis, tardive dyskinesia, tardive akathisia, tardive psychoses. These things can begin slowly, but are not easy to reverse. To be honest, I suspected you would be a lifelong resident. That does not give me any pleasure to say, you understand, it's simply the truth. But this . . ."

He leaned forward so suddenly as if to pitch straight out of his chair. Maybe he was trying to get a reaction. But I did not flinch. I got the feeling that I'd flustered him, and that I was peeking through his carefully polished exterior to what really lived underneath.

"You're not fooling with us, are you?" he said, looking me in the eye. "Because we're experts here. We'll see through it. You're a bright young man, and you've passed all our tests with flying colors. I just find it all . . . hard to swallow."

I held his gaze. "No, sir," I said. "I'm not fooling you. I do believe I'm better now, thank you."

Although he did not know it, Tessa sat next to me, holding my hand the entire time, and I felt safe enough to smile and nod and thank him again for his help.

A day after that, my mother came to check me out.

I wrote earlier about being at crossroads in life, and how hard it is to see them at the time. For a while I'd thought the crossroad in my own life was the day Tessa appeared to me, and I made the choice to take her in. Then I ended up trapped in the bomb shelter with those I considered my best friends. And after witnessing things that would defy belief, if I had not seen them with my own eyes, I had to shoot three of them, to stop them from killing me.

If that's not a crossroad, I don't know what is.

I also wrote that being friends means you might know something embarrassing about each other, or whom you have crushes on. But you don't know their most private thoughts, the things they don't share with anyone else, the things that make them bleed.

My best friends thought they knew me, but they were wrong. Hell, I didn't even know myself. That game I'd been playing, the one where I laughed at all the jokes and kept on going as if the entire world were a punch line, it was rigged. There were house rules, and I was just a guest with a line of credit that had run out.

But like my father said, life was about survival. The world didn't care if you lived or died; fate was strictly a human invention. Like it or not, I was the last man standing, and now I had a second chance to make things right.

As I left my house and climbed back into the Jeep, I thought about just lying down in the dirt and giving up. And then I thought about change, and second chances. I thought about crossroads. It was a hell of a long way to Alaska, but if I played my cards right, if I finally faced down my own demons and owned up to who I was and what I'd done, maybe I just might make it. And if I didn't, at least I'd go down knowing I gave it my best shot, on my own terms.

Dan's voice drifted back to me from the night before:

I want you to promise me that you'll do everything you can to survive. I don't want it to all end for nothing.

And so I climbed into that Jeep and I kept going, and I fought to the end for the sake of my friends.

They would have wanted it that way.

EPILOGUE

Saw the last nest outside of North Conway. These were smarter than the rest, moved more quickly. I think they were still alive, although their eyes were dead. Came at me through a used-car parking lot as I stopped to look for gas. There were four of them, and the hives were everywhere, across their faces and legs and arms, every bit of skin I could see.

They hit me using a pattern similar to the one the rats had used in the tunnel—one drew my attention while another flanked me as I bent over with the plastic tube in my mouth, sucking gasoline-flavored vapors from one of the car's tanks. As the gas came up and started pouring onto the cracked concrete and I coughed and spit, the first one, a girl of about fourteen in a skirt and Old Navy top, stepped out from between the cars parked right in front of me. I reached for my gun as she put her hands up and then I heard a noise from behind and turned and the second bastard had come wriggling underneath the car's chassis like a snake.

I shot him in the face, and when I turned back the girl had been joined by two others, a man and a woman, maybe her parents, I don't know.

It didn't matter. I managed to get all three of them before they spilled their black guts, but it was close.

After that I left North Conway, and I didn't see any more. There's a good foot of gray snow on the ground, but the Geiger counter says the fallout is safe enough for me to continue. I stole an oversize ski parka from a department store and managed to fit it over my suit. It's gotten a lot colder during the day, downright frigid at night, and I think I was right about the cold. I think it's keeping them dormant, like wasps at the end of fall as the frost moves in.

I've been picking up bits and pieces of voices from the radio for a few days now, but after I crossed the border into Canada, they got stronger. It's coming from the Doomsday Vault, and there are survivors, although I don't know how many. They say they have plenty of space, and heat, and food. They're asking anyone left alive to come. So we were right.

Thank God, we were right.

Passed Edmonton and holed up in the basement of a convenience store to rest for a bit. Almost out of gas. Have to siphon again and pray the Jeep will keep going. There's a lot more snow, and the roads are tough to navigate. Nearly got stuck twice. I may have to look for a different vehicle soon, maybe a plow or even a snowmobile, if it comes to that.

It's damn cold out here, and my fingers are cramped and aching, but I don't dare light a fire. I can't risk the smoke and the chance that I'm wrong about the infected going dormant.

I feel like the loneliest man in the world. The wind whips and howls outside like a living thing. There's nothing else alive out there, nothing that could be called human. The voices on the radio are all that's keeping me from ending things right now. There are a dozen ways to do it, and I've thought of them all. The easiest might be to just start walking until I feel like lying down and closing my eyes. The snow will take care of the rest.

But when I think of these things the memory of my friends comes in, and I see Sue and Dan and Jay and Jimmie cheering me on. I can't do it. I owe them too much.

* * *

Left the convenience store earlier this morning, into the teeth of another snowstorm. I can't seem to keep warm. It's not much farther now, according to the map, maybe a day or so of solid driving if I don't run into trouble. But the going's even worse, and I'm scared to death I won't be able to make it through the next couple of drifts.

Something I should mention, I guess. About an hour ago, as I was peering out through the spiderweb of cracks in the windshield, trying to keep to the road, an old friend came back for a visit.

I was driving past the remains of some kind of construction site, huge relics of machines rusting like the skeletons of ancient creatures long dead and gone, snow piled up against their massive treads. When I glanced in the rearview mirror, Tessa was sitting in the backseat.

But when I turned around she was gone.

She's only in mirrors now, and she doesn't speak to me anymore, just sits and watches. I imagine I see things in her eyes, whether it's anger or tenderness or something else, but it doesn't really matter. It's enough to have her there, even if somewhere in my mind I know she's not real.

I need the company.

One other thing. As I've gotten closer, the voices from the radio have become a steady stream. Mostly they just repeat the same things over and over, broadcasting their coordinates, the details of the situation here and instructions on what to do when faced with the infected. They don't seem to know much about why this has happened, or who was behind the attacks, or at least they're not talking about it over the air. I'm bringing them the binders we found, just in case the story needs to be told.

All this is fine, and I welcome the sound of human voices, I really do. But one thing in particular I heard recently has come to mean more than I thought it did. They've said something about a treatment for the infection. They've said that even if you have the hives, it's not too late.

And that's a good thing. Because I'm worried. I felt this itching, under my suit, and when I finally pulled over in a clear spot to check it out, I found a red patch in the skin on my arm, just below my shoulder and a couple of inches up from where Sue cut me with that knife.

There's a burning sensation that won't go away, and this maddening sound of whispers inside my head, only I can't seem to understand what they're saying.

At least, not yet.

☐ **YES!**

Sign me up for the Leisure Horror Book Club and send my FREE BOOKS! If I choose to stay in the club, I will pay only $8.50* each month, a savings of $7.48!

NAME: _____

ADDRESS: _____

TELEPHONE: _____

EMAIL: _____

☐ I want to pay by credit card.

☐ **VISA**   ☐ **MasterCard**   ☐ **DISCOVER**

ACCOUNT #: _____

EXPIRATION DATE: _____

SIGNATURE: _____

Mail this page along with $2.00 shipping and handling to:
Leisure Horror Book Club
PO Box 6640
Wayne, PA 19087
Or fax (must include credit card information) to:
610-995-9274
You can also sign up online at **www.dorchesterpub.com**.
*Plus $2.00 for shipping. Offer open to residents of the U.S. and Canada only. Canadian residents please call 1-800-481-9191 for pricing information.
If under 18, a parent or guardian must sign. Terms, prices and conditions subject to change. Subscription subject to acceptance. Dorchester Publishing reserves the right to reject any order or cancel any subscription.

GET FREE BOOKS!

You can have the best fiction delivered to your door for less than what you'd pay in a bookstore or online. Sign up for one of our book clubs today, and we'll send you *FREE* BOOKS* just for trying it out... **with no obligation to buy, ever!**

As a member of the Leisure Horror Book Club, you'll receive books by authors such as **RICHARD LAYMON, JACK KETCHUM, JOHN SKIPP, BRIAN KEENE** and many more.

As a book club member you also receive the following special benefits:
- **30% off all orders!**
- **Exclusive access to special discounts!**
- **Convenient home delivery and 10 days to return any books you don't want to keep.**

Visit www.dorchesterpub.com or call 1-800-481-9191

There is no minimum number of books to buy, and you may cancel membership at any time.
*Please include $2.00 for shipping and handling.